Miracle Fighter

Miracle Fighter

John Wooten

Miracle Fighter
Copyright 2015 by John Wooten

This is a work of fiction. Names, characters, places and incidents are products of the author's imagination and are used fictitiously. Any resemblance to actual persons—living or dead—is entirely coincidental. All rights reserved. No part of this publication may be reproduced, stored in a retrieval system, or transmitted in any form or by any means, electronic, mechanical, photocopying, recording, or otherwise, without prior written permission from the author. Criminal copyright infringement, including infringement without monetary gain, is investigated by the FBI and is punishable by up to five years in federal prison and a fine of $250,000.

Registered with The Writers Guild of America, West, Inc.
Certificate #1749181 issued to John Wooten for Miracle Fighter
ISBN: 1507547773
ISBN 13: 9781507547779
Library of Congress Control Number: 2015900678
CreateSpace Independent Publishing Platform
North Charleston, South Carolina

For my sweetheart, Nancy—the love of my life—for her support.

ACKNOWLEDGMENTS

Many thanks to Nancy for typing my dictation, and completing the first edit of my novel. I must also thank my wonderful family, children, and grandchildren who provide me with love and humor. I am so grateful to have you in my life.

In memory of my friend, Connell—Father Joe—Maguire. Special thanks for supporting me in this venture. My prayers are always with you.

With appreciation to Lori Oliveira, who went that extra step to help get this project underway.

Thank you to Dick Kulpa, AKA Captain Cartoon, the talented artist who created the digital images featured inside *Miracle Fighter*.

To Larry Small, my good friend and Blackbelt student of Jujutsu: thank you for taking all that physical abuse as my *uki* over the years.

Thanks to my friend Grandmaster Kenneth Miarecki, as I remember all the good times we shared together teaching and running seminars all over the country.

A huge thank you to my editor, Rosa Sophia; you are the best!

And a special recognition to Joe Sorota, who made this endeavor possible.

CONTENTS

1 Son of a Mobster 1
2 Seeing Is Believing 9
3 Wrong Place, Wrong Time 13
4 The Funeral 19
5 Boston Connection 27
6 Settling In Bean Town 33
7 Marenzano's Promises 39
8 Human Disposal 45
9 Photo Finish 51
10 Master of Masters 57
11 Love is In the Air 63
12 Family Secret 71
13 Vinnie's Birthday 75
14 Training for the Big Fight 81
15 Vinnie's First Pro Fight 89
16 Caught by Surprise 101
17 Family Skeletons 107
18 It Ain't Over Until It's Over 115
19 Right Place, Wrong Time 119
20 Code Blue 125
21 Road to Recovery 131
22 Snatch and Ridicule 139
23 Secret Identity 145
24 Payback Is A Bitch 153

25	Only the Strong Survive	157
26	Don't Get Caught With Your Pants Down	161
27	Brown Bag It	165
28	Such a Deal	169
29	Undercover	173
30	Meeting of the Minds	175
31	What Goes Around, Comes Around	181
32	A Fight to the Top	187
33	In the Dark of an Alley	197
34	Only God Knows	203
35	Penthouse Connection	209
36	Dream or Reality	213
37	A Cloud of Light	219
38	Bill of Good Health	229
39	Training at the Dojo	233
40	A Word of Wisdom	239
41	Press Conference	243
42	Terror In the Ring	247
43	Back In Bean Town	253
44	Arrival In Castellammare del Golfo	255
45	Messenger of God	263
46	A Matter of National Security	267
47	Lady of the Mountain	271

CHAPTER 1

SON OF A MOBSTER

She'd been digging through her purse, searching for change for the children—Mario and Maria—so they'd quit squabbling over the quarter they had for the candy machine in the convenience store.

That inconsequential memory was something she would always connect to the man who began to cross the street, a newspaper under his arm, just before a shot rang out and his brains were splattered across the asphalt.

Later, she would sit at home thinking, *I never found the change. I never found the change.*

But in those moments, her only thought was to gather her children, and return home.

They'd gone shopping in downtown Castellammare. She'd wanted her husband, Vinchenzo, to accompany her, but he was nowhere to be found. Her older son, Dominick, offered to take her, but of course, Vinnie, Mario, and Maria wanted to tag along.

"Now I have my whole family except for my husband, wherever he is. Let's leave right away and I will treat everyone to lunch."

"Yeah!" Mario shouted.

Maria asked, "Mom, can we have ice cream for dessert?"

"Certainly, whatever you like."

She might've thought how innocent the conversation was compared to the melee that played out in the street—if she hadn't seen this all before. The family they came from, the history they had, ensured Incoranata was no stranger to tragedy.

After all, her husband, Vinchenzo *the animal* Depasquale was Josepie Lamatina's underboss. Some of the most notorious mobsters were born in Castellammare del Golfo, Sicily, and Joe the Boss was one of them. As head of the five major crime families, many knew him as the Boss of Bosses, *capo dei capi*.

It was clear this had been a professional hit. Her thoughts revolved around her husband as a sick feeling rose in the pit of her stomach. She prayed he'd had nothing to do with it, but she knew one of the five families must have ordered the hit.

When Incoranata had dropped her purse in shock, Dominick had calmly scooped it up. Car horns sounded out, women screamed. The shooter had disappeared. Incoranata watched as blood pooled around the man in the road, and frantic onlookers shouted. Chaos had taken over in seconds. She tugged her other children closer to her, even Vinnie, who was becoming jaded in his teenage years.

Feet pounded as a man rushed out of the nearby barbershop. Incoranata caught a glimpse of Dominick's expressionless face as the man cried out, his eyes wide, "Can you imagine, this shooting in broad daylight? What balls they have! You know, that guy was in the barbershop." He brandished a trembling finger toward the man in the road, who was now being surrounded by officials who were directing traffic and blocking off the scene. "He told me he was late just a couple of days paying the *vig* on his loan, and for this they killed him, for just five hundred dollars?"

Dominick had offered a half-shrug, and spoke in a level tone. "He broke the rules and regulations with this thing of ours, and now he has paid with his life."

The other man swallowed slowly, paling. He turned and walked carefully back into the barbershop, terrified of Dominick.

Incoranata could tell her son hadn't meant for her to hear his words.

At home, she sat on the bed for over an hour, clutching her rosary tightly in both hands.

"I never found the change," she whispered, tears staining her cheeks. "Will my life always be like this? One horror after another?"

No one answered, and Incoranata wept.

Vinnie was already becoming a handsome young man at seventeen, with a wiry physique, muscular arms, and a face that made the girls in town swoon.

He quickly grew into a great boxer, with the help of his father, Vinchenzo, who managed the gym where he boxed, and a family friend whom Vinchenzo had strong connections with—Father Anthony.

Vinnie's first boxing match was scheduled for a muggy summer day, which increased his discomfort as he waited for the match to begin.

Mikey *the Ice Breaker* Ferrera was two years older than Vinnie, with three more years of experience under his belt. Vinnie's heart pounded and sweat beaded on his forehead as he watched his opponent prepare for the match on the other side of the gym. A lump rose in his throat, and he balked, suddenly worried he might lose, despite the fact he'd been doing nothing but training for months.

Vinnie learned that Mikey had won two out of five of his previous fights. Vinnie had a chance to beat him, but the chances were slim. As he waited for the match to begin, his nervousness increasing with each moment, he couldn't help but feel overwhelmed.

Remember, Vinnie, he told himself, you'll be okay. *Just remember what Father Anthony said. And remember the Virgin Mary . . .*

Vinnie had visited Father Anthony the day before, and the Father assured him he had nothing to worry about, blessed him, and sent him on his way.

That night, Vinnie had trouble falling asleep. Then he heard a woman's voice. She implored him to visit her on the mountainside before the fight, promising he would win the fight if he did as he was told. When he sat up in bed, he was sure he'd heard the voice, that it hadn't been a dream.

Who is she? He'd wondered what mountain she'd been referring to.

Then he had stretched out again, and quickly fell into a deep slumber.

On the morning of the fight, he'd overslept and woke frantically, rushed to get dressed, and grabbed his gym bag. Remembering the voice, he'd hurried out the door, not sure where he was headed. He'd gone straight to Father Anthony and told him what had happened.

The Father frowned, folding his hands before him. "It was probably a dream."

Father Anthony had shrugged it off, but Vinnie knew what he'd heard was real. He tried to ignore his annoyance at the Father, who probably thought he was crazy. The Father blessed Vinnie with holy water and gave him a pair of rosary beads.

When he'd left the church, Vinnie had wandered the streets looking for a sign, but nothing happened. Growing weary, he sat down on a rock.

He would never forget the man who'd approached him, an elderly gentleman with piercing eyes, clothed in a dark hooded cape, his face mostly covered by the scarf he wore. His gaze was hypnotizing, but frightening, and he looked like a phantasm, as if he'd materialized right out of the morning mists.

"I know who you are and I know who you are looking for." He pointed his staff and told Vinnie to walk until he reached a fork in the road. After turning left, he was to continue walking until he saw a fig tree on the left side of the road. Vinnie remembered his words clearly. "Then you will be at the side of a cliff. Do not move forward, just look straight ahead at the mountain. You will see."

When Vinnie arrived, he watched the mists rise from the valley below, and stood there for so long his legs grew tired. All of a sudden, a beautiful woman appeared, dressed in blue and white robes, her face concealed by a white veil.

"My name is Mary, the Mother of Jesus," she had said, her voice like soft music.

"I know who you are, I pray to you all the time." The energy pouring forth from her was so strong that it was a strain for him to speak. The intensity of Vinnie's emotions were almost too much to bear. Even as he recalled it, the strength of the moment nearly overcame him. The sight was too incredible to describe.

"That is why I am here now." Her lilting voice drifted over the misty valley.

"Why me?" Vinnie had asked.

"Never mind why. Just do what I say and you will win the fight. After you have won, you must promise to visit me every day at this location until the first snow fall."

"Thank you, Blessed Mother," Vinnie intoned, awestruck.

John Wooten

Miracle at Castellammare del Golfo

When he'd left and headed home, Vinnie wondered if Father Anthony would believe him now. He had to concentrate and prepare for the fight, which would take place that evening. The experience of the early morning had been so intense, he decided not to tell his family about it—not yet. It felt precious, too special to reveal, like a fragile gift that was best kept in its box. For now, Vinnie would keep it a secret. And he would win the fight.

Still thinking of the Virgin Mary, Vinnie entered the boxing arena with his father, Vinchenzo. Crowds of people were waiting for the fight to begin. The air in the arena was heavy and humid as father and son walked to the locker room where Father Anthony was ready to wrap his hands and put the gloves on.

"You're not going to believe what happened to me this morning!" Vinnie exclaimed, suddenly unable to contain the perfect memory.

"Vinnie, we don't have time for this," Anthony said, eyeing him with fatherly affection. "Let's get you out there and into the ring."

Determined, Vinnie forced himself to focus on the fight. Vinchenzo and Father Anthony walked him to the ring as the crowd roared. He spotted his family and friends where they sat waiting for the fight to begin.

The bell went off and the Ice Breaker landed multiple blows to Vinnie's head, one after the other. Disoriented, Vinnie heard a whisper in his ear.

Now, Vinnie!

He snapped out of it as a renewed sense of focus came over him and a burst of energy shot through his body. Vinnie remembered what the Virgin Mary revealed to him. He needed to overcome his emotions and deal with the fight at hand. Vinnie aggressively threw rapid punches repeatedly to Mikey's head and body. Mikey tried to block the punches, but they came too swiftly.

Vinnie hit the Ice Breaker with a left hook, so hard it knocked Mikey over the ropes and out of the ring. Vinnie's trainers, family, and friends rushed in the ring and lifted Vinnie onto their shoulders, yelling and cheering. Vinnie looked up toward the ceiling, thanking the Virgin Mary for his win.

"I will see you tomorrow, as I promised," Vinnie yelled out excitedly, not caring who heard him. They didn't need to understand; after all, the message was for him, not the screaming fans surrounding him.

After the crowd dispersed, Father Anthony approached Vinnie in the locker room, his hands clasped before him, a speculative expression on his wrinkled face. Vinnie shut the door to his locker and used a wet towel to cool the back of his neck. Father Anthony stepped up to him.

"Vinnie, I heard you thank the Virgin Mary for your win."

Vinnie nodded, gritting his teeth as he prepared to defend himself. "Yes, I know it was the Virgin Mary's voice I heard that night. Why don't you believe me?"

Father Anthony appeared resigned as he breathed out a deep sigh. "We need to talk, but not here. Meet me at the rectory in my office tomorrow after school at four. Besides, you need to enjoy your victory party."

Vinnie wondered if the Father had changed his mind. Did he believe him?

As the night darkened, the celebration of his win ended. He finally had a chance to rest. When he put his head on the pillow, he wondered how he would explain his meeting with the Virgin Mary to Father Anthony.

The next day after school, Vinnie showed up at the rectory. When he entered Father Anthony's office, he found him sitting in his swiveled chair, gazing out the window.

"Vinnie, have a seat." The Father turned and indicated the chair opposite his desk. "How do you feel after the fight?"

"Good!" He was tired, but he felt fulfilled. Even if his body had been aching, nothing could take away from the excitement of his victory.

Father Anthony gazed directly into Vinnie's eyes. "Okay, tell me the story from the beginning. I want the truth." His tone was firm and his dark eyes were piercing.

Vinnie stuttered a reply. "Well, it all started like this, Father Anthony . . ."

CHAPTER 2

SEEING IS BELIEVING

Vinnie awoke shivering. He reached for his blanket at the bottom of his bed, and wrapped it around his body, then stood to check the thermostat. He had to turn up the heat considerably. Stepping over to his window, he peered at the thermometer. The temperature outside was twenty-eight degrees. The wind howled in the distance as he gazed at the storm clouds, deciding to get an early start on his journey toward the mountain.

A short time later, as he advanced in the direction of the mountain, he got the distinct impression he was being followed.

He left town and walked up a hill, along a dirt path, shielding his face from the wind. Even his coat, scarf, and hat failed to protect his body from the chill. The frigid temperature tore through him as his teeth chattered. But it didn't distract him from the shadow he glimpsed from the corner of his eye. He saw it several times, but whenever he turned, the shadow disappeared. At first, he was frightened. Until he began to suspect who it was.

He continued along as if he hadn't seen it.

Finally, Vinnie arrived at the fig tree at the side of the mountain and patiently waited for Mary the Blessed Mother. Hours passed and there was no sign of her. As time passed, he became certain he wasn't the only one there.

He turned suddenly, catching a glimpse of a shadow he clearly recognized.

"It's *you*, Father Anthony, I saw you jump behind the rock! I know it's you, I saw your black robe. Now, come out from behind that rock," Vinnie snapped angrily. "You promised you wouldn't follow me to the mountain. *You promised!*"

Appearing crestfallen, Father Anthony stepped out of the shadows. "I'm sorry, I am only concerned for your well being. Vinnie, look...*nothing* is there." He indicated the mountain, where the mists slowly sunk toward the ground far below. "It is all in your mind, my son. Come back to the rectory with me and I will help you."

At that moment, a woman's voice echoed from mountaintop to mountaintop. She appeared on the mountainside surrounded by clouds, clad in a long blue robe with a white veil. A halo shimmered above her head. She was breathtaking, and bestowed upon the beholder an overwhelming sense of peace. She was so close, Vinnie felt as if he could reach out and touch her.

Father Anthony fell to his knees, gasping.

"Do you believe?" the woman asked, her face angelic and her eyes brimming with deep love for all that surrounded her.

"Yes, Blessed Mother, I believe!" Father Anthony exclaimed.

She continued, looking down upon them. "I have seven requests for you both. One request per year, which I will reveal to you now. During the first year, I want you to spread the glorious word of my coming to everyone. In the second year, you will receive ten million dollars anonymously. You will need to buy all the construction vehicles and equipment for the upcoming projects. The third year, you and the townspeople will construct twenty-one roads coming from all directions leading to the three heavenly mountains. In the fourth year, you will cultivate the sacred land and grow many succulent crops.

"In the fifth year, you will dig deep in the ground along the enchanted mountainside. You will find an abundance of oil and rich natural resources. Throughout the sixth year, you will all rest. Just come to the peaceful mountainside each day and pray to me. Then, in the seventh year, I will appear one last time. I am counting on you, Father Anthony, to execute my wishes, for Vinnie has a long journey ahead of him. He will not be coming back until the seventh year.

"Now leave in peace, and rush home to spread the word. Begin by telling the people to go outside at midnight. The night will become day and the temperature will rise to one hundred degrees. The day will become night and grow bitter cold below zero. When the townspeople see this miracle, they will believe."

Vinnie and Father Anthony rushed home to spread the news as snowflakes fell upon them. Only moments later, they glanced up and saw the sun was shining and there was not a cloud in the sky. The snow had stopped completely.

CHAPTER 3

WRONG PLACE, WRONG TIME

The next day, Josepie Lamatina and some of his crew were playing cards, drinking, smoking, and telling stories in the back room of his restaurant. Vinchenzo Depasquale was there, leaning back in his chair and eyeing the cards he'd been dealt, his brow furrowing. Three of Lamatina's loan sharks were also sitting around the table—Michael Defilipo, Anthony Saso, and Johnny Boy Desenza. Victorio Capaletti, Joe's number one zip, also sat with them. Ritchie *the Rags* Fabiano, one of his lieutenants, grumbled under his breath as he stared at his cards.

While they played, the room brimming with smoke, an unexpected visitor arrived. Dominick Depasquale, Vinchenzo's oldest son, stepped into the back room. One of the men shook his hand and gave him a shot of whiskey. At twenty-three years old, he was muscular, with olive skin and penetrating eyes. His black hair was combed straight back, and his gaze darted to each of the card players as he observed the game. He was warmly embraced by the crew, and invited to join.

Shortly afterward, Joe the Boss looked up from his cards as he scratched at the stubble on his chin. "Vinchenzo. Get the car."

The two men exchanged a knowing glance. Dominick looked up. Everyone had fallen silent. Where he sat in the metal folding chair beside Dominick, Johnny Boy had lit a cigar and was puffing on it thoughtfully.

By way of explanation, the boss added, "We need to take care of that... *little thing*," he explained, shrugging. "The rest of you can stay put and enjoy yourselves. You too, Dominick. We'll be back shortly to join you."

As they drove, Joe pointed across a dark street and told Vinchenzo to pull over.

"Run in and see Sammy, he has a bag for me," Joe ordered. He sat in the car with the window half-open, smoking a cigarette until Vinchenzo returned. When he sat back down in the driver's seat, Joe asked him to count the money. "There should be two hundred and fifty thou in there."

"It's all here, boss." Vinchenzo handed him the bag. "Where to now?"

"Joey Zaza's garage, to get this car checked out," Joe grumbled.

"Yes, boss, that's a very good idea, the car hasn't been running right for the last couple of days."

While Vinchenzo drove, Joe pulled a wad of cash out of the bag, not bothering to count it. He shoved it toward Vinchenzo.

"This is for you and your family."

"Oh, boss, you don't have to do that."

"Forget about it, what are friends for?"

Vinchenzo tucked the money away. "On the other hand, I'm sure Incoranata can find some use for the money."

"If she is anything like my wife, I'm sure she will," Joe said, cackling, then covering his mouth to cough loudly.

When they pulled into the parking lot at Zaza's, Vinchenzo climbed out and embraced Zaza in a warm hug, clapping him on the back. He explained the problem with the car, and told Zaza it had to be done by that evening.

"Will that be a problem?" Vinchenzo narrowed his eyes, grinning at the same time, his hand on his friend's shoulder.

"No, of course not." Zaza shook his head. "Easy."

"Can you tell me how much it'll cost?"

"Cost?" Zaza spread his arms, then shook his head as if he didn't understand the word. "What cost?" He lowered his voice. "All the parts I have are from stolen cars. Forget about it, my friend." He stuck a thumb toward the parked car. "Anyway, Joe the Boss *gave* me all the stolen parts." He laughed loudly, and Vinchenzo chuckled. "No charge for my godfather," the mechanic continued. "I will personally give you guys a ride back to the restaurant."

"That sounds great, Zaza, thanks."

The two men walked toward Zaza's car, Joe on their heels.

The card game continued back at the restaurant. Hours went by uneventfully. When Dominick was in the middle of telling Johnny an amusing story about a stripper he'd been going out with, the phone rang, interrupting their conversation, and Zaza informed Vinchenzo the car was ready.

Dominick stood, dropping his cards on the table. He hadn't finished telling his story, but the card game was getting dull. "I'll pick it up," he said, slipping into his jacket.

"Hey, what about that story?" Johnny asked. "You were just getting to the good part."

"Next time." Dominick chuckled.

It was clear to everyone that Joe and his father had too much to drink. Ritchie the Rags offered to help, and drove Dominick to Zaza's.

Upon their arrival, Dominick thanked Ritchie for the ride, and Ritchie headed home. Dominick raised an eyebrow at the bemused expression on Zaza's face. The mechanic seemed surprised to see him.

"Can I get the key?" Dominick asked after a long silence. Zaza hesitated. Frustrated, Dominick snapped, "Is there a problem?"

"Oh, no, no, no, of course not," Zaza said, finally handing him the car key. Dominick practically had to snatch the keys away from him. He eyed him suspiciously before he turned and walked toward the car. Dominick climbed into the driver's seat, then glanced out his side view mirror, watching Zaza as he quickly closed and locked his garage door.

Dominick didn't have time to question the mechanic's behavior.

When he turned the key, the car exploded in flames, igniting the gas pumps.

As the night went on, the card game ended, and the crew dispersed and went home. Vinchenzo and Joe were still waiting for Dominick to return the car. It was taking too long, and they were both concerned.

A cold sweat crawled up Vinchenzo's spine as he thought of his eldest son, and prayed he was safe. A terrible feeling rose in his gut as the bile in his stomach churned. There wasn't much that fazed him, but when it came to his family—his *children*—he would have done anything to protect them. He had a terrible feeling, and it worsened moment by moment.

"Vinchenzo, call Dominick on his cell phone, will you?"

"Sure, boss." Remaining calm, Vinchenzo dialed the number and waited. After a long pause, he gave up and said, "There's no answer." He wondered if Joe could see the fear in his eyes.

"Try Zaza's garage then."

Vinchenzo got the same results. He shook his head. "Nothing."

"Try Zaza on his cell phone," Joe said as he tapped his fingers worriedly on the scratched wood surface of the table.

Vinchenzo could tell his boss was growing impatient. After another long pause, Vinchenzo said, "No, nothing there, either." He set his phone on the table and glanced up. "I hope my son is all right."

"I hope so too," Joe said quietly.

Their gazes met, and for a brief moment, Vinchenzo thought everything would be fine. He pictured Dominick returning, sitting down with the family for dinner. All the normal things people took for granted. In that fleeting second, he was certain his son would be returned to him.

Until a shrill scream tore through his ears, and he gasped, shooting up from his seat. Joe stood more slowly, but both men were startled by the cry.

When Vinchenzo peeked out the window, his eyes widened and he shouted frantically. "It's my wife and children!" Vinchenzo flung open the door and Incoranata collapsed into his arms, hysterical.

"Vinchenzo, Vinchenzo, our son is dead, our son Dominick is *dead!*"

Vinnie stood close to his mother, and Mario and Maria clung to her, sobbing.

"Our brother is dead." Little Maria wept uncontrollably.

Vinchenzo cried in despair, and Incoranata banged her fists against her husband's chest, her eyes brimming with tears. He wrapped his arms around her, pulling her close.

"It was no accident!" she yelled.

Joe watched with interest, remaining calm. "How do you know that?" he asked, cocking his head to the side.

"There was an explosion…at Zaza's garage." Incoranata took several deep breaths, trying to compose herself. "Dominick…he was in your car when the bomb exploded. The hit was not for my son, the hit was meant for *you* and my husband. All because of this *thing* of yours, I lost my son. Joey Zaza was killed just thirty feet from the car. The police think he had something to do with it, but he couldn't get away in time."

Vinchenzo turned to Joe. "It must be the Burtucci family."

"Yes, I think you are right," Joe said solemnly. "You must take your wife and children home. You will need to start planning the funeral arrangements. I will get to the bottom of this and find out who is responsible for your son's death."

As he left, Vinchenzo turned swiftly toward Joe, his body trembling with fury and grief. "When you find out who killed my son, it will be *my* finger pulling the trigger."

CHAPTER 4

THE FUNERAL

It was a dreary day with a light drizzle of rain. The cemetery was crowded with hundreds of people, not all of them friends or family. A number of mourners had gathered around the casket, and they screamed, moaned, and yelled as they prayed for Dominick Depasquale.

Nearby, Vinchenzo, Incoranata, Vinnie, Mario, and Maria were huddled together weeping as a line of people paid their respects one by one. Father Anthony was getting ready to conduct the funeral service along with Father Antonelli. The mourners joined Incoranata and prayed with her. But their dramatics upset her, and she became visibly agitated and frantic.

Her power to concentrate on the funeral and her family diminished as her confusion deepened. She struggled, then screamed and shoved the mourners away, just as Dominick's casket was lowered into his grave.

None of this can be true. My son is not dead.

She flashed back to that moment in the street, when she'd seen a man die over a measly five hundred dollars, and she saw blood—*everywhere*. The blood of strangers, the blood of her son.

What kind of life am I living?

Bursting forward, she jumped into the grave on her son's casket and slammed her fists against the hard wood, then pried at it, trying to get one last glimpse of him.

He cannot be gone, he cannot be gone.

Strong hands wrapped around her arms. They pulled at her, and she shrieked for them to let her go. But it was no use.

Vinchenzo, Joe, and several other soldiers of the Lamatina crime family reached down and swiftly pulled Incoranata out of the grave, holding her and trying to comfort her.

She slumped against her husband, her energy dissipating. She felt as if she had nothing left. Then she remembered her other children—Mario, Maria, and Vinnie. And she pressed close against her husband, knowing she had to be there for her family. She could not let this destroy her.

She refused to give up.

Soon, everything had calmed down, and the cemetery workers slowly started shoveling dirt into the hole. Many people remained to console the family. The graveyard was quiet, and a menacing darkness seemed to sink around the mourners, filling them with dread.

From behind a tree, a man appeared with a hooded raincoat, staring directly at Joe. A dark shadow, barely discernible, surrounded the perimeter of his wiry body. Joe focused on the eyes of this stranger, and saw his milky white skin and the dark circles that surrounded his piercing gaze. The stranger moved slowly and purposefully toward him, and he felt an evil presence as he realized he was frozen in place.

The man stopped about ten feet away, and Joe watched the face of this stranger drastically change into that of a demon.

He knew this face, he knew this *being*. This creature of darkness.

Within the blink of an eye, his face changed to resemble a human again, and he reached into his raincoat, pulled out a gun, and shot Joe the Boss in the chest.

As Joe fell to the ground, pain lancing through his body, he knew without a doubt who'd shot him.

His killer was Satan himself.

Mourners screamed and threw themselves to the ground for cover. Vinchenzo, thinking quickly, ran after the stranger, while members of Joe's crew crowded around him, protecting the wounded man. Vinchenzo wielded his gun and shot the stranger in the leg. He tried to shoot him again, but his chamber was empty.

After a long struggle, Vinchenzo picked up a large rock and attempted to hit the man over the head. He halted suddenly when his enemy looked him directly in the eye.

"I am the one responsible for your son's death." He sneered, then laughed hysterically.

Vinchenzo balked, his heart hammering against his ribcage. He shook his head, blinking, unsure of what he was seeing; did this man resemble Satan? Before he could collect his thoughts, the stranger's face had changed back. Vinchenzo attacked, smashing the rock over his head, crushing his skull. He and one of Joe's men dragged the body to Joe's feet, dropping him there.

"This is the man who is responsible for my son's death," Vinchenzo announced grimly. "He is also the one who shot you."

Joe grabbed Vinchenzo's hand as the rest of the crew gathered around. Vinchenzo knelt beside him.

"You're going to be fine, boss," he urged.

"No—"

"Don't talk, you're going to be okay, I hear the sirens, we'll get that bullet out of you." Vinchenzo looked down at the wound, knowing it was bad; he didn't want to admit the truth, not even to himself.

"*Listen.*"

Vinchenzo acquiesced. "Yes, I am listening." He squeezed the man's hand, which was clammy and cool to the touch.

"These are my wishes," Joe continued, his voice weakening. "I am dying. You…you will become the new Don." His grip seemed to loosen, but then he tightened his fist again until his knuckles were white. Vinchenzo held his fingers tightly, looking down at the man he'd worked with for so many years. Joe's left hand was over his chest, stained with his own blood. "The rest of my men will work under you, as under boss, *consigliere*…captain and your soldiers.

There will be no changes in my line of command except for you, Vinchenzo Don Depasquale…my successor and…best friend." Joe's voice was growing weaker. All the men leaned closer, listening raptly.

"Now, *all* of you…Remember. Vinchenzo, send your wife and children out of the country, as they will be in grave danger. Many men from the five families will be killed during this power struggle. My crew…will arrange passage for your family out of Sicily…to the United States. Vinchenzo, remain here to run our business. I will guarantee your family's safety. Go with my men…they will lead you through the caves of Castellammare del Golfo.

"Your family will go to Rome, and Angelo DeNucci will meet them. He will have…new passports…for them." Joe coughed. "He will drive your family to the airport and see them off. When they are…in New York, Paul Festa will bring them to the train station, and they will go to Boston, where my friend Salvatore Marenzano, head of the New England La Costa Nostra, will meet them. He will…make sure they have a place to live, money…clothing. When the time comes, you will need to contact the New England boss.

"Remember, Vinchenzo, they *cannot* use their real last name of Depasquale. Do you understand…all this?"

"Yes, Joe," Vinchenzo said, his voice quiet, calling him by his first name and squeezing his hand gently.

Someone yelled out. "The sirens are getting closer, it must be the ambulance and the cops!"

Vinchenzo held Joe close to him, grasping his hand tightly. He knew his friend was not long for the world, as much as he didn't want to admit it.

First Dominick, now Joe—who'd always been a confidant, a man he could trust with his life. The anger and sorrow rising within him reminded him of Incoranata's outburst; Vinchenzo held himself together for his family. He *had* to.

Joe looked at him one last time.

"You must…go, Vinchenzo, go…" He took his final breath and died in Vinchenzo's arms.

The crew got up quickly, grabbing Vinchenzo and his family. They hurried to the caves, and the Depasquale family began their journey.

During their escape, they heard strange howling sounds. Vinchenzo was the first to see the face of Satan in a mirage. The skull began to bleed and deteriorate before his eyes. He thought he was hallucinating in the midst of his grief, until Incoranata and the children saw it, too. They were told by Satan to return to Castellammare del Golfo or they would die.

Vinnie tugged his rosary beads out of his pocket and began praying fervently to the Blessed Virgin Mary, telling everyone else to do the same. Satan was driven away, and at last they arrived on the other side of the mountain.

John Wooten

Vinchenzo kissed his wife, holding her close.

"I love you," he whispered, pulling her against him.

"I love you too, my husband," she replied, wiping away her tears.

He hugged each of his children and said his goodbyes, then watched his family board the boat to Rome with a heavy heart.

CHAPTER 5

BOSTON CONNECTION

Safe in Rome, Incoranata and the children received their new passports with their new name—Russo. In Boston at last, a man clad in very fine designer clothing, accentuated with gold and diamond jewelry, met with them, his hands clasped before him. The rings on his fingers glimmered under the light—especially one ring in particular that Vinnie was quick to notice. The well-dressed benefactor stared at the bewildered family and smirked, extending his hand.

"I am Josepie Lamatina's friend, Salvatore Marenzano, and I am known as Don Marenzano. I head the New England crime families. I was sad to hear of Joe's passing, and of Dominick's." He turned to Incoranata, his eyes downcast. He took her hand in his, squeezing gently. "I am sorry for your loss and all your pain and suffering. I hope the accommodations I set up for you and your family will be adequate."

"Thank you." Incoranata's voice was soft. She forced a smile. "I am sure it will be just fine."

Marenzano turned to the oldest son. "You must be Vinnie. I heard you like to box."

"Yes, sir," Vinnie replied.

"Well, I own a couple of boxing gyms," Marenzano boasted, putting an arm around the young man's shoulder. "Would you like to see them?"

Vinnie's eyes brightened. "When?"

"Soon enough." Marenzano patted him on the back, then released him and turned to the younger children. "You must be Mario and Maria." They both nodded in earnest. Marenzano turned to five of his goons and yelled,

"Don't just stand there, take my friends' luggage and bring them to the limo." He glanced back to the family. "I will arrange to have you taken to your new home and some of my crew will help you get settled. First, who is hungry?"

"We are!" the children shouted excitedly. Vinnie remained silent.

"I know a good Italian restaurant," Marenzano said, winking. They all laughed good-naturedly. "No, it is *really* good, I own it."

"What is it called?" Vinnie asked, still wondering about the ring on Marenzano's finger.

"Marenzano's Fine Italian Cuisine."

"Sounds lovely." Incoranata smiled widely, seeming to relax for the first time in days.

The limo pulled up to the restaurant, and the driver got out and opened the door for the passengers. A Lincoln Continental slid up behind the limo with five members of Don Marenzano's crew. Incoranata and the children stepped out and stared in awe at the large sign, the beautiful shimmering lights, and the quaint atmosphere of the high class establishment.

"Don Marenzano, nobody would miss this place for sure, not with that huge sign," Vinnie breathed.

"If you think *that's* big, wait to you see my menu." Marenzano signaled for his men to go in to the back room of the restaurant. "I will call you when I need you," he told them.

They stepped into the building, while Vinnie stayed close to his mother. The last few days, he'd been growing more perceptive to her grief over Dominick. His own heart ached, but his mother's heart had been broken. She was such a strong woman, smiling despite everything, but Vinnie could see her pain. He gently squeezed her hand as they stepped through the restaurant, and she reciprocated. He just wanted her to remember he was there for her—even though he didn't know how to act in the wake of this loss, either.

Once they were inside and seated, the waiter brought the menus, which were just as large as Marenzano had promised. They were difficult for the children to hold; Mario's cheeks flushed in embarrassment when he dropped the menu and had to fetch it from beneath the table.

Little Maria spoke up, leaning her head to the side so she could see the Don. "Don Marenzano, you should have a smaller menu for children. The menu is so big and heavy, I can hardly hold it up."

Marenzano leaned against the table and winked at her. "Maybe you should come to my gym where we can make you stronger, this way you would be able to hold up my menu without any trouble." Everyone laughed.

Incoranata widened her eyes at the selection. "I'm having a problem deciding what to order. There are so many choices."

"Allow me to order for you and your family," Marenzano suggested. He called the waiter over to take their order. "My usual for all of us."

"Of course," the waiter said, bowing slightly and rushing back to the kitchen.

While waiting for the food, Vinnie stared at Marenzano's unusual ring. Marenzano caught his attention, and Vinnie realized he'd been caught looking. Vinnie's cheeks flushed.

"It's all right," Marenzano said, sensing Vinnie's nervousness. "Do you like my ring?"

"I really can't see it that good from here," Vinnie admitted.

Salvatore took off the ring and slipped it on Vinnie's finger. Seeing it up close, Vinnie knew right away it was the face of Satan. As he recalled what had happened during his family's escape, the voice of the devil rang out in his head.

It's too late for you and your family, I own you!

Vinnie's mother began to shake him, and he glanced up as though in a trance. She desperately tried to remove Don Marenzano's ring from Vinnie's finger. She tugged the ring off his finger, and Vinnie shook his head as if to clear it. Salvatore reached over to regain possession of his ring, just as Vinnie grabbed the Don's left hand and saw the tattoo across his knuckles: *666*. Vinnie snatched his hand away.

"What's wrong with you?" Marenzano snapped.

"I'm sorry, I…I am thinking of my brother's death and worried about my father. I'm not myself. Forgive me."

"I am so sorry for his behavior, Don Marenzano," Incoranata intoned.

"Forget about it, I understand what he is going through. Vinnie and I are going to become good friends, aren't we, Vinnie?"

"Yes, Don Marenzano. *Dohveh eel bahnyoh?*"

"In back of the restaurant on your left." Marenzano waved his hand in the direction of the men's room.

Stepping away from the table, Vinnie took a moment to clear his head. He was truly shaken, and suddenly unsure if his family was safe with Don Marenzano. While on his way, Vinnie noticed a small statue of the Blessed Virgin Mother, sitting on a decorative shelf amidst bottles of wine. He quickly glanced up, made the sign of the cross, and recited the Hail Mary. Upon finishing his prayer, he whispered to the Virgin Mary, "Did you see what happened at the table? I know you said you would always be with me, but I am still fearful."

Vinnie continued to the men's room, the hair on the back of his neck standing on end. He was paranoid, worried now about his family and Marenzano's presence in their lives. When he went into one of the stalls in the bathroom, he was surprised to find old fashioned pull chain toilets in the beautiful restaurant.

While washing his hands, Vinnie allowed his paranoia to get the best of him. He decided to stand on top of the toilet seat and pad down the tank for a gun. He didn't find one.

Maybe I'm worrying too much. But look what happened to my brother.

He left the men's room, noticing other doors in the narrow hallway and wondering what was behind them. The restaurant was vast, seeming to take up much of the city block it was positioned on, so it didn't surprise Vinnie to see so many back rooms. He decided to open one of the doors. He peeked in and saw some of Don Marenzano's men drinking and playing cards. He quietly closed the door without being seen, then went to the next door in the hall. Inside, there was a large bar with strippers dancing on poles, and customers watching.

His paranoia was replaced with interest, and he began to think he was going to like it there. Opening a third door, he saw what appeared to be countless stolen items, and overheard men talking as they haggled over televisions, cell phones, and other equipment.

There was so much hidden there, he wondered what was behind the next door. After carefully opening the final door, he found a liquor store with a back room, and a man tied to a chair. He was being beaten and tortured by three of Marenzano's thugs.

"Please, don't hit me again, please!"

"You owe us twenty thou large, and you're five weeks late on the vig, so pay us, mother fucker. How do you like not having fingernails on your hand? How would you like to lose your fucking fingers next, you stupid fuck?"

"No, no, not my fingers," the man shrieked.

"Then take this pen and sign the deed to your house over to me now."

The man signed the deed as he was told.

His heart pounding, Vinnie closed the door rushing back to the table. "Sorry I took so long. I feel much better now."

"Your timing is good, the food just arrived," Marenzano said. "*Mangiare!*"

Much later, when they'd finished their meal, Marenzano stood up and wiped his mouth, then tossed the cloth napkin on the table.

"Now, let us take you to your new home." He signaled to his driver, Vito, and instructed him to pull the limo in front of the restaurant. He leaned forward and whispered, "Vito, tell the boys to follow close in the Lincoln."

Outside the restaurant, Marenzano said goodbye to Incoranata and her family.

"You're not coming with us?" she asked.

"No, I have a great deal of work to catch up on. I will visit you and your family later this week. Enjoy your new home!"

Incoranata thanked him with tears in her eyes.

Vinnie breathed a sigh of relief as he watched Marenzano leave. They climbed into the limo, and his mother patted him on the knee.

"Oh, my dears, I think we're going to be okay," she said.

Vinnie thought of the ring, and the *666* on Marenzano's knuckles. He wasn't so sure.

CHAPTER 6

SETTLING IN BEAN TOWN

The beautiful old brick row home was theirs to keep. Incoranata's heart was full to the point of bursting. She missed Dominick so much, and could still feel him around her as though he'd never gone. And she wished her husband were there, more than anything.

Some things cannot be, she reminded herself, while she admired the wide front porch. They stepped inside, and Alfonzo *Money Bags* Sacramone gave the family a tour of their new home.

"Here are your keys," he said, handing them to her on his way out. "We took the liberty of filling your refrigerator and cabinets with food and cleaning supplies. But you don't have to clean now. The boss had about eight bimbos, *excuse me*, Incoranata, I mean eight girls clean your house."

Incoranata raised an eyebrow and shot Money Bags a glare. "Yeah, it really looks it," she replied, her voice edged with sarcasm. She glanced up at the tall man while clearing her throat, then added, "Alfonzo, are you forgetting something?"

"Ah…Ah, oh yeah, you want me to tuck you guys in for the night?"

"I don't think so, Alfonzo. We can do that ourselves, but thank you."

"In that case, I guess I will be leaving now." The big man shrugged his wide shoulders.

"Just a minute, Mr. Money Bags, where's the money I was promised?"

"Oh, yeah, yeah, yeah." He wiped the sweat from his forehead with the back of his hand. "Oh, Incoranata, I thought you meant something *else.*" He winked, but it looked more like he was experiencing a nervous tic.

"Do not flatter yourself, Money Bags." Incoranata's stomach turned at the very thought.

Wordlessly, he handed her the money. She smiled curtly and slammed the door once he'd stepped outside. She turned to the children, shaking her head.

"Do you believe that guy? What a nerve."

They all laughed.

"Ma, forget about it," Vinnie said, patting her on the shoulder. "He is just a *stupido*."

"Whatever you do, don't tell your father how forward Mr. Money Bags was, he'll shoot him for sure. I hope all Americans are not as *stupido* as Alfonzo," she added, ushering them into the kitchen.

The warm, bright light illuminated the wide space. Incoranata was impressed by the recently redone kitchen with its smooth granite countertops, beautifully crafted wood cabinets, and brand new sparkling appliances. Their old house in Sicily hadn't been this well-equipped. She was startled from her thoughts as the children hopped up on the stools which were positioned around the kitchen island, the little ones *oohing* and *ahhing* over everything in sight.

"Do you know something, Ma?" Vinnie said, sitting down at the table. "Nobody is as slick as us Sicilians. You ought to know that. Dad conned you into marrying him."

Incoranata laughed and rolled her eyes, tapping her fingernails on the cool countertop. "You know, Vinnie, the worst thing is that Alfonzo is *not* an American. He is nothing but a damn *Napledan,* which is worse than any of them."

She paused for a moment, staring toward the floor, and suddenly started sobbing, her body trembling. The children gathered around her, consoling their mother.

Now that they'd arrived, it was as if all her walls were tumbling down, and the grief within her was strangely palpable—like a *thing* she could reach out and touch. It wrapped around her, making the tears come faster. She felt as if she were falling apart.

"I'm sorry," she said through her tears. "All of a sudden, I am very depressed thinking about your father, home alone without his family, and all the problems with the mafia wars."

"Dad is a grown man and knows how to take care of himself," Vinnie reminded her.

"Children, do you think you could all sleep in my bed tonight? Just as you did when you were younger?"

"Yes, Ma!" Maria exclaimed. "It'll be fun!"

Once they were all tucked in, they reminisced.

"Tell us about Dad," Mario said, tucking his head against his mother's shoulder.

Incoranata smiled fondly. "I remember when your father and I were holding hands and walked from his family's home to my family's home. I turned around and noticed we were being watched by each of our families. They would follow us where ever we went. They were never more than fifty feet away from us. That is how it was in the old days, when your father and I were growing up."

Maria tugged on Incoranata's arm. "Ma, are the stories true, the ones Daddy use to tell us when we were little kids sitting on his lap?"

"Yes, most of them. Sometimes he exaggerated."

"I thought so," Mario grumbled. "I didn't believe *everything* Daddy told us. I'm not stupid."

"Yes you are," Maria taunted, leaning up to sneer at her brother.

"No, I'm not."

"Yes, you are!"

"No, I'm not!"

"That's enough, stop!" Vinnie snapped. "Calm down. Let's say a prayer to Mary, the Blessed Mother, to watch over our father and protect our family."

They prayed and soon fell asleep. They awoke the next morning, showered, and got dressed before sitting down to breakfast in their new home.

After breakfast, the doorbell rang. Incoranata opened the door to find a strange man standing there. He was short and stocky, with a pudgy face and a receding hairline.

"Let me introduce myself," he said. "I am Frankie Manzini, and I am employed by Salvatore Marenzano."

"What do your friends call you?" Incoranata asked, her hand still on the door.

"My friends call me Frankie *the Cat* Manzini."

"How did you get that name?" Incoranata asked, smirking.

"It is very simple, I go to people's houses when I know they are not home."

"I see, kind of like a cat burglar." She nodded. "Are you limited to just houses?"

"No, I do jewelry stores also."

"That's good to know." She chuckled. "So, why are you here?"

"I am supposed to take you and your children to register for school. Afterward, I will bring you to the mall to shop for some new clothes."

"That sounds wonderful. Let me get the children ready. We'll only be a few moments. Come on inside."

"Thank you." The Cat stepped into the house, and Incoranata closed the door after him.

The next day, Frankie drove Vinnie to the boxing gym. Vinnie was excited to box, but wary about being around Marenzano. The man worried him, but he had to keep that to himself.

"Are you looking forward to going to school?" Frankie asked.

"I am always interested in furthering my education," Vinnie replied distractedly, his mind still flashing back to the ring on Marenzano's finger. He watched as city life flashed by—people walking along the streets, some kids playing basketball in a small park, a woman scolding her children in front of a convenience store. This place was so different from home.

"What education are you most interested in?" Frankie asked.

Deciding to lighten the conversation, Vinnie proclaimed, "Women!"

Both of them laughed as they arrived at the gym. "Let me show you around and introduce you to the right people."

Once they'd explored the place, Vinnie was so impressed he'd almost forgotten his worries. "The boxing gym is so huge, like a picture I saw of Madison Square Garden. I've never seen eight boxing rings under one roof," he gushed. "The locker rooms are big and don't even smell. The urinals don't have piss piled up to the brim, like other gyms. People really flush the toilets and urinals around here!"

"If that's what you're impressed with, I'm worried about you, kid." Frankie handed him his gym bag, a donation from the Don. "Everything you need is right here. So, put on your new gym clothes and start working out. See that old black man with the white hair? His name is Whitey. He is going to be your trainer."

"What is his real name?"

"I'll let Whitey tell you. Now, go in the locker room and change. Marenzano will be here soon."

Vinnie did as he was told, and began hitting the heavy bag. Then he went to the speed bag. The workout centered him, bringing his mind back into the zone where he was most comfortable, where his thinking was clearest.

He allowed his thoughts to dissipate as sweat beaded on his body. He let everything go.

This is exactly what I needed.

Maybe his mother was right. Maybe they would be okay, after all.

Marenzano watched Vinnie from his loft over the gym, where he could observe everything that went on below. Whitey stood beside him, studying each move Vinnie made.

"What do we have here?" Marenzano eyed Whitey. The old man cocked his head and squinted, wrinkles crawling across his leathery face.

Whitey turned and looked at the Don. "*What do we have here?* I'll tell you what we have here. We have a damn champion on our hands. That's what we have, providing you keep him away from certain aspects of your business. Vinnie hits like a mule and he's faster than a jack rabbit."

"Frankie told me Vinnie has women on the brain," Marenzano said, ignoring Whitey's comment about his business.

"You know women and boxing don't mix," Whitey said coolly.

Marenzano patted Whitey's shoulder in a reassuring manner. "Everything's under control. Don't you worry. I'm gonna go talk to our *damn champion*."

Marenzano went downstairs and greeted Vinnie by putting his arm around him. "Vinnie, follow me to my office." As they headed up to the loft, he continued, "I watched you for about an hour while you worked out. You have a great boxing future ahead of you. Whitey agrees with me." Marenzano scrutinized Vinnie's attentive expression as they stepped into the office and shut the door behind them. "I am going to buy you your own car. This way you can drive yourself to school, the gym, and run errands for your family. Besides, you need a car to take out the pretty girls. You know what else I am going to do for you this weekend? I am going to take you to a couple of night clubs and introduce you to some hot girls who work for me."

"Don Marenzano, I'm not twenty-one yet!"

Marenzano shrugged his big shoulders. "Yeah, but the Boston license I'm getting for you will show your age as twenty-one."

"Aren't the girls over twenty-one?" Vinnie seemed skeptical.

"Not exactly. Some of the girls have the same type of identification you will have. After the night clubs, I will bring you to one of my gambling establishments to teach you how to operate one. You'll need to earn some extra money to take all those girls out, right?"

Frankie stepped into the office and folded his hands in front of his bulky frame.

"Frankie," Marenzano began, clapping Vinnie on the back, "Take this young man home so he can get a good night's sleep."

"Thank you, Don Marenzano, for everything!" Vinnie hugged the Don excitedly and kissed him on the cheek. Marenzano hugged him back, laughing.

"Sure, kid, sure. See you later."

Vinnie headed out with Frankie, and went home.

CHAPTER 7

MARENZANO'S PROMISES

When Vinnie rushed into the house, he told his mother about Marenzano's promises—the car, the hot girls, and the job at the casino.

He wanted to believe there was more to Marenzano than he'd seen at the restaurant. Maybe he didn't have an alliance with the devil, maybe it was just for show. He told himself that, but he wasn't sure he believed it. Boxing was important to him, and Marenzano was paving the way; he had to remind himself of that fact.

"What do you think, Mama?" Vinnie asked excitedly, sensing she would disapprove.

Incoranata folded her arms over her chest and frowned. "I think you need to go slow with this Marenzano guy. I am not one hundred percent convinced that he can be trusted, and I think you feel the same way. You're my baby and I don't want anything to happen to you."

"Ma, I'm going to be eighteen in a few weeks," Vinnie said, rolling his eyes.

"Go slow, anyway, Vinnie. For me, please." She embraced him, holding him close, and he relented.

"I'll be careful, Ma. I promise."

"Good boy. Go to bed now. Get some rest."

"Yes, Ma."

The next morning, Vinnie went to school, then headed to Marenzano's gym as soon as the last bell rang. When he arrived, he gasped when he saw a brand new Cadillac Escalade, the black paint job shining, parked in front.

Is that mine?

For a moment, the memory of Marenzano's ring flashed across his mind. His mother's words of the previous night returned to him, and he thought of the Blessed Virgin Mary. No one had ever given him a car before. He wondered if Marenzano would expect anything of him in return.

Setting these thoughts aside, he went in and headed to the locker room to change into his workout clothes. He began by skipping rope, but was soon interrupted abruptly by Whitey.

"Stand up straight and look right into the camera!" There was a flash.

After the picture was taken, Whitey snapped, "Go back to work."

"But what was that—"

"Back to your workout, Vinnie," Whitey retorted as he turned his back and walked away.

After skipping rope and punching the heavy bag, Whitey yelled out, "Get up in the ring. I have someone that wants to spar with you. His name is Jackie."

Vinnie spotted the man as he walked near them both; Jackie was lean and muscular. By his build, Vinnie guessed he was quick. *Hopefully not quicker than I am.*

"Do you want me to go easy on this kid, Whitey?" Jackie asked.

"No, I want you to let into him like you were fighting Sugar Ray Leonard for the title."

"Okay, boss, it's his funeral."

Whitey snickered at the comment. The bell rang and they started fighting. Jackie began by whaling lefts and rights at Vinnie, but Vinnie evaded him by bobbing in and out so fast with his footwork, that Jackie had a hard time landing blows to Vinnie's head. At the end of the third round sparring match, it was obvious Jackie was exhausted, with blood dripping from his nose.

Vinnie was unscathed and not even out of breath.

Jackie sneered at Whitey as he wiped the blood from his face. "You have a damn champion on your hands."

"Don't you think I fucking know that, you dumb ass? Why the hell do you think I put him in there? Get yourself in the locker room and take a good look at your puss in the mirror. It looks like Sugar Ray did a number on your face. See Bobby and he will patch you up. Take a few days off to recover, then I want to see your ass back in here." As Jackie wandered off, Whitey yelled out to Vinnie. "Come here! I have your new driver's license and the keys to your new Escalade parked in front of the gym."

Vinnie realized why Whitey had taken a photo of him earlier. He'd learned to drive in Sicily, and before Whitey let him go, he reminded him that driving in America might be a bit different. He told him to be careful, and pay close attention to all road signs. This would be a new adventure for him, and he was liable to become overexcited. Vinnie listened intently and assured his trainer that he would be careful. Without further conversation, he grabbed the key, and headed outside.

He found Marenzano standing in front of the Escalade.

"Thank you, thank you, Don Marenzano! You are a man of your word."

Marenzano leaned in and placed a firm hand on Vinnie's shoulder. Vinnie caught a glimpse of the ring, and felt his heart rise into his throat. "I always keep my word, Vinnie, but don't you ever try to fuck me. No one fucks Salvatore Marenzano and lives to talk about it. *Capisce*, Vinnie?"

"*Capisce*, Don Marenzano."

"Now go and have yourself a good time, but get in early. Remember what I said."

"Yes, Don."

As he climbed into the driver's seat, Vinnie thought again about his mother. She was not convinced Marenzano could be trusted, and deep down, Vinnie wasn't sure either. The devil ring popped into his mind from time to time, but he shoved it away with thoughts of the Blessed Virgin Mary. He reminded himself to just enjoy his new life, and do his best. As long as he did his best, Marenzano would have no reason to be angry with him. *Right?*

Vinnie sped off and decided to take a little tour of downtown Boston in his new SUV, with the windows down and radio blasting. After a short drive, Vinnie arrived home and showed off his new Escalade to his mother, brother, and sister, then drove them around the neighborhood. Afterward, Vinnie took them home to eat dinner, relax, and retire for the evening.

The following morning, Vinnie took Mario and Maria to school, then continued on to high school. He felt like a big shot in his new Escalade.

After leaving school, he offered to take three of his classmates—beautiful girls—to watch him work out at the gym. First, he needed to pick up Mario and Maria and drive them home. Afterward, he and the girls headed to the gym, laughing and having a great time. Vinnie walked in with the girls on either side of him—Tara, a platinum blonde in tight jeans and a sweater, the gorgeous auburn-haired Jenny from his English class, and raven-haired Cheryl, whom he'd met during lunch hour.

All the guys stopped what they were doing, their jaws dropping, to gaze upon the girls.

Vinnie changed quickly in the locker room and began his training. When he was finished, Vinnie introduced them to Whitey, as well as Bobby, another trainer.

Whitey eyed them all with a degree of discontent. "You know, I don't usually like girls in the gym, because they distract the fighters. But since you're friends of Vinnie's, you're welcome anytime."

Bobby puffed up his chest and grinned. "Yeah, the next time you come, I'll show you how to wrap a boxer's hands."

Tara tossed back her mane of curly hair. "Sure, Bobby, that'll be cool!"

Vinnie headed to the locker room to shower. When he was done, he said goodbye to Whitey and Bobby.

Vinnie turned to the girls, who were giggling amongst themselves. "How'd you like to get something to eat?"

"Yes, I'm starving, where should we eat?" Jenny asked.

"How would you like to have authentic Italian food?"

"Yeah, sure!" All the girls nodded excitedly.

"Great, I'll take you to my house. My mother is the best cook in the universe," Vinnie bragged.

At the house, Vinnie introduced his new friends to his mother. They all had a good time and enjoyed his mother's delicious dinner. After taking the girls home, Vinnie went to sleep that night with a full stomach, and rested well.

The next day at the gym, Vinnie finished his workout. Just as he was about to walk off to the locker room, Marenzano called to him.

"Vinnie, come on upstairs a minute, I've got something for you!"

Once they reached his office, Marenzano pulled two new suits from the closet. "These are for you, Vinnie. Remember, it's Friday, and you're going out with me and some of the guys. No man that works for me and parties with me is going to wear a suit that costs less than a thousand. You need to look good when you are with Salvatore Marenzano!"

Shortly thereafter, they both climbed in the limo along with some of his crew. They decided to eat somewhere else that night, instead of Marenzano's Italian Restaurant, and chose Anthony's Pier Four. When they finished eating, their next stop was one of Marenzano's nightclubs in Kenmore Square, near Fenway Park in Boston.

Afterward, it was off to Landsdown Street to another one of Marenzano's nightclubs. It was getting late, but Marenzano waved a hand and winked conspiratorially.

"One more place, Vinnie."

Vinnie was growing nervous as the limo brought them into a seedier part of town, and they turned a corner into a dark alley. Heading down the alley, they parked in between a couple of abandoned buildings. He remembered his mother's warning about Marenzano, but he promised himself he would get through this night the best he could—without disappointing the Don.

"Everybody out," Marenzano announced.

Dutifully, Vinnie climbed out of the limo and into the dark. After standing there for ten minutes or so, he was growing increasingly uncomfortable, unsure of what would happen next.

The sound of a deep grumbling engine came from the other side of the wide alley, and bright headlights blinded Vinnie. A tractor trailer pulled up and cut the lights, making him blink to readjust his eyes. The back door of the tractor trailer opened and a ramp was extended.

Vinnie was expecting the worst. Men with guns. The end of his life at only seventeen. Joining Dominick on the other side. His mother sobbing at his funeral.

When the inside of the truck lit up, and he saw what was really going on, Vinnie laughed in relief and slapped his thigh.

"It's a casino on wheels!" he gasped.

Marenzano clapped him on the back. "Yes, Vinnie, it's a real traveling crap game." The Don eyed him with suspicion, obviously picking up on Vinnie's unrest. "What's a matter, did you think you were gonna get wacked?" All the men laughed, and Marenzano slipped five one-hundred dollar bills into Vinnie's palm. "Go ahead, take a shot and try your luck."

"Okay, I'm going to place this on the black at the roulette table," Vinnie declared with complete certainty.

"Why are you doing that?"

"The color of the new Escalade you gave me is black," Vinnie explained. The wheel spun and Vinnie yelled out, "Come on, *black!*"

The ball landed on the black and he doubled his money. Exuberant, Vinnie jumped up and down. Marenzano stopped him before he could get carried away.

"Okay, now we can go home," the Don said.

"But we just got here," Vinnie breathed, aghast.

"Kid, what you've got is beginner's luck. Don't worry, Vinnie, one day soon, you will be running one of these floating casinos. I brought you here so you could see what it was like. I'd like you to manage one." He put his arm around Vinnie in an almost fatherly gesture as he led him back to the limo. "What do you think?"

"It's amazing!" Vinnie exclaimed.

Marenzano laughed loudly. "Glad you like it, kid."

It was late in the night when the limo dropped Vinnie off in front of the gym where his SUV was parked. Until that point, he hadn't realized how tired he was. Climbing behind the wheel, he turned the key in the ignition, and drove home.

CHAPTER 8

HUMAN DISPOSAL

Vinnie showed up at the gym the following day around four o'clock. As he headed toward the locker room, Whitey approached him.

"Marenzano wants to see you upstairs in his office before you change."

"Okay, thanks, Whitey!"

When Vinnie opened the door to Marenzano's office, the Don was on the phone.

"Don't worry about it," Marenzano was saying into the receiver. "I will send three of my guys over right away." He hung up and turned to Vinnie. "I want you to skip the gym today and do me a favor. I want you to go to Benidito's Disposal Company with Frankie. It seems Mr. Benidito has suddenly got a case of amnesia. He owes me this month's payment of thirty-five hundred dollars plus the juice."

"What do you want me to do, Don Marenzano?"

"Forget about it, Frankie will show you everything when you get there."

Vinnie did as he was told and left the gym with Frankie, despite his discomfort with the situation. In the back of his mind, he questioned Marenzano's intentions, but he knew better than to argue. After all, no one ever crossed the Don.

They headed to Benidito's Disposal Company in Rocksbury. Vinnie didn't know what to expect. Upon entering the main office, he jumped back when Mr. Benidito dashed under the counter to reach for a shotgun. He watched as everything unfolded before him; Frankie was too quick to the draw, and before Benidito realized what was happening, he'd gotten the drop on him with a 357 magnum pointed right between his eyes.

"Vinnie, take his shotgun," Frankie ordered.

His heart pounding, Vinnie jumped forward and grabbed the shotgun, then aimed it at Mr. Benidito. He was impressed with the steadiness of his own hands, and the calm way he handled himself.

"I am going to give you one last chance to tell me where the thirty-five hundred dollars, plus the juice, you owe Marenzano is located. If you don't, you and your disposal company are history."

Vinnie leaned over to Frankie and whispered, "What do you mean by that?"

Unlike Vinnie, Frankie didn't bother to keep his voice down. "I mean, Vinnie, I am going to blow this mother fucker's head off from here to Chelsea."

"Oh, I see," Vinnie muttered, trying to hide his apprehensiveness.

"Take it, take it all, just don't kill me!" Mr. Benidito begged, his hands in the air. "The money is in the safe, I'll give you the combination."

When the safe was opened, Frankie ordered Vinnie to put all the money in a bag, over fifteen thousand dollars. Mr. Benidito was trembling where he stood, his face flushed.

Frankie leaned in close to him. "The next time you owe us money, you better pay on time. You might not be so lucky in the future."

Frankie made a quick phone call to Marenzano, listening closely to the Don's new instructions. They were to leave Benidito with something to remember. Frankie handed his 357 magnum and the shotgun to Vinnie and told him to put them down on the table behind him. He ordered Vinnie to remove his coat and place it on the table also. Frankie came up behind Benidito and put him in a full nelson.

"Vinnie, Marenzano wants you to get a workout before you return to his office, since you had to skip the gym today," Frankie explained. "He wants you to make believe Mr. Benidito is a heavy bag, like the one in his gym. Start now, I am timing you." In Frankie's grasp, Benidito whimpered and begged. "Get your workout on Benidito's face and body."

Vinnie felt uncomfortable, but he didn't want to admit it. The bottom line was that he couldn't defy Marenzano; his life was at stake if he dared to refuse. So, he began striking him reluctantly.

"Stop fucking around, you are hitting him like a little girl," Frankie snapped. "Hit the Benidito bag the same way you do it at the gym."

Knowing he had no choice, Vinnie started striking Benidito, hitting him harder with continuous blows to the face and body.

After a little while, Frankie said, "Stop, that's enough." He dropped Mr. Benidito to the floor, and the bloodied, bruised victim moaned and groaned where he lay. Vinnie grabbed the money and his coat while Frankie got the guns. They departed swiftly and headed back to Marenzano's office.

Vinnie opened the bag of money on top of his desk. Marenzano handed a stack of hundred dollar bills to Frankie and Vinnie.

"There's twenty-five hundred dollars apiece for you guys."

"Thank you, Don Marenzano," both men answered simultaneously.

"The two of you look like hell, as if you were in a blood bath. Now go home, shower and change, be back at seven o'clock tonight. After all, I need to show my appreciation by taking you both out to a good Italian restaurant. Then, off to one of my gentlemen's clubs. From the look of you guys, I think you both need to get laid."

"I'm up for that boss," Frankie said, grinning.

"Not too sure about that, Frankie." Marenzano cackled. "Last time I set you up with one of the broads from my club, she told me you couldn't get it up."

"Maybe he needs testosterone hormone shots," Vinnie suggested. Frankie grumbled to himself while Vinnie and the Don laughed heartily at his expense.

When Marenzano was alone, he put the rest of the cash in the safe and locked it. He heard someone coming up the stairs, and then a knock at the door. Without delay Marenzano grabbed his gun and cocked it.

"Who's there?"

"It's me, Whitey."

"Come in." He kept his gun cocked, even after Whitey had stepped into the room. The old man didn't flinch.

"What's a matter boss, why do you have your gun pointed at me?"

"Forget about it, you can't trust anyone these days."

Whitey nodded and shut the door behind him. "Yeah, I know what you mean."

Marenzano set his gun on the desk and slumped into the leather chair behind him. "Well, what do you need, Whitey?" he asked as he folded his hands over his stomach.

"You can't be taking Vinnie out of the gym, he needs to train."

"He did train earlier today," Marenzano said, remembering the blood all over Vinnie's hands.

"What do you mean?" Whitey narrowed his eyes.

"Instead of the heavy bag, he worked out on Mr. Benidito."

"Why do you get this kid involved with this thing of yours?" Whitey snapped.

"This thing of mine is my fucking business, not yours." Marenzano rose from his chair and slammed a fist on his desk. "You are out of line, and if you stick your nose where it doesn't belong, *you* can end up like Benidito. Now fuck off!"

Whitey shook his head in disgust and went off down the stairs, an old man who wasn't afraid to speak his mind, even to the Don. Marenzano had to admire him for that much.

The Don waited patiently for Frankie and Vinnie to return. Once they were back, he told Frankie to get the limo while he spoke to Vinnie.

"After dinner we are taking a ride to Providence, Rhode Island. We are going to a strip club owned by a friend of mine. You are going to enjoy this place, but first let's *mangiare*. I'm starving."

"I'm starving, too," Vinnie said.

Frankie shouted from the bottom of the stairs, "The limo is ready, boss!"

They headed downstairs and Marenzano said, "Frankie, take us to the new Italian restaurant called *La Famiglia*."

"Yes, boss!"

During dinner, Vinnie asked, "Who owns this restaurant?"

"I do," Marenzano said proudly. "What do you think of the name?"

"One thing for sure, I know you picked it out," Vinnie said, chuckling. "Let me pick up the meal tonight, in appreciation of everything you have done for me."

"Forget about it," Marenzano said, waving his hand. "None of my men pay when they eat at my restaurants. You are kind of tax exempt, if you get what I mean."

"Yeah, Don Marenzano, I understand, kind of like the IRS."

"Vinnie, do you know what FBI stands for?"

"Yes, the Federal Bureau of Investigation."

"No, I'll tell you what it stands for, *Forever Bothering Italians*." Marenzano nodded toward the other side of the dimly lit room as tasteful music floated through the air. "Vinnie, see those three guys sitting at that table with the cheap polyester suits and preppy haircuts? That's the FBI. Those fucking pieces of shit. They have the nerve to come in here to eat my good Italian food, and tomorrow they will be back arresting some of my crew." He leaned in toward Vinnie and Frankie. "I want you to meet my new cook, Alberto." Alberto had emerged from the kitchen at Marenzano's request, and greeted the men. "Did you take care of my three special guests at that table?" Marenzano asked.

"Don't worry, boss, I took care of them." The corner of Alberto's mouth quirked upward in amusement. "I took really good care of them."

"Alberto, tell my friends exactly what you did for our three guests."

"First, see the guy with the gray suit eating veal parmesan? I have a sinus infection, so I spit up some green *lugers* right into his dish."

Marenzano grinned. "I hope you mixed it up real good." Everyone laughed.

Alberto turned to Vinnie. "Notice the guy with the blue suit."

"Yeah?"

"Well, my bus boy, Sonny, discovered this morning he has the clap." Alberto snickered. "We shared the clap with the guy in the blue suit when we grated on his parmesan cheese."

They broke out in laughter again.

"What did you do with the guy wearing the tan suit?" Frankie wondered.

"We gave him something quite special. My other bus boy, Ralphy, called in sick today. He has diarrhea. He was kind enough to send us a sample, so use your imagination."

Marenzano shook his head. "It's a good thing we are finished eating. Fuck the FEDS, let's go!"

Frankie, Vinnie, and Salvatore traveled to Providence, Rhode Island, to Angels Gentleman's Club. While inside the club, Marenzano ordered champagne for their table.

He sent over a stripper named Silver Lace and she started giving Vinnie a lap dance. At twenty-one, she had luscious curves and generous cleavage. She took Vinnie by the hand and brought him to one of the private booths, stripping down totally nude. Vinnie pulled out some cash to tip her and she shook her head.

"Your money is not good here," she whispered while grinding her pussy against him. "Especially for one of Marenzano's soldiers. Where do you live, Vinnie?"

"With my family in Boston," Vinnie said. His gaze roamed her body; he wanted her, but he knew not to touch.

She smirked, seeming to notice the hunger in his eyes.

"Next Saturday is my night off." She handed him a piece of paper, as if she'd long since planned to invite him over. "This is my phone number and address. You're taking me out, so pick me up at six o'clock at my place. Maybe, if you are good to me, I'll let you stay the night."

After leaving the club, Salvatore told Frankie to drive them back to the gym. When they arrived, he told Vinnie to meet him in the gym the next day at twelve o'clock.

"I am taking you to Suffolk Downs. One of my horses will be running in the first race," Marenzano boasted.

"What's the horse's name?"

"The horse's name is Pasta Fazool."

"Go figure," Vinnie said, laughing.

CHAPTER 9

PHOTO FINISH

On race day, Vinnie showed up at the gym to work out at nine in the morning. Afterward, he showered and got something to eat, then returned to the gym. When he walked in, Whitey caught his eye and waved to him.

"Come here, I want to speak to you." Whitey ushered him to a corner and leaned close, his hand on Vinnie's shoulder. "I know you think Marenzano is a great guy." Whitey glanced around quickly to make sure they weren't being overheard. "I am going to tell you a short story about him and you can be the judge."

He hesitated, and Vinnie frowned. "Well? What is it?" He didn't want to tell Whitey about his uncertainties; he wasn't sure he could formulate it into words. He only knew the worry that niggled at the back of his mind.

"It is not a story I would tell just anyone, but you need to know. Just prepare yourself."

"Okay, I'm listening."

Whitey kept his hand on Vinnie's shoulder as if to steady him—just in case the story hit him hard. "Before you arrived in Boston, Marenzano's mother died. After she died, he tried to take the rings from her fingers, but they were so swollen he couldn't get them off. So, he took a meat cleaver and thought nothing of chopping her fingers off right in the basement of the funeral home."

Vinnie gaped. "*What?*" he hissed, glancing about. They were still alone.

"Even after he chopped off her fingers, one ring was stuck on the knuckle of her middle finger. I'm not kidding, Vinnie." He shook his head, cringing in revulsion. "He put it in his mouth and started chewing down to the bone to remove the ring, then placed them in his pocket. The mortician saw everything, and he wanted to know what he should do about the chopped off fingers. Marenzano threw several hundred dollars on his mother's body, and told him to sew her fingers back on. 'Do a good job,' he said, 'after all, you only have one mother.' That's what I heard, and it's no joke. All the truth."

Bile rose in Vinnie's stomach. He couldn't imagine doing something like that to his own mother, and he knew he would never be able to look at Marenzano's pearly white smile the same way again.

"Well," Whitey said, releasing a ragged breath. "I guess I gave you something to think about."

"I...I can't believe it," Vinnie mumbled in shock. "Thank you, Whitey. I'll watch my back." He glanced up and saw Marenzano walking in on the other side of the gym. "Here he comes. Thanks again."

"Sure, kid."

Marenzano crossed the gym, beckoning to Vinnie. "Let's go. Frankie is waiting for us in the limo. Hurry, I don't want to miss the double."

Vinnie and Whitey exchanged a glance before the old man walked away, leaving Vinnie with the Don. Soon enough, they arrived at Suffolk Downs just in time for the Daily Double. Marenzano, Frankie, and Vinnie waited in line to get to the window to place their bets. The entire time, Vinnie couldn't get the story Whitey had told him out of his head. The images it created in his mind were revolting, and he did his best to force them away.

Suddenly, an announcement was given. *"There is a jockey change on the ten horse in the first race. Pasta Fazool will now be ridden by Frank Amonte."*

Marenzano was growing annoyed at the long lines. Another announcement echoed around them. *"There are only three minutes to post time, get your bets in now!"*

"Don Marenzano." Vinnie coughed, covering his mouth. "How are we going to get our bets in, with only three minutes left to post?"

Marenzano narrowed his eyes. "I didn't come all this way to bet on my horse for nothing, *capisce?* Frankie, Vinnie, follow me."

Marenzano walked up to the third person in line from the window. "Do you know me?" he snapped. "Do you know who I am? Do you know what I can do to you?" The stranger trembled, nodding yes to each of his questions. "Then go to the back of the fucking line. If anyone says anything to you, just tell them you were holding my place while I went to the *bahnyoh*."

Vinnie leaned over and whispered, "Your horse is going off at forty to one. I don't think anyone is betting on him."

"Keep your fucking mouth shut and let me place my bets."

Vinnie gulped and stepped back; once again, the story Whitey had relayed came flooding back, and his stomach turned. Bile rose in his throat, but he fought it back. *Who is this man? What should I do? How can I ever trust him around my family?*

Soon, it was Marenzano's turn to bet with two minutes to post. "I want two one hundred dollar bets to win on the ten horse in the first, and two fifty dollar double wheels with the ten horse with everything in the second." Marenzano handed Vinnie and Frankie their tickets. "Now go watch the fucking race and leave me the fuck alone."

Turning back to the teller, he growled, "Now that I got that over with, maybe I'll have time to make my own bets. Give me two thousand to win, two thousand to place, and two thousand to show on the ten horse in the first race. I want two one hundred dollar exacta boxes in the first race, ten with the one, and ten with the six. Give me a two hundred and fifty dollar double wheel, ten with all. One more bet, give me a fifty dollar tri-wheel, ten one all, ten all one, ten six all, and ten all six."

"Will that be it for you, Don Marenzano?"

"Yes, here's a hundred dollar tip for you. If you're smart, you'll bet on my horse, Pasta Fazool, instead of pocketing the money. Keep it to yourself."

"Thank you, Don Marenzano."

Just then, another announcement was given. *"The horses are in the gate, and now they're off!"*

Vinnie and Frankie watched from where they stood in the crowd.

"How long is this race?" Vinnie asked, shoving his hands into his pockets and fidgeting anxiously.

"A mile and a sixteenth." Frankie pointed across the sea of people. "Look, there's Don Marenzano. Watch his face. His heart must be pounding."

Vinnie thought he saw Marenzano staring at his devil ring, his lips moving in a subtle chant. *But that's ridiculous,* Vinnie thought. *Right?*

"At the quarter turn, Pasta Fazool is running fifth out of a pack of ten."

Vinnie and Frankie screamed, "Go, Pasta Fazool, go!" Vinnie had to admit to himself that at least the race was a distraction; he didn't want to think about the horrors he'd learned about Marenzano. He wanted to enjoy this day, and he was determined to do so.

"The horses are coming to the last quarter pole. They are approaching the wire. Here comes Pasta Fazool. It's Pasta Fazool! It's Money Train! No, it's Pasta Fazool! No, It's Money Train! The horses approach the wire. The race is over!

"Ladies and Gentlemen, please hold all your tickets, it's a photo finish. The judges are now examining the photo."

Eight minutes passed and the judges had a winner. *"Wait a minute, Ladies and Gentlemen, the stewards have posted an inquiry. It seems as though the veterinarian was advised by the stewards to test both horses for any enhancing drugs. A result will be ready momentarily."*

Ten more minutes went by. Vinnie ground his teeth in anticipation.

"Under the advisement of the stewards and track veterinarian, Money Train has been disqualified. The third horse winner, number six, It's So Easy, takes second place. The one horse, Devil's Advocate, takes third place. The ten horse, Pasta Fazool, takes first place. Pasta Fazool pays eighty-two dollars to win, thirty two dollars to place, and eighteen dollars and forty cents for show. The Daily Double six hundred sixty-six. The Exacta ten and six pays three hundred and forty dollars. The trifecta pays six thousand, six hundred sixty-six dollars and six cents."

Marenzano punched the air with a fat fist, and Frankie and Vinnie shouted with glee.

"Let's go to the clubhouse, boys!" Marenzano yelled, clapping them both on the back.

Marenzano ordered champagne, lobster, caviar, and king crab. The joyous celebration helped calm their nerves, especially for Marenzano, who had appeared on edge all day. While they drank champagne, a strange man moved intently toward their table. Sensing trouble, Frankie shot up while grabbing his gun from the inside of his coat. Marenzano immediately gripped Frankie's forearm, pulling him down.

"Don't worry, this guy is a friend of mine."

"Don Marenzano, no disrespect, but you have some strange looking friends," Frankie mumbled.

"I'll second that," Vinnie said, as the thin, balding, sharply dressed man with beady eyes approached them.

Marenzano stood up to greet him, then glanced at Frankie and Vinnie. "I want you both to meet my dear friend, Mr. IRS."

"IRS?" Vinnie asked.

"Don't worry, he is not an IRS agent. He is really called a ten-percenter. He has fifty phony driver licenses, one from each state, as well as a different social security number from every state."

IRS grinned at Vinnie, baring his crooked teeth. "This is how it works. You and Frankie give me your tickets, and I cash them in at the IRS window. I take ten percent and then I duke the teller fifty bucks for each of you. I come back to your table and hand you the cash. The same thing is done for Don Marenzano. This way, nobody pays any taxes. Then, I'm happy, you're happy, the teller is happy, and the only IRS you will ever have to be concerned about is me."

The three men handed their tickets to Mr. IRS. Fifteen minutes later, he returned with their money.

"Don Marenzano, it was a pleasure to work with you again," he said, nodding. "Frankie, it was nice to meet you. I hope to see you again soon."

"I can't speak for Frankie, but you will be seeing more of me at Suffolk Downs," Vinnie added. Marenzano laughed.

"Have a good night gentlemen," Mr. IRS said, turning to leave.

"*Ciao,* baby, until next time," Marenzano said, slumping into his seat. He motioned to the waiter for the check.

The waiter stepped up to their table, shaking his head. "Don Marenzano, my manager, Mr. Bucci, informed me that your dinner is complimentary. Congratulations on your big win."

"Tell your Mr. Bucci I am very grateful." Marenzano stood up and handed the waiter three hundred dollars. "Congratulations to you."

The waiter's cheeks flushed. "Oh, thank you so much, Don Marenzano, my family will appreciate it!" The waiter pocketed the money and rushed off to the kitchen.

Marenzano wiped his hands on his napkin and tossed the napkin on the table. "Let's go home."

Back at the gym, Marenzano insisted Frankie should take the night off. "Go do what you got to do, whatever that is."

"Frankie, you have enough money to buy a thousand testosterone shots," Vinnie said, chuckling.

"Yeah, Vinnie!" Marenzano laughed. "Maybe this time he'll actually get a hard-on."

Frankie grumbled under his breath as he left the gym.

"Listen," Marenzano began, putting his arm around Vinnie, "you have a great deal of money there. Make sure you give some to your mother and save some to impress Silver Lace on Saturday night. Stash the rest somewhere in your house, where no one else can find it. Remember, don't go to the track without me, I only bet on sure things. Act smart, Vinnie, be like me and use other people's money, not yours. Now get the fuck out of here and go home."

Vinnie chuckled. "Yes, Don Marenzano. Thank you."

CHAPTER 10

MASTER OF MASTERS

On Saturday morning, Vinnie was having breakfast with his family. Incoranata, proud of her beautiful new kitchen, had kept it sparkling clean. They sat at the large oak table, which was so smooth Vinnie could almost see his reflection in the shining wood grain. He was grateful his family had a home, but his worry regarding Marenzano continued to keep him on his guard. He was always careful, just as he promised Whitey. To do anything else would surely risk his siblings, and his mother.

"What are your plans today, Vinnie?" Incoranata asked, scooping the last few crumbs off her plate.

"Why, Ma, do you need something?"

"Yes, I do. I need you to take Mario to his Jujutsu class."

"Where is it?"

"It's in Sommerville. Mario has the directions."

"What's the name of the school?"

"It is not a school, it's a Dojo," Mario shouted.

"The name of the *Dojo*—" Incoranata said, eyeing her youngest son pointedly—"is the World Academy of Self-Defense."

"What the hell does Dojo mean?" Vinnie asked sarcastically, rolling his eyes.

"Boy, Vinnie, you're stupid," Mario retorted, sticking out his tongue and showing the chewed-up eggs in his mouth.

Vinnie shook his head at his little brother's immature behavior.

"The two of you need to respect one another," Incoranata snapped, slamming her fork down on the flowered placemat. "No arguing!"

Vinnie felt his face flush as he ran his hand through his hair. He had to look after them, and be the one they could count on—especially since Dad wasn't around. "Yeah, Ma, you're right. I'm sorry, Mario." Vinnie glanced over at his little brother. "Are you finished eating?"

"Yes, I am."

"Then, let's go to the Dojo."

While they climbed out of the SUV in Sommerville, Vinnie said, "What's your teacher's name?"

"Grandmaster John Wooten," Mario said proudly.

"Where have I heard that name before?" Vinnie thought for a moment. "I think I heard Salvatore Marenzano mention this guy. Yeah, Wooten, he knows this guy. I guess the Don has plenty of respect for him. He was some kind of special forces recon guy. Marenzano told me he has more medals than he knows what to do with. I want to come in with you and meet him."

They stepped into the Dojo and Mario yelled out, "Hello, Grandmaster Wooten! This is my brother, Vinnie."

The large, muscular man approached them. He had dark brown hair and piercing blue eyes.

"It's a pleasure to meet you, Grandmaster Wooten," Vinnie said. "I have heard many good things about you."

"I have heard good things about you, too." Grandmaster Wooten had a firm handshake. "I've been told you're a talented boxer. Is that right?"

"Yes, I hope so, Grandmaster Wooten."

"Well, Vinnie, it was good to meet you. Now I have to teach my students, so sit down and enjoy my Jujutsu class if you're interested. It'll take an hour and a half."

O Soto Gari

Curious, Vinnie sat and watched intently while Grandmaster Wooten instructed his students. He easily tossed them through the air while demonstrating moves. It was clear to Vinnie he could have tied just about anyone up in knots. The big man commanded the class with authority, and everyone listened intently to his words.

Near the end of class, Vinnie raised his hand to get Grandmaster Wooten's attention.

"How do you think this Jujutsu stuff would do against a boxer like me?"

Grandmaster Wooten grinned. "Well, Vinnie, why don't you remove your coat and shoes, then step on the mat. I will be glad to show you."

The students gathered around Grandmaster Wooten and Vinnie. The Grandmaster told Vinnie to throw a series of right and left punches to his face, as fast and hard as he can.

"Start now, Vinnie," Grandmaster Wooten shouted.

Vinnie threw at least twenty shots to the Grandmaster's face, but he wasn't able to hit him, not even once.

Breathing heavily, Vinnie exclaimed, "What was that you did with your fist?"

"It is called Chinese boxing, Wing Chun Kung Fu, and JKD, which stands for *Jeet Kune Do*, the way of the intercepting fist. Now, let me show you a little of *my* style." Grandmaster Wooten raised a bushy eyebrow.

"What's that called?"

"*Woojujutsu* Jujutsu System of Systems, it means fighting without fighting. I took all the other bullshit out of all the different styles and kept the good shit. That's why my system of fighting is superior. It consists of the big ten."

"What's that?" Vinnie asked. All around him, the students listened intently.

"Kicking, punching, blocking, throws, chokes, locks, arm bars, sweeps, grappling techniques, and weapons. How to use the weapons and how to take them away."

"Oh, wow! I would like to see some of that," Vinnie said excitedly.

"Okay, Vinnie, throw some more series of punches to my face."

Before Vinnie knew it, Grandmaster Wooten had executed all ten of his principles, and Vinnie was flat on his back on the mat, in an arm bar gasping for air.

When he was able, Vinnie yelled, "That's enough!"

The class burst out laughing.

Knife Disarmament

"You're boxing is good for the ring, but when you want to learn how to defend yourself in the street, you know where to come."

Vinnie struggled to get off the mat to put his shoes and coat on. The class ended, and he thanked Grandmaster Wooten, shaking his hand with admiration.

The grandmaster turned to walk away, then called out to Vinnie over his shoulder.

"What is it Grandmaster?" Vinnie asked.

"You should choose your friends better."

"What do you mean by that?"

"One word—Marenzano. Speak to Whitey sometime, when you guys are alone. Ask him to tell you the story about me and Marenzano. A word to the wise!"

"Thank you, Grandmaster," Vinnie replied, puzzled. His concern regarding Marenzano increased, and in that moment he made a vow to keep his family safe from any dangers the Don might bring them. No matter the cost.

While Vinnie drove his brother home, he marveled about his experience, amazed he hadn't been able to hit the Grandmaster—not even with a single punch.

CHAPTER 11

LOVE IS IN THE AIR

Vinnie arrived home with Mario, and quickly prepared for his date. After he finished his shower and got dressed, he shouted out to his mother, "Ma, I'm leaving now. I have a date in Providence, Rhode Island. Don't wait up for me."

"Why?" Incoranata peered around the corner from the kitchen, eyeing her son suspiciously.

"I won't be coming home tonight, I'm staying with a friend so I don't have to drive home late."

"What's her name?" She frowned.

"Silver Lace."

His mother balked. "What kind of a name is Silver Lace? Don't tell me she's one of those dance hall girls or something."

"No, Ma. She goes to a ballet school." Once she appeared to accept the ruse, Vinnie said goodbye to his mother, and closed the door.

Marenzano sat down behind his desk and picked up the phone.

"Is Vinnie on his way to your place?" he queried, when Silver Lace answered.

"Yes, he should be here any minute."

"Remember what I told you, don't disappoint me," he said persuasively.

"I have everything under control."

"Okay, call me tomorrow and let me know what happens."

Marenzano hung up and leaned back in his chair. He looked forward to hearing her news the next day.

Vinnie stopped at a florist and picked up a dozen red roses. When she answered her door, he handed her the roses and admired her curvy figure, ample breasts, and the silky red dress that accentuated every part of her incredible body. Her dark brown hair appeared soft to the touch, and cascaded gently across her shoulders. He'd seen her naked at the strip club, but now she looked different; something about her was increasingly compelling, and he couldn't look away.

"Wow, what a dress. You look gorgeous," Vinnie breathed, whistling under his breath.

Silver Lace smiled fetchingly. "You look pretty good yourself," she said, giggling. "Where are you taking me out to eat tonight?"

"How about Federal Hill?" Vinnie hoped this would dazzle her.

"You really know how to treat a woman," she said, raising an eyebrow.

"Let's eat at *Congillies*, it has the best Italian food on the hill. Besides, it's very romantic."

In the restaurant, two men played instruments accompanying an Italian singer. The maitre d' escorted the couple to their table, and the singer walked over and sang a beautiful love song to Silver Lace called *Al di La*. They held hands under the candlelight. Vinnie realized he was quite taken by her, and he wondered where this feeling was coming from. He'd never met a girl he was so comfortable around, and he hoped this was the beginning of something special.

"Are you enjoying yourself?" he asked a while later. They'd been eating their dinner, and Vinnie took her hand again, gently caressing her fingers. She blushed, and it was the most endearing thing he'd ever seen. Her eyes were bright, beautiful—he was captivated by her.

"The food is absolutely delicious and the love songs brought tears to my eyes. Being here with you…this has been the most incredible night I have had in a long time. I've never felt this way, but it's almost as if I've known you forever." Her eyes brimmed with moisture, and he brushed a thumb across her cheek, gently wiping away a tear. "Oh, Vinnie, when you hold my hand, I get a chill running up and down my back. You make me feel like a real woman. Ever since I met you at the club, I can't stop thinking of you. And, I mean...I see a lot of men at the club. But you...you're *different*."

"I can't stop thinking of you, either." Vinnie's heartbeat quickened.

They leaned close and kissed for the first time. She was so soft, and he could taste the Italian spices on her lips. Her breath caressed his cheek. He had never wanted any girl as much as he wanted her. When they parted, Vinnie said, "You are a great kisser."

"So are you," Silver Lace whispered, not bothering to hide her arousal.

"I'd like to know your real name." He placed a gentle kiss on her bare shoulder.

"My real name is Incoranata, but I prefer to be called Mary."

Vinnie's eyes widened in surprise. "My mother's name is Incoranata!"

"I know."

"Allow me to guess...Marenzano told you." When she nodded, he intoned, "Wow," as he shook his head in disbelief. "Three women named Mary in my life."

"So, who is this other Mary?"

"It's the Blessed Virgin Mary, she's the other woman in my life. I pray to her every day."

"Oh, thank God!" Silver Lace placed her small hand over her heart. "I thought for a minute you had another girlfriend named Mary."

"No, I don't have any other girlfriends." He smiled playfully. "Just you. What would you say to going clubbing in downtown Providence? There's a new disco that just opened called Juke Box Saturday Night."

"Okay, great!" Silver Lace exclaimed.

They danced the night away, and the club closed at two in the morning. She introduced Vinnie to two other couples she knew, and they all decided to go out for breakfast. After eating, they said goodbye to her friends.

Before getting in Vinnie's SUV, Silver Lace wrapped her arms around him and kissed him long and passionately, wrapping her legs tightly around him.

She pressed her soft body against him, pushing his back against his car, then ended the kiss.

"Come on, you're staying at my place tonight," Silver Lace whispered huskily.

"Yes, let's go," Vinnie agreed, kissing her again.

When they arrived, Silver Lace wasted no time, immediately tugging at the buttons on Vinnie's shirt, then undoing the belt of his pants. Their kisses became more passionate, and deeper, before Silver Lace led Vinnie by the hand to the bathroom. The hot shower turned the bathroom steamy, and they lost themselves in the moment.

In the bedroom, Vinnie noticed the statue of the Blessed Virgin Mary on her dresser. Silver Lace caught him staring at it, her arms around him as they stood there naked.

"There seems to be more about you than you're telling me," she said softly. "What happened in Sicily, and why did you move here without your father?" She wrapped a robe around her body, and he tugged a towel around his waist, suddenly lost in thought.

"I can't talk about my father and family right now. What I can tell you is about my encounter with the Blessed Virgin Mary." He explained the details leading up to his vision. "Do you believe me?"

Instead of answering him, she walked across the room for a box of wooden matches to light a candle beneath the statue. Then she took Vinnie by the hand and they both sat down on the edge of the bed, and gazed upon the statue of Mary. All of a sudden, teardrops appeared to fall from the eyes of the Virgin Mary, slowly trickling down the front of the statue.

Vinnie and Silver Lace were mesmerized. They both stood up simultaneously to touch the teardrops, then made the sign of the cross and stepped back. They stared at one another and decided to go in the other room and get dressed. Then they embraced and held each other tightly.

"I knew you were going to be a special person to me, but nothing like this," Vinnie said, kissing her gently on the lips.

"I feel so connected to you right now," she replied. "I think our relationship will be a special one. You are a good man, Vinnie, and I know I can spend the rest of my life with you. Come in the bedroom with me. We can fall sleep together with our clothes on."

Neither felt comfortable being intimate since the Virgin Mary was with them. They laid in bed and fell asleep in each other's arms. When Vinnie and Silver Lace awoke in the morning, they showered separately and got dressed.

"Tonight, you are coming to my house and eating real homemade Italian food," Vinnie told her proudly.

"I would like that."

"There is one thing, though. I never told my mother you are a stripper. She thinks you are a ballet dancer. My mother is old-fashioned in her ways."

"I understand." She slipped her hand into his, shrugging. "I can't blame her…I mean, if she finds out and she's upset."

Vinnie frowned, nodding. "Well, we'll deal with that when it happens."

Just before leaving, they said a pray to the Virgin Mary. Time passed quickly, and they were soon driving to his home in Boston for Sunday dinner with his family.

As they pulled up into his driveway, both looked at each other and said almost simultaneously, "I think I am falling in love with you."

Warmth spread throughout Vinnie's body as he pulled her close and claimed her lips, reveling in the softness of her embrace. Her adoration was clear in the way she touched him.

They cuddled close for a long moment. Then, they held hands while walking up the stairs and into the house.

Vinnie's mother, brother, and sister greeted them as they entered.

"Ma, meet Mary." Vinnie squeezed her hand gently.

Incoranata frowned, appearing baffled. "Mary? I am confused, I thought your name was Silver…something."

"That's my nickname. You and I have the same first name, Incoranata."

"I like her already," his mother proclaimed, patting her on the arm. "What is your last name?"

"My last name is Vincente. My parents are one hundred percent Sicilian."

Mario tugged on Vinnie's coat, wanting to be introduced.

"This is my younger brother, Mario," Vinnie said reluctantly.

"You're hot, how old are you?" Mario asked boldly.

"Too old for you, my little man," Mary said, wagging a finger. Everyone laughed.

"This is my sister, Maria," Vinnie said.

"Hi, Mary, I guess there are two beautiful girls in the house now." Maria giggled.

"No, *three*. Your mother is a beautiful woman, too."

"I like her even more!" Incoranata exclaimed. "Now, follow me into the dining room for Sunday dinner."

They all sat down at the table. Vinnie's mother told him she needed his help in the kitchen.

When she'd gotten him alone, Incoranata leaned in and whispered, "Watch out for this girl."

"Why, Ma? What do you mean by that?"

"When a girl has hips and a butt like hers with no stomach and real big breasts, not fake, she's a prime candidate to get pregnant. Just don't make me a grandmother any time soon."

"Yes, Ma." Heat flooded his cheeks as he averted his gaze.

Vinnie and his mother brought the food to the dining room table. They enjoyed the big Italian feast and told stories about their lives in Sicily. After their meal, Vinnie left with Mary and took her home to Rhode Island. Outside her condo, they kissed passionately and held each other tight.

"I'll see you next weekend," he said, placing a soft kiss on her forehead.

"I'll miss you," she replied, frowning.

"Don't worry, I'll call you when I get home." He gave her another quick kiss on the cheek and stepped back to his car, waving goodbye once more from the street.

During his drive home to Boston, his cell phone rang.

"Vinnie, it's me, Silv—I mean, Mary."

"Are you okay?" Vinnie asked, worried something might have happened after he'd left.

"I'm fine, it's okay. I just…Vinnie, I've decided to quit dancing once I find another job."

"Wow, really?"

"I'm doing this for us, Vinnie. I mean…I know we haven't known each other long, but I know you're the man for me. As long as…am…am I the woman for you?" Her voice quivered as if she were worried he might turn her down.

"Yes, Mary." His heart pounded, and his whole body tingled with the recollection of her touch. "Yes, without a doubt, you're the woman for me." He thought he heard a relieved sigh on the other end of the line.

"I…I know the Virgin Mary would prefer it this way, too. I'll quit dancing. Maybe I can find another job in Boston and move there."

"That sounds fantastic," Vinnie said excitedly. "I can help you move when the time comes. Mary, I love you. Never forget that. I'm so proud of you. I just know we'll be happy together."

"I love you, too, Vinnie. Remember to call when you get home, so I know you're safe…"

CHAPTER 12

FAMILY SECRET

Marenzano anxiously called Silver Lace on Monday morning to see how her weekend with Vinnie went.

"I knew it was you, Dad," Mary said.

"How did it go last night?"

"Well, it didn't progress the way you wanted."

"What do you mean by that?"

"Dad, I think we should talk in person."

"Meet me at the gym at one o'clock to discuss this over lunch," he replied, eager to know the outcome.

When she arrived, she stepped into his office and he shut the door to ensure they wouldn't be overheard. "Before we go to lunch, tell me what happened between the two of you."

"Okay, Dad, let's sit down…and please don't say a word until I'm finished."

An hour passed by as Mary explained the details. While Marenzano listened raptly, he twisted the devil ring around his finger, a sinister expression on his face. When she wasn't looking, he slipped the ring off and placed it inside his desk.

"Now, it is your turn to talk," Mary said. "I have never known you to lie to me, but some of what you told me is hard to accept."

"Vinnie must never know you are my daughter," he said firmly. "It would destroy my marriage if the affair becomes known. I don't want to sound insensitive, but what happened between your mother and I occurred before I got married. God Bless your mother's soul. I have taken care of you for twenty-one years, and I have given you everything within my power. I am pleased you are going to stop stripping." His brow furrowed and he thought deeply for a moment, uncomfortable with their discussion about the strip club. "I admit... going to that club and seeing you there was never easy for me. Especially because we have to hide the fact we know each other. You have no idea how many times I wanted to *destroy* any man who got near you." He grimaced, clenching his fist. "As your father, it always bothered me. So, as I said, I am glad of that."

She nodded solemnly, but said nothing, her long hair slipping around her face.

"I also accept the fact you want to move to Boston, and I will set you up in an apartment in one of my buildings. I will continue to pay for your college education. I can get you a bartending job in one of my clubs in Boston." He had offered her a job in the past, but she'd insisted on making money her own way—by stripping. He would never be able to express how glad he was that she was abandoning that path. "I am going to resume supporting you for at least one year after you graduate college. Then, you are on your own. As far as Vinnie is concerned, I understand why you could not execute my wishes." He paused, then added, "I have concerns about this Blessed Virgin thing of yours."

"Dad, she is not a *thing*, she is the mother of Jesus," Mary said, an expression of displeasure on her face after hearing her father's comment.

"All right, calm down." He rolled his eyes, then shrugged in resignation. "Come, we'll finish our discussion over lunch, I'm starving."

After school, Vinnie drove to the gym and began his fierce training. Afterward, he found Whitey and pulled him aside. "Can I talk to you for a moment?"

"Yes, what's on your mind?" Whitey asked.

"When am I going to have my first pro fight?"

"Two months from now. You will have your first fight at the TD Garden Arena in Boston with Sean *the Man* Riley from Southie. Get a load of this, Vinnie. He has ten wins under his belt, no losses, nine TKOs, and one decision. Sean has a jaw like the Rock of Gibraltar."

Vinnie shook his head in awe. "Well, this guy is about to lose his first fight."

Whitey chuckled in appreciation of Vinnie's resolve. "Next Saturday is your eighteenth birthday, and Marenzano is planning a big birthday bash with your mother. I believe your girlfriend, Mary, is also involved. You're not supposed to know about it, so don't say anything. They will have my head on a platter if they knew I told you."

Vinnie wasn't interested in the party. Instead, he asked, "How do you know about Mary?"

"There isn't much that happens around here that I don't know about."

Vinnie laughed. "Whitey, I have one more question for you." Vinnie cocked his head and crossed his arms over his chest. "What is your real name?"

Whitey shrugged. "I don't know."

"I'm confused. Why wouldn't you know your real name?"

His eyes took on a distant look, and his expression became grim. "Well, a white man and woman found me in a trash receptacle when I was a baby, as they were dumping their morning garbage. Another man from the second floor of their building saw them, and ran outside when he realized what they'd found. The couple didn't want to take me because I was black, and they were worried what people would say." Whitey spoke nonchalantly, as if the story didn't bother him at all. "The man who'd seen them offered to take me instead."

"Who was he?" Vinnie asked, intrigued.

"Don Marenzano's father."

"Oh my God," Vinnie breathed.

"That's why they just call me Whitey." He shrugged.

At that moment, Marenzano and Mary walked into the gym. They both greeted Vinnie and Whitey.

"Are you finished with your training?" Mary asked, slipping her hand into his.

"Yes, I am."

"Good, let's go downtown to the cafe and have some espresso." She grinned excitedly. "I have some wonderful news to tell you."

CHAPTER 13

VINNIE'S BIRTHDAY

Saturday was a big day for him. He was eighteen now; he had become a man. As usual, he drove to the gym to work out and train. Afterward, he heard Marenzano shouting out to him. "Vinnie, are you finished with your training?"

"Yes, Don Marenzano."

"Come up to my office, there is someone I would like you to meet."

Vinnie climbed the stairs two at a time and stepped through the entryway, nodding to a tall, bulky man in a black suit. He had dark eyes and wavy black hair.

"Vinnie, this is Pauly the Prison Boy," Marenzano said, as he leaned against the front of his desk.

"Nice to meet you, Pauly."

"Same here," Pauly said, slumping into a large armchair near the window that overlooked the gym.

"Why do they call you the Prison Boy?" Vinnie wondered as he took a seat.

"I've been in and out of prison since I was a young boy." For a moment, Pauly had a faraway look on his face, as if he were thinking of all the crimes he'd committed when he was young, and how he'd arrived in that moment, in that chair, in the Don's office. It had been a long journey.

"Yes, you have been in prison more than you've been out on the street," Marenzano commented. "I think he must love it in there or somethin'. Must be the good food." The Don cackled and the two men joined him, chuckling good-naturedly. "Listen, Vinnie, I need a little favor from you. I want you to go with Pauly. I need you two to take care of something for me. Go to the Chelsea Market Place and find Barnetta's Fruit Company. Here's the address and the key to their eighteen-wheel tractor trailer. You'll see the Barnetta's Fruit Company name on the truck. It has Florida plates. You will need a pair of bolt cutters to enter the locked gate. When you locate the tractor trailer, use the key to open the back gate door of the truck. Inspect the tractor trailer to make sure it is fully loaded with fruit and then lock the truck door. Pauly, you drive the truck to my warehouse. Vinnie, tag along behind the truck in Pauly's car and make sure you're not followed. Park the car in my warehouse alongside the truck."

"Don Marenzano, what if someone spots us and writes down the plate number?" Vinnie asked worriedly.

"Forget about it! It's not a hot plate. The plate came off another car with the same make, color, and year as Pauly's car. If a cop runs the plate, it will come up legit. Okay, that's enough questions. We're wasting time. After parking the vehicles at my warehouse, shut off the lights and lock them up. Walk six blocks down to L Street and Broadway. Go in O'Toole's Tavern and have a drink." For a moment, Marenzano appeared contemplative. "No, have a few drinks, because by the time you complete the job, you'll need a few. Wait inside until one of my guys meets you there."

Anxiety twisted Vinnie's gut, but he tried not to show it. "Who are you sending to pick us up?"

"Don't worry about it, that is for me to know and for you to find out," Marenzano retorted, brandishing a fat finger at Vinnie. "Now get going."

Pauly and Vinnie arrived safely at O'Toole's Tavern, relieved the job was completed without any problems. An hour passed as they downed a few drinks. Vinnie's heart finally stopped racing, and he leaned against the bar, exhausted.

A strange man dressed in a black topcoat walked in the tavern and approached them.

"Are you Vinnie?"

"Who wants to know?" A cold sweat broke out on the back of his neck.

"My name is Patsy and that must be Pauly sitting next to you. Don Marenzano sent me to pick you guys up."

Apprehensively, reluctant to trust anyone, Vinnie and Pauly followed Patsy to his car, then noticed a man sitting in the passenger seat. They climbed into the back of the little car, and no one said a word.

Finally, Pauly cleared his throat and spoke up. "Aren't you going to introduce us to your friend. Patsy slowly turned his gaze toward the back seat and winked at Pauly.

"Excuse me for my rudeness, this is my friend Rocco."

"Good to meet you guys," Rocco said, his voice gravelly.

"Yeah, good to meet you, too," Vinnie said.

Just before the men arrived at the gym, Patsy called Marenzano. "It's me. Everything is clear on my end." Patsy listened for a moment, then said, "Right, boss."

He hung up the phone, then pulled into the alley behind the gym and cut the engine. He sat there for at least thirty seconds without uttering a word. In the dead silence of the car, Vinnie was growing nervous, and his stomach fluttered. He hid his discomfort behind his tough-looking exterior, but he couldn't help but wonder what was next.

Suddenly the phone rang, and it was Marenzano.

Vinnie leaned forward in his seat and thought he heard the hushed tone on the other line, Marenzano's order to Patsy.

"Pop goes the weasel."

Patsy flipped his phone shut and slipped it into his pocket. "Boss says we gotta wait for him until he gets here."

Again, more silence. Vinnie swallowed, then licked his dry lips. The dim light in the alley cast a sickly yellow glow on the trash cans, debris, and his own hands where they sat linked in his lap. Without warning, a loud bang resounded when the back door of the gym was kicked open and Marenzano barreled out. The light from the doorway shone on Rocco's face.

In a movement so quick Vinnie barely saw it, Pauly wrapped piano wire around Rocco's neck, ripping through his throat, cutting off the blood flow to his carotid arteries and breaking his windpipe. There was a hissing, choking sound as Rocco shook, fought for his life, and gasped his last breaths.

Marenzano walked casually over to the car, his hands wrapped around the neck of an enormous, filthy rat. Without preamble, he stuffed the rat down Rocco's mouth, and it swiftly clawed down his throat, ripping its way through his esophagus.

Then he pulled a roll of electrical tape out of his pocket to secure Rocco's mouth, capturing the rat inside him, leaving only the tail showing.

"Patsy, get Rocco outta here and dump 'im in the trunk of the car."

"What should I do with him?"

"Take this rat mother fucker to Chelsea Market and hang him by his feet right underneath the massive fucking lighted sign for Barnett's Fruit Company. Then, you and Pauly drop the car off with your buddy who runs the crime investigative clean-up team. They'll get rid of all the blood and evidence." Marenzano leaned toward the window, looking past the body, and said, "Come on, Vinnie, you did a good job. Congratulations, kid, you just assisted in your first homicide."

Vinnie's throat felt dry. A cold, clammy feeling crawled along his spine. "I...I'm confused," he said, climbing out of the car and walking over to Marenzano.

The Don patted him on the back and put his arm around his shoulder. "Forget about it! This is nothing you should worry about. Rocco's dead, everybody's happy. Anyway, it's your birthday." The two of them walked in the back door of the building and down a long hallway until they reached the gym. Inside, Vinnie was horrified, but he hid it well.

Marenzano opened the door to the gym and flipped the light switch on.

Suddenly, lights blared, and a crowd of people raised their hands and yelled, "Surprise!"

They sung *Happy Birthday* to Vinnie while the band played. There were over two hundred people there, including Vinnie's family, Mary, his friends from school, everyone from the gym, and Marenzano's crew. It was a stark contrast to the brutality he'd just witnessed, and he barely said a word as people patted him on the back, hugged him, and welcomed him into their warmth.

He was able to relax after a while, thrilled with the festivities and the vast gathering. A buffet was set up with a great assortment of delicious Italian food and drinks. Halfway through the celebration, Patsy and Pauly showed up, greeting Vinnie and wishing him a happy birthday.

"Did you take care of that thing you were supposed to do?" Vinnie asked, a drink in his hand.

Patsy nodded. "Just watch the news tomorrow morning. It'll be on every channel. I wouldn't be surprised if it makes the front page of the Herald or the Globe." Patsy and Pauly laughed, exchanging knowing glances.

Vinnie wasn't laughing. The cold sweat had returned, and he wandered through the crowd, distressed and distracted. He had seen things most guys his age only saw in the movies. He wondered how it would affect him, and he wondered why he felt so twisted up inside. He thought of the Virgin Mary, her warning, and how quickly he'd become a part of Marenzano's crew. There was no escaping that, he knew.

Vinnie picked up a bottle of Tequila and poured two shots, one for Mary and one for him. He knew she was watching him, peering at his expression as if trying to figure out what he was thinking.

"You should be happy on your birthday," she said perceptively.

"I am happy, just overwhelmed with this huge crowd," he lied. He thought for a moment, then mused, "I wish my father were here." *So I could see him on my birthday, or so I could ask for his advice?* Vinnie wasn't sure.

"He would be here if it were possible," Mary said, caressing his arm affectionately before sipping her drink. "I have a feeling you will see him soon."

"I hope you're right. I miss my father terribly."

Vinnie heard a familiar tune, and realized Mary had instructed the band to play the song they heard on their first date. *Since I Fell For You* filled his ears, and Mary embraced him, gazing into his eyes. He relaxed again, but his worrisome thoughts didn't leave his mind.

"They're playing our song, Vinnie." She led him out onto the dance floor they'd set up in the gym, and they moved to the romantic music. Soon other people joined them, and the evening's festivities were brimming with love, good cheer, and happiness.

Later on, Vinnie's mother commanded their attention. "Everyone, it's time to bring out the cake and light the candles!"

The cake was enormous and resembled a boxing ring with two fighters, one that looked like Vinnie. His mother lit the candles, and the circle of friends and family sang to Vinnie again. He made a wish and blew out the candles. Shortly after, Incoranata announced that it was time to open the presents.

He could tell she was trying to hide her tears, knowing her son was now a man. She had made her worries about Vinnie's relationship with Marenzano quite clear, knowing in her heart the Don was no good. Vinnie quaked in his shoes as he tried to enjoy himself, while images of the evening flashed back to him and the memory of Rocco's murder replayed itself in his mind. Marenzano's chilling words continually returned to him: *Congratulations, kid, you just assisted in your first homicide.*

What if someone found out?

The party ended soon after the gifts were opened. Incoranata suggested Mary leave her car at the gym and stay the night at their house. Some of Marenzano's crew helped Vinnie put the gifts in his SUV, and they all left for home.

CHAPTER 14

TRAINING FOR THE BIG FIGHT

Vinnie was at the gym training for his first professional fight. Whitey increased his vigorous training to four hours per day, even though Vinnie was still attending school. His strenuous training for the big fight began early in the morning with miles of road work, ending at the gym for a quick shower and off to school.

When classes finished, he returned to the gym to jump rope, hit the speed bag, and pulverize the heavy bag. Somehow, he managed to get good grades at school, despite his exhaustion. At the end of the day, he was in the ring with his sparring partners for several grueling rounds of fighting.

Late in the day, Whitey took Vinnie on a short trip to Harvard Stadium, where his endurance training consisted of carrying a hundred and eighty pound sand dummy on his back while running up and down the stadium stairs.

Battle at the Stadium

This intense training continued for nearly two months. In the interim, Vinnie graduated high school with honors. He had no thoughts of attending college at that time, since his mind was set on becoming the greatest boxer of all time.

Even with how busy he was, Vinnie still found time to see Mary, and they grew closer as each day passed. Three days before his first pro fight, the anxiety and anticipation was at an all-time high.

At Vinnie's house, Whitey sat with him during breakfast for a short meeting.

"Are you ready, son? Are you ready to kick his Irish ass all the way back to Ireland?" he asked.

"At least to South Boston," Vinnie replied with a grin.

"That's what I want to hear! You're a damn wrecking machine, anything that comes in your path, you destroy. Just like the naval destroyer I was on during the Vietnam war." Whitey paused, his gaze meeting Vinnie's. "You have become like a son to me, like the son I never had. This calls for a celebration. Do you have a bottle of that special Italian wine?"

"Yes, can I have a glass with you?"

"Sure you can, a small glass of wine occasionally is fine when you are in training. The wine will calm your nerves."

Vinnie's eyes lit up. "I have just the bottle of wine for us. My mother has a good vintage down in the basement. I'll go get it."

Whitey knew who was waiting in the basement, but Vinnie had no idea. He flipped the switch and walked down the creaking, dusty stairs. He took the bottle from the wine rack. As he turned to go back upstairs, his father, Vinchenzo, was standing there.

Vinnie startled, then shouted out, "Dad!" He rushed forward and the two men embraced.

"My son, it's so good to see you. I hope I didn't scare you, I wanted it to be a surprise—"

"No, it's great, I'm so excited to see you! We were so worried about you, not knowing if you were dead or alive." Vinnie couldn't suppress his tears. "The whole family was praying for you."

"This is a happy occasion, not a time to cry," Vinchenzo said, trying to console his son.

"Dad, I have someone upstairs, Whitey, my boxing trainer from the gym. Do you want him to know you're here?" Vinnie wasn't sure why, but his father appeared slightly amused.

"It's all right, I want to meet Whitey."

Vinnie and Vinchenzo climbed the steps to the kitchen where Whitey sat at the table, his hands clasped before him. When Vinchenzo looked at Whitey, both men burst out laughing.

"Wait a minute, do you know each other?" Vinnie asked, confused by their reaction.

"We got you, didn't we?" Whitey said, putting his arm around Vinchenzo. "This kid of yours, he's a damn good boxer, but pretty easy to fool!" Both men laughed again.

"Yeah, you got me good, but remember payback is a bitch," Vinnie said, snickering.

Vinchenzo gazed at his son, admiring the man he'd become, while the three of them enjoyed the wine.

"You didn't think I would miss this, did you? What kind of father would I be, if I did not show up?"

"I'm so glad you're here, Dad."

"Me too, son." Vinchenzo patted him on the shoulder. "Listen, I need a favor from you both. Whitey, I don't want you to tell anyone I am here, *especially* Marenzano. Thank you for picking me up at South Station when my train arrived."

Whitey shrugged. "No big deal. I won't tell a soul."

"Thank you." Vinchenzo turned to his son. "Vinnie, your mother, Mario, and Maria are shopping. They took the MTA subway to Boston, and they should be back soon. I want to surprise them, the same way I did with you, so don't tell them I'm here, eh?"

"I won't, Dad."

Whitey chuckled and shook his head. "It's good to see you two together. I'm leaving, got a lot of catching up to do at the gym." He patted Vinnie on the back. "See you tomorrow."

"Bye, Whitey."

"Remember, Whitey—" Vinchenzo stood from his chair, setting his empty wine glass on the table. "*Don't tell anyone*. Marenzano will find out soon enough, *capisce?*"

"*Capisce*," Whitey said, nodding.

Vinchenzo took the three wine glasses and washed them at the sink, knowing Incoranata might be suspicious if she saw them. He didn't want anything to ruin the surprise.

"Dad, I need to talk to you before Mom comes home." He eyed his father with a curious expression.

"Yeah, son?"

"Dad, straight up—are you on the lam?"

Vinchenzo put the glasses away, shaking his head. "Your father does not run from anyone or anything. You should know better than to ask me that." He turned, wiping his hands on a dish towel. "Now, I want to tell you something son. You are aware I am the Boss."

"Yes, Dad, I remember. Joe the Boss made you his successor right before he died."

"Yes, but you're not aware of everything that has been happening in Sicily. I will clue you in, there has been plenty of bloodshed among the five families, many who have died. I am lucky to be alive. None of my crew has died, but some were injured by hostile gun fire. Vinnie, I am the *Capo dei Capi* of all the five families."

"What exactly does that mean?"

"In English it means I'm the head of all five families. But there's still unrest due to renegade family members who have exiled and united, attempting to form a sixth family with a new commission. We cannot allow this to happen. We're stronger and more organized as the five families than the renegades can *ever* be." Noting Vinnie's confused expression, Vinchenzo raised a hand and added, "It will all become clear in a moment. I'll explain the rest. The only problem is the renegades are like terrorists without a headquarters. They aren't in one place long enough for us to destroy them. In time, we will break them up, but until then it's not safe for my family to return to Sicily. Understand?"

Vinnie nodded. "Yes, Dad."

"I will get word to you when that time comes." He paused. "First, Vinnie, I need to speak to you about Salvatore Marenzano. Do not interrupt until I finish. I know every move you have made with Marenzano and he has gone too far."

Vinnie gulped. "Dad—"

"Silence. Don't ask how I know. I just *do*. I am showing up at your fight and sitting next to him. I am going to give him an offer he just can't refuse.

This fucking bullshit with you and Marenzano will stop. You are *my* son. You are here to take care of our family in my absence and further your boxing career. I *do not* want my son to become a full-fledged gangster." Vinchenzo leaned in close, his gaze sharp. "*Capisce?*"

"*Capisce*, Dad!" Vinnie exclaimed, his eyes wide.

Vinchenzo knew his son well, and he had a feeling Vinnie didn't want any part of Marenzano's dealings. Which could only mean one thing: he was afraid to mention it. Fury boiled in Vinchenzo's belly at the mere thought of anyone bothering his children.

"Vinnie, do you have any questions for me?"

"No, I...I'm just very proud of you, Dad." Vinnie's eyes were downcast. He sighed heavily and leaned against the kitchen counter. "I'm relieved you're taking care of this. I have to admit, I've been so stressed out about my involvement in Marenzano's jobs. I did what he told me because...I just...I didn't know what else to do." Vinnie looked up, shrugging. "He told me no one fucks with him and lives. Dad...I know you didn't come alone."

"Smart boy," Vinchenzo said proudly. "I brought three of my best zips along with me. If I get any shit from Marenzano, he will be the first on my list. I hope for his sake he wears a diaper under his fancy pants. When I sit next to him at the fight, he is going to shit himself. Don't worry, Vinnie, my zips will be behind me. After the fight, Marenzano and I will take a little ride with my men and have a *talk*. I guarantee you, Marenzano will not be calling you to do any more of his fucking bullshit jobs." He placed a hand on Vinnie's shoulder. "Last, but not least, I would be lying to you if I said the only reason I came here was to see my family and watch my son's first pro fight."

"What's the other reason, Dad?"

"The Blessed Virgin has appeared to me. She told me to leave Sicily and go to my family. Vinnie, she said you needed me. Moments after she appeared, the fighting and the bloodshed stopped. Then, just a few days after, I was appointed *Capo die Capi*."

Vinchenzo could see his son's excitement at learning the Virgin Mary was still watching over him and his family. Suddenly, they both heard a car pull up out front.

"Dad, they're here! Quick, go down to the basement."

He was already headed in that direction. Smirking at Vinnie, he disappeared into the darkness, shutting the door behind him.

Elation pounding in his chest as he tried to appear nonchalant, Vinnie greeted his mother at the door, helping her with the groceries. Mario and Maria joked around, playing and laughing, then running into the other room. Incoranata sighed heavily as she and Vinnie lugged the packages into the kitchen and deposited them on the countertop.

"Ma, can we have some wine with dinner tonight?" Vinnie asked casually, knowing she would want to get it from the basement herself.

True to his assumption, she said, "Sure. I'll go down and get a bottle." Incoranata started toward the door in the corner. "You can start setting the table with your brother and sister."

Vinnie nodded, hiding his excitement well. He crept over to the door of the basement, listening closely. Mario and Maria had skipped into the room, jabbering amongst themselves; Vinnie shot them both a glare and told them to hush.

Within a moment, he heard his mother's footsteps. His heart pounded as he awaited the inevitable, a grin plastered across his face. Then—

"*Ahh!*" Incoranata shrieked, then shouted, "Vinchenzo!"

Mario and Maria ran over to Vinnie, unable to keep quiet.

They heard their mother's sobs as she exclaimed, "Oh, Vinchenzo, Vinchenzo, it's really you!"

CHAPTER 15

VINNIE'S FIRST PRO FIGHT

On the morning of his first professional fight, Vinnie started his day with a hearty breakfast.

"Ma, I'm going to take a long walk along the Charles River. I need to chill out before my big fight tonight."

As his mother collected the dishes, his father asked, "Would you like some company?"

"No thanks, Dad." Vinnie stood from his seat at the table. "Don't be offended, I just need some time to myself to clear my head."

"I'm not offended, I totally understand."

"Well, maybe you should take your girlfriend, Mary. She will relax you," Incoranata suggested, chuckling as she submerged the dirty dishes in soapy water at the sink.

"Oh no, oh no! Are you kidding, Ma? She will drive me crazy. I need peace and tranquility." Suddenly, Vinnie realized he shouldn't have mentioned anything in front of his little brother and sister.

"Why don't you take me and Mario?" Maria asked excitedly, bouncing in her seat. "You never take us anywhere."

"Yeah, Vinnie, you never take us anywhere," Mario whined.

Incoranata and Vinchenzo exchanged an amused glance across the room, and Vinnie frowned. After a moment, he shrugged, aware he'd been defeated. "All right, what the hell. I walked into that one. Maybe it's a good idea, I don't get to spend much time with you guys anymore. Anyway, it'll give Mom and Dad the opportunity to spend time alone together." When he saw his mother and father grinning, he rolled his eyes and added, "I don't want to know! Okay, guys, let's get in the car and drive to Boston."

"Yeah, let's go!" Maria jumped out of her seat and ran to the front door. "Come on, Mario, I'll race you to the car."

It was a gorgeous sunny day with a light breeze. Puffy clouds floated above them as they walked along the banks of the Charles River. They had fun, laughing and joking, and playing Frisbee. Afterward, Vinnie laid a blanket on the grass by the river, and they reminisced about old times in Sicily.

As Vinnie stared out over the water, glimmering under the sunlight, he recalled an old song and nudged little Maria.

"I remember hearing it a while ago. It's about the Charles River," he said.

"Can you sing it to us?" Maria asked as a group of ducks flew low and landed on the water, sending ripples toward the shore.

"I will try, but I only know some of the words. It goes like this…"

Maria and Mario joined in and they all sang the song together. After a while, Vinnie stopped singing, but the children had memorized the song and repeated it throughout the day.

"Can you open the back of your SUV?" Mario asked, tugging on his older brother's arm.

"Yes, but why?" Vinnie reclined on the blanket, turning his head to look at Mario.

"I saw two empty cans there. Maria and I want to fill the cans with the muddy water from the river."

"Why?"

"When we go home to Sicily, we want to show our friends the dirty, muddy water," Mario explained.

Vinnie still didn't understand. "What are you going to do with it after you show your friends?"

"We are going to sell the muddy water from the river."

Maria bounced up from where she'd been laying on the blanket. "We're going into business together and become rich!"

Mario rolled his eyes. "Whatever."

Vinnie climbed to his feet to retrieve the cans, and the children filled them up, chattering enthusiastically about their plans. The blanket was folded up, and they climbed into the Escalade. While Vinnie drove them home, he reflected on his decision to take his brother and sister along. It had turned out to be a great time, and had kept his mind off the fight.

Time passed quickly, and Vinnie was soon preparing for the evening. He grabbed his gear and gym bag, then kissed his mother on the cheek, and embraced his family before leaving. Realizing he'd forgotten something, he ran up the stairs to his bedroom and knelt on the floor to pray to the Virgin Mary for help and guidance.

Then he drove to the gym to meet with Marenzano, Whitey, Mark, and the rest of the crew. Everyone climbed into the limo and left for the TD Garden Arena. Upon arrival, they walked through a long winding corridor to Vinnie's locker room. There, Whitey gave Vinnie a pep talk while Mark wrapped his hands.

Don Marenzano embraced Vinnie and kissed him on the cheek. "Remember, Vinnie, there is an extra twenty-five thousand for you if you can knock this bum out in the first round."

"Oh, is that right? If I get an extra twenty-five thousand, you must be getting a great deal more."

Marenzano grinned devilishly at Vinnie and lightly smacked him on the face with a right and a left. Then he grabbed Vinnie's cheeks, and said, "Is this guy smart or what?" He released him and added, "I need to go to my seat now. Good luck and I'll see you at the end of the fight."

Vinchenzo watched as Marenzano headed to his ringside seats accompanied by two of his henchmen, who took their places on either side of him. The crowd had gathered and the air was thick with excitement and tension.

He approached slowly, stepping through the crowd. Just as he'd anticipated, Marenzano was shocked by his sudden appearance. He shot to his feet as Vinchenzo neared, and the two men locked gazes.

Vinchenzo stared into his eyes while waving two ringside tickets. He crossed the row, closing the space between them, the tickets still raised before him.

"Don Marenzano." He paused, his eyes narrowed. "Your henchmen can move to the row in front of you. I have tickets for these seats."

Marenzano said nothing as Vinchenzo's zips took their seats. One of the men sat on the other side of him, while the other zip sat just behind him. Then, Marenzano lowered on to his own seat.

Vinchenzo turned to him and leaned close to whisper. "Just listen, don't talk. Every time you talk, you put your foot in your mouth. I appreciate all you have done for my family, but what I do not appreciate is getting my son involved with your business. Like when you had my son beat that disposal guy half to death, and then he witnessed a hit by your guys. He did not tell me any of this; I have my own ways of finding out. Also, how about the hijacking of the truck. Following Vinnie's fight, you and I, plus my two zips are going back to your gym to have a sit down while your two henchmen wait outside. How dare you involve my son in such treacherous activities. Maybe, just maybe, If you do not lie to me, I might spare your life."

Vinchenzo glanced down, noticing Marenzano had peed himself. He whispered in his ear again. "How does it feel to be on the other side of the coin for a change?"

Pandemonium broke out as the fighters approached the ring. The almost electric atmosphere was thrilling; Vinnie had never been more ready or more excited for anything in his life. His heartbeat quickened as the announcer's voice boomed across the arena, and he spotted his father in the audience beside Marenzano—just as he'd promised. Vinnie couldn't contain the amused grin that spread across his face.

"Good evening ladies and gentlemen, welcome to Saturday night boxing extravaganza, fifteen rounds of professional boxing, brought to you by TD Bank Garden Arena in Boston, Massachusetts.

"I proudly present in this corner, six-foot-one, weighing in at two hundred and one pounds from Boston's North End, Vinnie Russo, the Sicilian Fighting Machine. This is his first professional fight."

The crowd went wild, chanting, "Vinnie, Vinnie, Vinnie!"

"And, in this corner, five-foot-eleven inches tall, weighing in at two hundred and five pounds from South Boston, Massachusetts, with six wins and no losses, is Sean the Man Riley!"

The crowd roared enthusiastically.

"Our referee is Gus Mareno. Now, the singing of our National Anthem."

Both fighters stood with their right hands across their chests, showing allegiance to their country and flag.

"Okay, fighters, meet with me in the center of the ring. You know the rules, no hitting behind the head, and no hits below the belt. I want a clean fight. Touch gloves and return to your corners. Wait for the bell to ring for the start of the first round and come out fighting. May God Bless you and the United States of America."

The crowd was merciless, and the arena was filled with excitement, loud cheering, and stomping of feet. The bell rang and the two boxers came out fighting.

Sean *the Man* Riley aggressively threw rapid punches to Vinnie's body, and Vinnie just stood there taking punch after punch. Then he stepped away from his opponent and lifted up his gloves, motioning to Sean.

"Can't you do better than that?" Vinnie taunted.

Without warning, Sean burst forward, pushing Vinnie into the corner against the ropes, and continued to deliver numerous punches to his head and body, while Vinnie blocked, receiving the punishment over and over.

How much could a man endure?

It was now two minutes and thirty-six seconds into the first round, with only seconds left to the bell. Vinnie still hadn't thrown a single punch to his opponent. In a flash, the bell rang and the fighters returned to their corners.

Just before Vinnie sat on his stool, he glanced at his father at ring side. Vinchenzo held up his right arm, making a fist with his thumb up. With his left hand, he showed Vinnie two fingers representing the second round. Then he turned his thumb to the down position. This was a signal for Vinnie to take Sean out in the second round.

Vinnie removed his mouthpiece, while Whitey and Mark worked on cleaning up his face and body.

"What the hell are you doing out there?" Whitey hissed. "This guy has been working you over like a piece of meat."

"Forget about it," Vinnie snapped, annoyed. "Do I look like I'm in any pain?"

"Well, you got me worried. You haven't thrown a single punch or scored any points yet. The entire round went to your opponent."

"Whitey, don't worry," Mark said. "I think I know what Vinnie is up to." He placed the mouthpiece back in Vinnie's mouth.

Vinnie grunted in Mark's ear. "He's going down now."

The bell rang and Vinnie came out like a completely different fighter, bouncing around with his gloves down by his side. He continued to taunt his opponent, which angered Sean, who quickly attempted to throw a left and right punch at Vinnie's head and body. This time, he couldn't hit him. Amazingly, two minutes into the second round, Vinnie still hadn't delivered one punch to Sean. But Sean hadn't been able to connect any punches to Vinnie either.

The crowd stopped screaming and stomping their feet for a split second and even the shouting from the fighter's corners ceased. Vinnie threw a left hook from his side, so fast and furiously that not even the judges noticed what happened. All anyone could see was Vinnie, *the Sicilian Fighting Machine*, standing directly over Sean, who was knocked out stone cold with blood trickling out of his nose and ears. Sean's mouthpiece had flown completely out of his mouth and across the ring to the lap of one of the judges.

Vinnie spat out his own mouthpiece and placed his hands over his head in triumph. An uproar broke out in the crowd, while Whitey and Mark ran into the ring to celebrate Vinnie's victory.

"We have a unanimous winner at the end of the second round by TKO, with only one incredible punch which was so fast like lightning, the judges and spectators including myself couldn't see or believe it, until we watched the instant replay in slow motion of that invisible punch landed by Vinnie the Sicilian Fighting Machine Russo."

Following the announcement, two TV anchors sat side by side discussing the fight, continuously playing back that infamous punch that put Sean *the Man* Riley in Never-Neverland.

"Maybe the referee was right, Vinnie should change his name to the Sicilian *Invisible* Fighting Machine."

The other anchorman glanced at his partner. "You know, in Sicily, the Sicilians are known for their expertise with knives."

"Yeah, they probably could stab you so fast, you won't know what hit you."

"I think you are right, he probably acquired it from his Sicilian heritage." Both men laughed.

Vinchenzo overheard the conversation and approached their booth just as they were finishing up. He leaned over and pulled the plugs from the speakers.

Before the anchormen could question him, he leaned in close and snapped, "I am one of the Sicilians you were talking about from the old country. We don't appreciate the comments you made about our heritage." He pulled a switch blade out of his pocket and flashed it in front of their eyes. "Do you get the point?" Then he tucked the weapon back in his pocket. *"Capisce?"*

After Vinchenzo's brief detour, he went to his son to congratulate him on his exceptional victory.

"I will meet you at the celebration party," he said. "First, Marenzano and I have some unfinished business."

"Is everything okay, Dad?"

"There is nothing for you to worry about, everything is under control. I will see you in a couple of hours. By the way, I heard they want to change your name to *Sicilian Invisible Fighting Machine.*"

"Yeah, Dad, I heard that, too. What do you think?"

"Well, if the shoe fits, wear it!"

Vinnie laughed, then hugged and kissed his father. Vinchenzo left his son to clean up and get dressed, then he and his two zips accompanied Marenzano and his henchmen to the boxing gym.

When they arrived, Vinchenzo ordered Marenzano's men to wait in the car.

One of Marenzano's henchman stepped up next to his boss, looking nervous. "Is this cool with you?"

"It's all right, there is no problem here," Marenzano replied, reassuring his crew.

"You guys have no choice but to wait here, *capisce?*" Vinchenzo warned.

They entered the gym and went to Marenzano's office. One of Vinchenzo's zips guarded the front door, while the other zip guarded the back door.

When they were both seated, Vinchenzo glared at Marenzano. "What the fuck were you thinking when you got my son involved in your business? You were instructed to take care of my family so they would not want for anything. You went too far, stepping over your bounds with my son's life." He paused. "This is what I expect of you: Make sure Vinnie has the best training possible. Watch over him like a hawk and *never* involve Vinnie in family business again. My son is a very special boy."

Marenzano nodded. "Yes, I agree with you, Vinnie *is* very special." He leaned forward against his desk, his brow furrowing. "Is it true about your son's visions of the Virgin Mary?"

"Yes. I also witnessed the miracle, and so did Father Anthony."

Marenzano stared at Vinchenzo in awe, while making the sign of the cross. When his hand moved over his chest, Vinchenzo saw his ring and nodded toward it.

"May I see that, Salvatore?"

Marenzano nodded and slowly pulled the devil's ring from his finger, handing it to Vinchenzo.

"You know, I used to think you and I were alike." Vinchenzo shook his head in disgust. "But after looking at your ring with the devil's face, I see how evil you really are."

"But, Vinchenzo, how could you make judgment of me entirely on my ring alone?" Marenzano asked, clearly flummoxed.

"It is not the ring itself, but what it represents. Evil breathes evil." Vinchenzo placed the ring on the desk just as Marenzano slowly opened the top drawer of his desk, attempting to reach inside.

Vinchenzo immediately pulled his gun and aimed it at Marenzano's head.

"Don't move," he growled. "Now slowly push your seat back, stand up and walk to the front of the desk." Vinchenzo stepped around to the desk drawer and sat down, the gun still pointed at Marenzano. He opened the drawer the rest of the way. To his surprise, there was no gun. Instead, he found a hammer. "What the fuck were you going to do with this? Before you answer, make fucking sure you tell me the truth or I am going to clip you between the eyes as sure as I can see you."

"Don Depasquale, with due respect, how long have we known each other?"

"Too long!"

"No, not too long, only thirty years. Did I ever fuck you once in thirty years?"

"You have never been on the chopping block until tonight!" Vinchenzo shouted.

He threw the hammer across the room and told Marenzano to pick it up. He reluctantly did as he was told. "My old friend, would you like to see what I was going to do with this hammer?" Marenzano hefted the weight of the tool in his hand.

"That depends." Vinchenzo narrowed his eyes at him, ready to fire his weapon if need be.

Marenzano said nothing. Instead, he picked up the devil ring and placed it in the middle of the desk as Vinchenzo cocked the trigger of his gun. Then he lifted the hammer over his head, bringing it straight down on the ring. Vinchenzo raised an eyebrow in surprise; he hadn't expected this.

Marenzano pounded on it until it was destroyed, then he continued to smash everything on the desk, releasing pent-up rage on everything within sight—pens, pencils, an inbox filled with paperwork, a crystal paperweight, a boxing trophy. His temper was getting out of control, so Vinchenzo shot his gun into the ceiling to get his attention. Plaster showered over them, and Marenzano stopped, sweat beading on his forehead as his chest heaved.

He dropped the hammer to the floor. The two men locked gazes.

"I guess you are telling me by your actions that you just wanted to use the hammer to destroy the ring. I can take this as the truth, *or* give you an academy award for your performance as best actor of the year," Vinchenzo said calmly.

Marenzano placed his hands on the front of his desk, Vinchenzo still seated behind it. "If you can't trust me as your friend, how can you trust me with your family?"

Vinchenzo stood up, leaning over the desk. He went and picked up the hammer, then slammed it down between Marenzano's hands and started laughing uproariously. Then he slipped his gun back in his holster, and the two men walked toward each other and embraced as friends. The sudden quiet probably made Vinchenzo's men think someone was dead.

A fist pounded on the door, and one of his zips yelled out, "Don Depasquale, Don Depasquale, are you all right?"

The door opened and Vinchenzo announced, "Yes, we're all right, just practicing anger management. Go inform Marenzano's men everything is fine and we will be out shortly."

Vinchenzo chuckled when he overheard one of his men say in Italian, "These guys are fucking crazy!"

Vinchenzo turned to Marenzano and winked. "By the way, I hear your daughter Mary is a beautiful girl."

Marenzano balked, his face pale. "How did you find out?"

"I know *everything*."

"Does Vinnie know?"

"No, he doesn't."

Marenzano breathed a sigh of relief, his shoulders slumping. "Let's keep it that way for now."

"Of course, my friend, of course."

Soon, everyone left in the limo for Vinnie's celebration party. When they arrived, Don Depasquale told both crews to go inside and eat, drink, and enjoy themselves.

"Salvatore and I will catch up with you inside." He put a hand on Marenzano's shoulder. "Before Vinnie and Mary's relationship becomes more serious, I think my son should know Mary is your daughter."

Marenzano frowned, then acquiesced. "I think you're right. Let me be the one to tell him."

Vinchenzo asked one of his men to find Vinnie and Mary. "Tell them to meet us outside in front of the house, so we can speak to them privately."

When they arrived, Marenzano introduced Mary to Vinchenzo.

"I've heard so much about you, but you're more beautiful than I'd imagined," Vinchenzo said, kissing her on both cheeks.

"Thank you," Mary said, blushing.

Marenzano cleared his throat and began. "Vinnie, there is something you should know." He paused. "Mary is my daughter."

Vinnie's eyes widened in shock, and he turned to Mary with a curious expression on his face. "Why didn't you tell me?"

Mary's eyes widened, seeming surprised her father had divulged the information. "My father didn't want me to say anything. No one knows I am Salvatore Marenzano's daughter. It needs to remain a family secret," she insisted. "My mother is not my father's wife, and if it gets out, it would destroy his marriage." She wrung her hands in distress.

Vinchenzo looked at his son and said, "Do you love Mary?"

"Yes, I love her very much," Vinnie said, gazing adoringly into her eyes.

"I am very much in love with your son." Mary smiled as she embraced Vinnie.

"Don Marenzano, maybe you will be my father-in-law someday soon," Vinnie declared, snickering.

"I couldn't ask for a better son-in-law than you, Vinnie," Marenzano said proudly, clapping him on the back.

Vinchenzo smiled, content this was all working out. When he thought back to Marenzano pissing all over himself at the boxing arena, he was surprised at how well things were coming together.

Placing his arm around his son, he intoned, "I can see the two of you really love each other. I cherish the idea of you becoming my daughter-in-law, Mary, once you finish college and Vinnie becomes Heavyweight Champion of the World." He chuckled and patted his son on the back. "Now, let's go inside and celebrate Vinnie's victory with our family and friends. Come, drink, and *mangiare!*"

CHAPTER 16

CAUGHT BY SURPRISE

Six months later, Vinnie and Mary were sitting outside a quaint café next to Boston Harbor, making their wedding plans. Time had flown by. Vinnie had become an even more talented boxer, and Mary was doing well with her schooling. Every day, their love grew, and they knew in their hearts they wanted to spend their lives together.

They held hands across the table. Mary gently caressed his fingers. "I love you," she whispered.

"I love you, too," he replied affectionately.

"I know your father wants us to wait until we're more settled before we get married, but I…" She giggled softly. "I just can't wait to marry you, Vinnie."

"Yes, your father wants us to wait, too."

"Vinnie, where would you like to get married?" She leaned her head to the side, and a gentle breeze tousled her soft brown hair.

"In my home town of Castellammare del Golfo in Sicily." He squeezed her hand, lost in the beauty of her eyes. "I would like Father Anthony to perform the ceremony."

"I think that's a great idea. I would love to see the town you grew up in, and especially the mountainside where you first saw the Virgin Mary. Is your family's house still there?"

"Yes, my father is still living there. I wish he could have seen the last three fights I won," Vinnie said wistfully.

"I know, but he will come again when the time is right."

"Yes, I know. I just miss him."

They were quiet for a while, reflecting. A waitress brought their check, and refilled their coffees. Mary sighed and leaned her chin against the palm of her hand.

"I wish I was already finished with college," she mused. "At least I've completed my second year and kept a near-perfect grade point average. When I start the new semester, I want to change my major to Sports Management." Her wide eyes sparkled. "This way I can help you in your boxing career, and maybe become your agent and manager."

Vinnie chuckled. "Why would you want to do that?"

"I can spend more time with you, and help you invest our money sensibly for future endeavors."

"Typical woman, you are saying *our* money and we are not even married yet!" Vinnie joked. Mary laughed and leaned across the table to kiss him gently on the lips. "That's why I love you," he added. "You know, I've been in Boston for over two and a half years now. I really like living here. Those Patriots are great! Aren't they?"

"Yes, but so are the Celtics, Bruins, and Red Socks," Mary reminded him. They both laughed, and Vinnie paid the check. "Let's take a walk along the harbor," she suggested, slipping her hand into his.

"Okay, that's a good idea, but first I need to put more money in the meter. I better hurry, I can see the meter maid coming down the street. Wait here, I'll be right back."

As Vinnie walked briskly toward his Escalade, a black Mercedes swung around the corner and came to a screeching halt in the middle of the street. Two windows rolled down on the passenger side, near where Vinnie was walking. Suddenly, multiple shots rang out from the black Mercedes, aimed toward the cafe. As adrenaline coursed through him, Vinnie's first thought was Mary and her safety. Ducking down, he turned and saw that she'd thrown the metal café table on its side and was hiding behind it. Knowing she was okay, Vinnie ran toward the Mercedes just as the windows went back up and the car sped off, burning rubber.

He pivoted around and ran to Mary, finding her curled up in a ball holding a large silver salad bowl over her head. Behind her, the windows to the café were shattered, and people were beginning to crawl out of hiding. A woman emerged from behind the door to the café, sobbing, and someone rushed to her, holding her steady, having noticed her arm had been grazed by a stray bullet. Sirens rang out in the air.

Vinnie lifted Mary into his arms, embracing her, trying his best to comfort her. It seemed as if they'd been firing directly at her. She trembled in his arms, sobbing and shrieking as she fisted her hands in Vinnie's coat. *Why would anyone want to hurt my Mary?*

"Why, w-why…were these hoodlums shooting at me?" she cried out. "I never did anything to anyone. Oh, Vinnie, what's going on, can…can you explain it to me?"

"Calm down, Mary, they're gone." Vinnie held her clenched in his arms as she cried hysterically. The sirens were growing closer. "Baby, I'm worried… I think this was retaliation against your father and you were the target." He rubbed her back gently, trying to soothe her.

His words only seemed to upset her further, and she sobbed uncontrollably. "My father and this…t-thing of ours…"

Her words echoed in his mind, reminding him so much of similar words his mother had spoken in the past. His heart ached, knowing his family and the woman he loved were in danger.

A realization came over him. He grabbed Mary's fists and held her, looking into her red-rimmed eyes. "I want to tell you something. What you just said to me is the same thing my mother said to my father when my brother Dominick was killed. Maybe that's why I love you so much." He looked up as patrol cars and ambulances arrived, and cops began to block off the street. "Listen, I have the plate number to give to the cops, so don't worry." Vinnie's memory was impeccable, and he'd long-since filed the information away in his mind. He kissed her gently on the lips.

"Vinnie, I don't feel well," she mumbled, slumping against him.

"Here, honey." He quickly pulled a chair over and helped her sit down. A waiter rushed over to see if they were all right.

"I think she just needs to rest. This was very scary for her," Vinnie explained.

"Yes, yes," the waiter said, nodding his head. "But…are you sure?" He leaned over Mary, peering at her. She was clutching her stomach and slipping off the chair.

Vinnie hurriedly knelt down and realized blood was trickling out from under her shirt. She'd been so hysterical, slumping over, that he hadn't noticed it until now. Terror and dread shot through him.

Please, God…no…don't let this happen…not to my Mary…

He tugged her hands away from her body and lifted the bottom of her blouse to find a wound on the perimeter of her stomach. She'd been shot.

His heartbeat quickened and panic thrummed through him. She'd been operating on pure hysterics, adrenaline. The paramedics rushed over and began working on her. Vinnie was in a haze, shoved to the side, as everything spun around him, cops rushing by, interviewing witnesses, other paramedics checking on anyone else who might have been wounded.

Meanwhile, they started an IV and took Mary's blood pressure—ninety over fifty. Vinnie's heart was in his throat.

"Your girlfriend is bleeding internally," one of the men said. "We need to get her to the hospital immediately or she could die."

"I'll come with you," Vinnie croaked, his face pale, a cold sweat working its way across his back and neck.

She was lifted onto a stretcher and quickly placed in the ambulance. Vinnie jumped in and held her hand tenderly, talking to her as the vehicle sped down the road toward the hospital.

She signaled for Vinnie to come closer. He leaned over her and she whispered, "I love you. P-please c-call my father…I…I can't feel my legs!"

One of the paramedics assured her, "Everything's going to be just fine, Miss. Hang in there."

Vinnie wanted to believe him. All he could do was pray.

The ambulance squealed to a halt at the Massachusetts General Hospital, and Mary was rushed upstairs to the operating room. Vinnie paced up and down the hall outside the entrance to the O.R., trembling, sweating, and terrified he would lose her. He called Marenzano and struggled to get each sentence out, explaining what had happened. Then he paced more, waiting to hear from the doctors.

Finally, Marenzano arrived, flanked by two henchmen. He walked up to Vinnie and embraced him, then looked him in the eye and asked how his daughter was doing. Vinnie did his best to explain her situation, and went into more detail about what happened at the café.

"I…I just can't think of anything other than…" Vinnie paused, running his hands through his hair, his scalp moist with sweat. He moved in close so no one would hear him. "I think someone's trying to get revenge on you by going after her."

"No one knows she is my daughter," Marenzano hissed, wringing his hands in agitation.

"Are you sure?" If no one knew, it might become clear soon; just by being here, Marenzano was risking unintentionally revealing his secret.

"Yes, I am sure," he whispered hoarsely. "Why would anyone want to shoot her?"

"I have the plate number. I memorized it as the car was driving away. It's a black Mercedes."

Marenzano narrowed his eyes. "Give me the number."

Vinnie told him the sequence, and Marenzano scribbled it down on a piece of paper. Then he walked to the end of the hall and handed the information to one of his henchmen.

"Find out who did this," he told him, tugging the man over to a corner of the hallway where no one but Vinnie would overhear them. "Don't kill them just yet, but tie them up and hold them in our warehouse. Don't do anything to these men until I arrive, *capisce*?"

They both watched as the henchmen departed.

After a long wait, two doctors emerged from the O.R., talking in hushed tones. They removed their masks.

"She came through the operation," one of the doctors told Vinnie.

"How is Mary?" Vinnie asked anxiously.

"She's in critical condition. I'm afraid I cannot tell you more than that."

Before Vinnie could ask why, Marenzano interrupted. "Is she going to live?"

"We cannot discuss her condition with you, only with family members."

"Do you know who I am?" Marenzano growled, leaning in so close the doctor could probably smell his breath.

The doctor frowned, not bothering to hide his irritation. "Yes, I know who you are. I read the Herald and the Globe. I've also seen you on all the TV stations in the Boston area, and I am *not* impressed."

Marenzano's temper boiled over and he reached into his holster for his gun. Vinnie quickly grabbed his arm to stop him, holding him firmly.

The doctor sneered. "If you make another move like that again, we will call security to have you removed from the hospital."

Marenzano gritted his teeth. "I'm sorry."

"Mr. Marenzano, it's better if you both wait downstairs since you are not family."

Marenzano started to turn away.

"You need to tell the doctors the truth," Vinnie implored him. Both doctors watched them curiously, confusion painted across their faces.

Marenzano tightened his fists, as if holding on to whatever restraint he had left. Infuriated, he snapped, "I *am* family!"

After a long pause, during which he seemed to be thinking it over, Marenzano finally admitted, "What I say is the truth. Mary is my daughter."

"Why does she have a different last name?" the doctor asked.

"It's none of your fucking business."

The doctor frowned. "Fine. There is nothing else we can do right now except wait and pray. If there is any change in her condition, we will let you know. Once she gets out of recovery, the nurses will bring her to the Surgical Intensive Care Unit. When she is brought to SICU, both of you will be able to see her. My advice to the two of you is to go down to our chapel and pray for her recovery."

The doctors turned and left, walking down the hall in the opposite direction.

Wordlessly, Vinnie and Marenzano took the doctor's advice. They went to the elevators, which would take them downstairs to the chapel.

CHAPTER 17

FAMILY SKELETONS

Just as Vinnie was about to step into the chapel, Marenzano placed his hand on his shoulder.

"I have a better idea," Marenzano said. "The doctors told us it will be some time before Mary gets out of recovery. Take a ride with me, and I'll show you a very special place."

They climbed into Marenzano's car and drove to East Boston, then went through the Callahan Tunnel.

"Where are we going?" Vinnie asked.

"Trust me, we are almost there," he replied. "Okay, here we are in Orient Heights."

"What's so special about this place?"

"Wait until we get to the top of this hill, and you will understand why I brought you here."

When they reached the top of the hill, Vinnie gazed upon an enormous statue of Mary the Blessed Mother. His eyes widened in awe. They parked and climbed out of the car.

"Thank you for bringing me here," Vinnie breathed.

"This is the Madonna Queen of the Universe National Shrine," Marenzano explained, his hands tucked into the pockets of his coat. "It's a replica of a statue in Rome. They were both made by Arrigo Minerbi, a Jewish-Italian sculptor, to show his gratitude to the Catholic Church for protecting him and his family from the Nazis during World War II."

"Wow." Vinnie nodded, amazed. The shrine stood upon an incredible globe.

"The shrine was built by the Don Orione Fathers in 1954." He paused as he looked up at the magnificent statue. "You know, Vinnie, originally the statue sat way on top of the pedestal. It's so tall, planes almost hit the statue. They had to take it off the original platform so they could lower the Madonna."

"Wow, I can see the Logan Airport from here," Vinnie exclaimed. The city of Boston stretched out below, and the waterfront glimmered under the light. The view was breathtaking.

"At night, the Madonna is lit and you can see her for miles around."

Vinnie and Marenzano lit candles and knelt to pray for Mary's recovery.

Hours passed. Mary was finally out of recovery and had her own room in the SICU. She was still unconscious, and she looked so helpless laying there, tubes attached to her body, an IV in her arm, oxygen being pumped into her. It was painful to see her that way, and the sight tugged at Vinnie's heart. Both men wept and took turns kissing her on the cheek and talking to her.

Vinnie spoke about how they met, all the good times they had together, and about their upcoming wedding. He reassured Mary she would be all right, and he was waiting to hold her in his arms again.

Marenzano interjected, reminiscing about the times he'd spent with Mary, from when she was a little girl and through the years until she became a beautiful young woman. He held his daughter's hand close to his chest, weeping with anger.

"What kind of a coward would do this to my beautiful little girl?"

Suddenly, his phone rang. He listened to the voice on the other end, muttered a clipped reply, and turned to Vinnie. "I am going to the warehouse to find out who these fuckers are that shot Mary. I want you to stay with her. Call me if there is any change in her condition. I'll be back soon."

Vinnie nodded and watched him depart, then sat quietly staring at Mary's closed eyes, her hand tucked into his own.

When Marenzano reached the parking garage at the hospital, four assailants with black hoods grabbed him and threw him into a van before he could fight back. He was driven to a building that appeared to be some kind of makeshift safe house, and told to sit down and shut up by one of the assailants.

Unlike when Vinchenzo had approached him, he managed not to piss himself. More than anything, he was furious. And he was too upset over Mary's predicament to worry about himself.

"You don't know who we are, but we know who you are." The man's voice was gravelly, as if he'd spent many years chain-smoking.

"Yeah?" Marenzano retorted contemptuously.

"We know the young girl who was shot is your daughter."

"How do you know that? Who the hell are you people?"

"Listen, your daughter is in great danger and you are a marked man, so yelling won't help your situation."

"What do you mean I'm a marked man?"

The man with the scratchy voice seemed to be the one who was in charge. He did all the talking.

"When you got married, you cheated on your wife and got another woman pregnant. You paid her off to keep her mouth shut. Your big mistake was thinking she would keep quiet forever. At the time you got her pregnant, she was married, but you fucked her anyway. Her husband believed Mary was his daughter until his wife revealed the truth during an argument. He beat his wife half to death. In a rage, he went to Roxbury to pay four gangbangers a large sum of money to shoot and kill you and your daughter."

"That bastard!" Marenzano shrieked. "Where is Mary's mother now?"

"She is under protective custody, receiving medical attention."

"Where is her husband?" he snapped, agitated.

"We don't know, we have our men looking for him now as we speak."

"Where are the four hired gangbangers?"

"We don't know that yet, either. Vinnie gave the cops a description of the vehicle, but he did not have the license plate number."

Vinnie had lied to the police; he'd given Marenzano the plate number, which he'd memorized. *What idiots these men are.*

"By the way, the man who put the hit out on you—do you know what this guy does for a living?" one of the men asked.

"Yeah, I have lunch with this fucking guy every fucking day and I play strip poker with him every Friday night," he quipped sarcastically.

"Don't be a wise guy, Marenzano."

"He is a made guy with the Gambino crime family," one of the other men offered.

"What is his name?"

"Jerry Vincente. Do you know him?"

Marenzano's pulse raced, but he kept his expression stoic. "Yeah, I know him."

"Do you want police protection?"

"Who the fuck are you guys, anyway?" Marenzano shouted. He blinked when sweat dripped into his eye from his forehead.

"Let's put it this way, we are *Forever Bothering Italians.*"

"I want to see your badges!" Marenzano retorted sharply.

All four men slowly removed their black hoods and flashed their badges.

"FB-fucking-I," one of the agents said. "You do understand English, don't you?"

"Not all guineas are stupid," another man said. "Is that right, Marenzano?"

"Fuck you, fuck your mother, and fuck the FBI," Marenzano growled. "I don't need you." The FBI agent in charge handed his card to Marenzano. He read the card out loud, "Special agent, James O'Shea."

The agents exchanged glances of mock amazement. "I can't believe it, this guinea can read."

"I should have known, another fucking Irish pig! Just like the one you busted a couple of years ago in Southie. He was a rat and a pig just like you."

James O'Shea shook his head. "Get this fucking guinea out of here, he makes me sick. Bring him back to his car at Mass General."

At the hospital garage, Marenzano was shoved out of the vehicle. As he dusted off his suit, one of the agents warned him to watch his back. "You know how to contact us, if you change your mind." They drove off into the night, taillights and headlights creating flashes of shadow in the dark garage.

Instead of going into the hospital, Marenzano jumped into his car and sped down the road. He dialed his cell phone.

"Plan A is not good," he said in a clipped manner. "In lieu of that, go to Zebra House. I am hot, I'll explain later. I will meet with you guys when I can. I have J. Edgar Hoover on my tail."

He hung up and headed for 95 South toward New York City, then he called a sit down with the Gambino crime family regarding his daughter's assailants.

Upon arrival in the Big Apple, Marenzano met with members of the commission. He knew Jerry Vincente was a made man, and he couldn't whack a made man without asking the commission first. The problem was, two wrongs didn't make a right. Marenzano was married when he'd had sex with Jerry's wife, and this was not tolerated.

But that was twenty-two years ago, and at that time, Jerry Vincente *hadn't* been a made man. This technicality could be argued.

Don Chico slammed his ham fist on the desk in his office. "You have a lot of fucking balls coming here by yourself, but you always had more balls than brains."

"Don Chico, with due respect, I am sure you and the rest of the commission have had adequate time to come to a decision," Marenzano began. "I would like to tell you my side of this problem."

"Not necessary," Don Chico shouted. He sat back in his chair. "Twenty-two years ago, you made a grave mistake, but it does not give Jerry Vincente the right to whack you and your daughter. Our prayers are with your daughter, Mary, for a speedy recovery. I want you to know, under no circumstances do we the commission condone this act, nor did we order this violence against you or your daughter. We sympathize with you and hereby order our commission to take care of this serious problem. Consider it done! However, you are forbidden to have any confrontation or to be seen with Jerry Vincente, and that goes for your crew, too. You must lay low, since you are very hot right now! Are you sure no one followed you here?"

"I was careful not to be followed," Marenzano assured him.

Don Chico nodded. "We are sending a van to pick up the four gangbangers you are holding hostage in your warehouse. We will drive them to the New Jersey Meadowlands. Trust me, when their bodies are found, you won't be able to recognize them. As far as Jerry Vincente is concerned, we know where he is held up. Don't worry, we will make it look like a suicide." Don Chico leaned forward over his desk. "I need one favor from you, Don Marenzano. When your boy Vinnie is ready to fight for the Heavyweight Championship, I want front row seats for everyone on this commission."

"Not a problem, I'll even throw in extra tickets for the wives," Marenzano offered.

"Fuck the wives, we get enough of their shit every night," Don Chico snapped. "Why don't you supply us with some bimbos for the weekend? I'm sure you have plenty of them at your fingertips." All the men laughed. "My guys will follow you in a van back to your warehouse in Boston to pick up the gangbangers. Now go in peace, Don Marenzano."

As he drove back to Boston, his phone rang. It was Vinnie.

"Where are you?" Vinnie asked, his voice edged with worry.

"Never mind where I am, it will be hours before I can get there. Why do you ask, is Mary all right?" For a split second, Marenzano prepared himself for the worst. When he heard Vinnie's reply, he let out a breath he hadn't realized he was holding.

"She just came out of the coma and was asking for you. I will be back around eleven tonight. Don't leave her side or allow anyone near her. She's still in danger." Vinnie paused. "By the way, there are two FEDS standing guard outside her room."

"Good!" Marenzano said, relieved. "Give Mary my love and tell her I will see her soon. Don't talk to those fucking FEDS."

"Don't worry, I know better," Vinnie assured him.

When Marenzano arrived at the warehouse, the van from New York behind him, he went inside and instructed his men to hand the gangbangers over to the Gambino crew. They tied and shackled them to the seats of the van and shoved black hoods over their heads.

Don Marenzano joked, "Have a safe trip, boys."

One of men from the New York crew leaned out the driver's side window. "They will think they're in paradise or wish they were, when we get through with them. *Buonanotte*, Don Marenzano."

"*Ciao*, baby." Marenzano watched the van drive away, then turned to his crew and thanked them. "It's time to go home to your families. I want you to stay off the phone and don't discuss any of this with anyone else in the crew. Just sit back and relax for a few days, consider it a vacation. If there is an emergency, call Vinnie, he will get in touch with me. Remember, stay off your phones."

Rico Delgado, one of the younger men on Marenzano's crew, spoke up. "What do you consider an emergency?"

"When your wife's pussy dries up, that's an emergency," Marenzano retorted sarcastically.

"Okay, okay," Rico said, chuckling. Everyone laughed, shaking their heads, but Rico appeared dumbfounded.

Marenzano stared at Rico. "KY Jelly?"

"Oh yeah, I get it, boss," Rico said, nodding.

Marenzano threw his hands in the air. "*Oh mio dio, lui e stupido*. Let me get out of here before I kill him."

He said goodnight to his crew and drove to the Mass General to see Mary. He stepped off the elevator and headed into the SICU unit. Suddenly, an alarm bell sounded off, flashing red. Doctors, nurses, and technicians scrambled and sprinted toward Mary's room. Marenzano had returned as promised, but he was shoved out of the room by one of the nurses.

"She needs to be tubed immediately!" someone shouted.

"Give me ten milligrams of epinephrine and two nitroglycerins sublingual, stat."

Marenzano listened near the door, wringing his hands, his heart in his throat, his mouth dry.

"Nurse, give me a pulse."

"Pulse is fifty. Blood pressure is ninety over sixty, and falling fast."

Marenzano covered his mouth and felt a clammy chill crawl up his spine.

"We're losing her…Hurry!"

CHAPTER 18

IT AIN'T OVER UNTIL IT'S OVER

A nurse ran down the hallway, then rushed Vinnie and Marenzano out of the SICU to the waiting room.

"What can you tell us, is she going to be okay?" Vinnie asked, his voice shaky.

"Calm down. We'll give you an update momentarily, just try to relax." She turned and headed back the way she'd come. All Vinnie and Marenzano could do was wait.

Thirty minutes later, the same nurse returned, looking relieved. "The doctors were able to revive her and the prognosis is better."

Both men breathed a sigh of relief.

"I will inform you about her condition periodically," the nurse promised. "Meanwhile, use these blankets and pillows to try to make yourselves comfortable. It will be a long night."

"Thank you," Marenzano said, accepting the bundle.

Three hours passed, and Vinnie and Marenzano were fast asleep in the waiting room. A doctor emerged and shook them both awake. Marenzano sat up, blinking, Vinnie beside him.

"I'm Doctor Joseph Tringalie. I have some news for you about Mary's condition."

They were both alert now, listening attentively.

"The good news is, we just removed the breathing tube and she is breathing fine on her own. As you know, when she was first admitted to our hospital, we removed the bullet from the side of her stomach. What you don't know is we found a second bullet wedged in her spine, located in a dangerous area. Mr. Marenzano, at this point, your daughter cannot feel her legs."

"Oh my God, can I see her now?" Marenzano stood, a cold sweat crossing his brow.

"No, she is currently being moved to the operating room. I have one of the best spine surgeons in the country being medevacked here. He is scheduled to arrive within twelve minutes."

"Doctor, please tell Mary I love her and I am praying for her."

"Yes, I will certainly tell her. I know it's been a long, frustrating night for you, but you should try to get some rest."

The doctor left the waiting area and headed for the operating room. Marenzano and Vinnie talked for a while, anxious about the outcome of Mary's operation, and eventually fell asleep, exhausted.

At eight in the morning, Marenzano awoke and went to get a cup of coffee in the cafeteria. As he trudged down the hallway, he thought of his daughter—and he thought of the Virgin Mary. Something had changed inside him, some darkness had passed. It was due to his daughter. His fear of losing her outweighed all else, and he was changing. He knew it was for the better.

In the mostly empty cafeteria, two orderlies left the room, chatting amongst themselves, having discarded a newspaper on a crumb-ridden table. Marenzano read the headline with interest.

Mafia hit man found in hotel room hanging by his neck.

The article said the police were calling it suicide.

Good, Marenzano thought. *Everything is working out perfectly. Now I just need my Mary to get better.*

He continued to read the article after fetching his coffee and stirring in the cream and sugar. A van had been found with four men inside who were chained to the seats and burned alive.

The Boston Globe featured the story of an extensive FBI probe with a link to organized crime. FBI special agent James O'Shea stated that the apparent suicide and burning of the four men could be associated with the New England crime boss, Salvatore Marenzano.

Marenzano grumbled to himself as he sipped his cup of steaming hot coffee.

He continued to read the article, which talked about his daughter and her condition. Then he flipped the paper over and saw a large photo of himself.

"Fuck," he mumbled, glancing around to make sure no one was there. "Oh my God, my wife gets the paper every morning. She'll kill me." He tucked it under his arm and headed back to the waiting room to consider his next move.

Vinnie skimmed the article, then glanced at Marenzano. "Maybe you should call the FBI and ask for protection from your wife," he joked.

Marenzano scowled, but before he could react, two doctors approached them.

One was a tall man with graying brown hair and glasses. He nodded in greeting and shook both their hands. "I'm Doctor King, and this is Doctor Roberts," he began, indicating his partner, who was stocky and balding. The other man said hello. "I have some good news for you," Dr. King continued. "The surgery was successful and we were able to remove the bullet from her spine. Mary is not out of the woods yet, though," he added when both Vinnie and Marenzano brightened. "The next twenty-four hours are critical to her recovery. Once she awakens, we will know if she regains the feeling and movement in her legs."

"Thank you both," Marenzano said. "When can we see Mary?"

"She will be in recovery for at least three to four hours before she can be moved to the SICU unit, then you can see her."

"Thanks," Vinnie said quietly.

The two men nodded and walked away.

Marenzano went to the sofa and collected his newspaper.

"Do you want to join me in the cafeteria for a bite to eat?" Vinnie asked.

"No thanks, I think I better go home and talk to my wife."

As he walked out the front door, Marenzano was met by eight men in suits flashing their FBI badges accompanied by U.S. Marshals. Special agent James O'Shea stood before them.

"We are escorting you to FBI Headquarters. There are many questions you need to answer."

Marenzano cursed under his breath, then walked between the agents as they led him to their van. O'Shea walked beside him, the sunlight glinting off his dark sunglasses.

"You have the right to remain silent, anything you say can and will be used against you in a court of law," O'Shea began, leading Marenzano into the parking lot. "You have the right to have an attorney present now and during any further questioning, and if you cannot afford an attorney, one will be appointed for you free of charge if you wish. Do you understand these rights?"

"No, I'm a guinea." Marenzano rolled his eyes. "I don't understand anything. I want my fucking lawyer before I say another word, you fucking FBI cock suckers."

O'Shea didn't say a word. He just shook his head as the other agents directed Marenzano into the van, and shut the door.

CHAPTER 19

RIGHT PLACE, WRONG TIME

The FBI Organized Crime Unit led by special agent James O'Shea and several U.S. Marshals escorted Salvatore Marenzano to the U.S. Marshal's holding center in the Federal Building. He was brought into a sparse room with a two-way mirror and handcuffed to the large table. Marenzano sat patiently waiting for access to a phone so he could call his attorney. Twenty minutes dragged by. Finally, O'Shea returned accompanied by two other agents and the United States Attorney General David Weinstein.

Mr. Weinstein was holding thick files of papers and a land phone with a long cord under his arm. He slammed the stack on the table and plugged the phone into an electrical outlet, then set the phone down hard next to the papers. Looking Marenzano straight in the eye, he tossed newspapers on the table.

"What do you know about these murders?" Weinstein snapped.

"I want my fucking lawyer," Marenzano growled. "Look what we got here, the Keystone fucking cops led by a Leprechaun and a Jew. What a fucking joke! You *are* a Jew, aren't you? The Jews killed Jesus and you want sympathy for the holocaust. You don't deserve any! You got what was coming to you for killing Jesus. Now, it's your turn. Weinstein, do you have a rebuttal?"

There was a brief period of silence as Weinstein glared at Marenzano. Then he got up from his seat and grabbed his stack of files. "This is what we get for saving your life. When I walked into this room, I had intensions of offering you a plea deal. Now you can go straight to hell! The deal is off the table. I have enough evidence in these files to put you away for five hundred years."

Marenzano leaned his head toward O'Shea. "Is this guy okay, or what? Doesn't he know Italians live forever?"

O'Shea shook his head. "You're not quite right."

"What do you mean by that?"

"It's true, Italians like *you* live forever." O'Shea leaned forward. "But not necessarily all Italians will live forever as they burn in hell."

Weinstein waved a hand in annoyance. "Let him call his lawyer. Bail is set at one million in cash. I am sure he will be out in an hour, anyway."

Once Marenzano was on the phone with his lawyer, Joseph Gandolini, he hurriedly explained his situation and where he was. "Hurry, get me the fuck out of here. These pigs make me sick." He hung up the phone and the FEDS unplugged it.

Before he was left alone in the room, Marenzano had to get the last word. As Weinstein was on his way out, the Don said smoothly, "Why don't you come to my restaurant on Hanover Street and have dinner…on me. We'll kinda make it like the Last Supper!"

Weinstein sneered. "Who's Last Supper, yours or ours?"

"I guess it's a matter of interpretation."

The door closed, and Marenzano was left alone.

An hour passed by before his attorney showed up and was ushered into the room.

"You're all set, let's get out of here!" Gandolini exclaimed. "But I want to see you in my office tomorrow afternoon at three o'clock sharp without fail."

"No problem!" Marenzano rose from his seat, more than ready to leave. "I need a lift to the Mass General where my car is still parked. Lend me your cell phone, I want one of my guys to meet us at my car."

"For what?" Gandolini raised an eyebrow curiously.

"You'll see."

Vito, one of Marenzano's crew, sped over from Prince Street in the North End to meet with him. Marenzano and his attorney arrived only a minute before him. He told Vito to sweep the car inside and out for any electronic surveillance devices.

Moments later, Vito discovered two different gadgets. The first was a tracking device that would have enabled the FEDS to follow him wherever he went. The second was a listening and recording device to intercept all conversations that took place in his car.

"Don Marenzano, after you were arrested, did the FEDS confiscate your personal belongings, including your cell phone?" Vito asked.

"Yes, they did."

"Open your car door and empty everything from your pockets…and I mean everything," Vito instructed. "Take all the contents of your pockets plus everything out of your wallet and place it on the seat of the car."

Vito swept everything. "Just as I thought. In back of your cell phone and in your wallet, I found these two chips." He went to the edge of the parking garage and threw the chips over the side. "You are clean now, but I should sweep your home as well. I'll follow you there. But before we go, I want to sweep your attorney and his car. After all, leave no stone unturned."

On the attorney's suit was a listening chip, and underneath his car, Vito found a tracking device to keep tabs on his travels.

"Okay, Don Marenzano, we can go and sweep your house now."

The attorney drove away and Marenzano and Vito left in separate cars. When they arrived, Marenzano found an envelope taped to his front door.

"It's from my wife." He stepped aside and ushered Vito in. "Go ahead and start, I'll be a second." An invisible weight sunk over his shoulders as he read the letter.

Dear Salvatore,

Your are a liar and a cheat! All these years, you have been lying to me. How could you do this to me?

I know all about Mary. I spent the entire afternoon at lunch with Mary's mother, your mistress, your goomah! She has revealed to me all the details of your affair. We are going over to the Mass General to see Mary. If you have any balls, cojones, you will meet us at the hospital. As far as you and I are concerned, we will take this up privately at home tonight. I don't want any of this brought up at the hospital in front of Mary or her mother.

I love you so much, Salvatore. How could you break the bond between us?
Love, Philamenia

Marenzano crumpled the letter up in his fist and slammed it against the side of the house. "First Mary's shot, and I'm put on Jerry Vincente's hit list. Then, I am arrested by the fucking FBI, and now this! What else is going to fucking happen?" He stomped into the house and yelled out to Vito. "I need to go to the Mass General, my wife is waiting there for me."

"Okay, boss!"

"Finish sweeping the house and I will catch up with you later."

Marenzano rushed to his car and sped to the hospital. This time, he parked on Beacon Hill and walked to the hospital to avoid the FEDS seeing his car.

On his way in through the lobby, Marenzano spotted another newspaper on the reception desk. The headline was written in large, imposing letters.

Federal Probe investigating allegations of misconduct from the FBI's Organized Crime RICO Unit, involving federal agents from Boston, Providence, and New York City.

There is evidence from the Federal Grand Jury coming down tomorrow implying collusion with members of organized crime, FBI, and other Federal agencies.

The paper had made his day.

Marenzano stepped aside to call his lawyer. When there was an answer on the other line, he didn't bother saying hello.

"Did you see tonight's special edition of the newspaper?"

"Yes, Salvatore, this is good news for you," his lawyer said, sounding pleased. "We will talk in person tomorrow at three o'clock."

"Sounds good, I'll see you then." Marenzano hung up and continued on his way.

As he approached the elevators, he saw an out of order sign hanging on the doors. Without thinking, he sauntered nonchalantly toward the stairs, swung the door open, and headed up. Footsteps echoed behind him, but he ignored them. When he reached the fifth floor, Marenzano froze.

A man shouted out, "Hey, Salvatore, long time no see." The voice echoed in the cavernous stairwell.

He turned around swiftly and eyed the bulky man behind him who wore a casual suit and heavy rings on his fingers. "Where do I know you from?"

"From my brother, Jerry Vincente, who you just killed."

"I didn't kill your brother, he committed suicide," Marenzano retorted.

"*Wrong.* However he died, the blood is on your hands. Now it's your turn to die, Marenzano!"

Despite the man's bulk, he moved quickly, and the gun was aimed at the Don before he could react. The bullet sailed through the air and hit Marenzano in the chest, then Jerry Vincente's brother tossed the gun on his victim and ran down the stairs, taking them two at a time.

A fleeting thought passed through Marenzano's mind as he strained to lift himself up, trying to reach the door to the SICU hallway.

How the fuck did he get a gun into a hospital?

He managed to pull the door open before collapsing on the floor. As he drifted into an unconscious state, alarms blasted around him. He heard the voices of the hospital staff as they ran toward him, while he lay in a pool of his own blood struggling for his life.

CHAPTER 20

CODE BLUE

Vinnie had stepped out of the waiting room when he heard the gunshot, and saw the victim being rushed down the hall. Confusion set in as he wondered how this could've happened in a hospital.

His eyes widened when he recognized the face of the man on the stretcher—Don Marenzano. He quickly rushed alongside them, shouting, "What's wrong, what happened? I'm a friend of his!"

"He's been shot, that's all we know," the doctor snapped. "Now get out of the way, we're in a hurry."

"Who the fuck shot him?"

"We found him in the hallway by the stairs," a nurse said quietly, falling back.

The doctors didn't seem willing to talk to Vinnie, regardless of the fact he and Marenzano had come in together in the first place.

A security guard stepped in front of him, gently pulling him back with a heavy hand. He escorted him to the waiting room.

"Sit down, Vinnie." The security guard pushed him onto the sofa.

"How do you know who I am?" He looked up at him, noting his dark brown hair and piercing eyes. He was perhaps a few years older than Vinnie.

"I listen to everything that goes on around here." He shrugged. "I know you're close to Salvatore Marenzano. I'm also close to him through my father, and he told me about you." He leaned forward, his eyes narrowing. "I need to tell you something right now. Get a handle on yourself and calm down, before I have to put one of my moves on you." He crossed his muscular arms over his chest. "Besides being a security guard, I am the assistant instructor under Grandmaster John Wooten. I am a fifth degree black belt in Jujutsu and a fourth degree in Judo. Twice, I have been the former National Judo Champion."

"Why are you telling me this? Am I supposed to be scared?" Vinnie growled.

"Watch your mouth or you will have a chance to find out."

Vinnie flipped off the security guard. "Fuck you, and fuck the horse you rode in on!"

There weren't many people in the waiting room, but they all watched in horror as the guard wrestled Vinnie to the ground and put him in a submission hold.

Vinnie shouted out in pain. "Let me go, let me go!"

"I want an apology first."

"Fuck you!"

The security guard cranked Vinnie's arm up, applying excruciating pain. "Fuck me, no…fuck you, Vinnie. Good thing we're in a hospital."

"Okay, okay, okay. I'm sorry!"

As soon as he'd gotten what he'd asked for, the guard let Vinnie go and helped him up off the floor. "By the way, my name is Michael." He reached out and shook Vinnie's hand while Vinnie used his other hand to massage his arm. "All I want is to find out who shot Marenzano." He spoke in hushed tones. "But keep it quiet, the cops are lurking around here and they don't want any amateur investigators on the case."

Vinnie nodded. "Right. We can start with the hallway by the stairs where he was found. How the hell did that guy sneak a gun in here, anyway?"

"They don't know. Somehow he got past the metal detectors."

Vinnie shook his head in amazement. "Damn."

"We need to hustle, the Boston police and the state police will be here any second," Michael hissed, keeping his voice down so the other people in the waiting room wouldn't overhear. "Once they arrive, we won't be able to get in there."

They rushed toward the elevators and the entrance to the stairwell Marenzano had been shot in. While exploring the steps, Vinnie waved his hand to get Michael's attention, then pointed at what he'd found on the floor. It was in the corner, obscured from view; someone passing by might not have seen it in the low light.

"That's not Marenzano's gun," Vinnie said.

"How do you know that?"

"He told me he would never own a thirty-eight because they suck." Vinnie leaned to pick it up, but Michael grabbed his arm.

"Don't touch it. You can't interfere with the evidence, it'll just complicate things. Come on, let's look some more." Continuing down the steps, they found a wallet laying in another dusty corner. "We can't touch this, either. Go to the top of the stairs to the fifth floor. Open the door and stand guard. Don't allow anyone down the stairs."

"Where are you going?"

"I'm running down to the first floor to make sure nothing else was left on the stairs." Michael sprinted down the steps, then returned a moment later to the fourth floor, where the wallet rested on the dusty step. "Vinnie, stay where you are on the fifth floor near the gun and I'll wait here by the wallet, so both of us can secure the crime scene until the police arrive."

"Okay, good idea!" They were quiet for a few minutes, and then Vinnie asked, "Hey Michael, how long have you known Grandmaster Wooten?"

"All my life."

"Really, how's that?"

"He's my father."

Vinnie raised an eyebrow and whistled in appreciation. "One thing is for sure, he taught you well." He rolled his arm in the socket and winced. "My shoulder still hurts."

"Since we're friends now, you can call me by my nickname."

"What's that?"

"Crank."

Vinnie grimaced. "Like the way you cranked my arm up?"

"Yeah, Vinnie, the way I cranked your arm up." Michael laughed.

"I'm glad you think it's funny, but I don't!"

Michael peered out a small window in the stairwell that looked out over the parking lot. "The Staties are here, along with the Boston Police."

"Staties, who's that?"

"In Massachusetts we have a slang word for the State Troopers. We call them Staties."

Soon the stairwell was bustling with activity. A heavy man in uniform took the steps two at a time and approached Michael, shaking his hand.

"I'm Trooper Walsh. What do we have here?"

"Man shot here in the stairwell, sir. My friend and I"—Michael pointed up toward Vinnie—"found a gun on the next floor, and there's a wallet here."

Trooper Walsh looked down at the evidence. "Did you touch, open it, or move the wallet in any way?"

"No sir, I know better."

"Good call," the trooper said, nodding.

He continued to the top of the stairs to the fifth floor. Vinnie extended his hand to introduce himself, but the trooper cut him short.

"You're that champion fighter Marenzano is bank rolling." His tone was reproachful. "It's too bad, Vinnie."

"What's too bad?" Vinnie asked, crossing his arms over his chest.

"It's too bad Marenzano has you under his grips."

"What do you mean by that?"

Trooper Walsh reached into his pocket and handed Vinnie a business card. The card read:

Trooper Jack Walsh, National Collegiate Champion Boxer, International Collegiate Champion, Two Time Olympic Champion, United States Navy All Time Champion, Navy Seal, and Massachusetts State Police Three Time Boxing Champion.

"Wow," Vinnie said in amazement. He tucked the card into his pocket.

"I watched you fight and you have great potential. When you are ready to switch sides, let me know."

"With all due respect, Trooper Walsh, right now I have a girlfriend in critical condition and her father is upstairs in surgery fighting for his life. Boxing is the last thing on my mind."

"I understand, Vinnie. I need you and Michael to leave the crime scene, so my men and I can begin the investigation."

"Of course, it was a pleasure meeting you."

"Same here," Trooper Walsh said as he got to work.

Michael and Vinnie walked back to the waiting room and one of the nurses headed toward them.

"I have some good news for you," she said, smiling. "Your girlfriend is out of recovery and has regained feeling and movement in both her legs."

Vinnie breathed a sigh of relief. "How is her father, Salvatore Marenzano?"

"I'll go up to surgery and report back to you on his condition." She turned, then said over her shoulder, "Mary has been asking for you, but don't discuss what happened to her father. She might not be able to handle it, and her condition could take a turn for the worst."

Two hours passed, and the nurse entered Mary's room to find Vinnie laying next to her with his head on the pillow, gently holding her hand.

"I hate to interrupt you two, but I would like to see Vinnie in the hall for a moment." She smiled sweetly at the young lovers.

Vinnie slid off the bed, gave Mary a kiss, and followed the older woman into the hall. "Good news. Salvatore Marenzano is out of surgery and the bullet has been removed successfully. He is in recovery under stable condition. When he's out of recovery, he will be brought to the SICU unit. However, under the circumstances, the doctor will assign him to the B-wing, the opposite end of A-wing where Mary's room is located," she added, pointing down the hall.

"Thank you, nurse."

"Please, call me Lynn." When she smiled warmly, laugh lines at the corners of her dark eyes turned upward.

"Thank you, Lynn, I appreciate all you've done for Mary." He couldn't suppress a yawn as he ran his hand through his messy hair.

"Vinnie, you look exhausted!" she intoned, shaking her head. "I was instructed to give this to you. Here is the key to Dr. Benson's sleeping quarters down the hall from SICU. He just got off duty and is off for the next three days. You can shave, shower, and get some sleep there. There is also a package of toiletries with everything you'll need."

"That's so generous of the doctor…are you sure?"

"Of course. That's just the kind of guy he is." Lynn winked. "Now, don't worry, either myself or someone from my staff will wake you in case of an emergency."

"Thank you so much for all your help and consideration," Vinnie said appreciatively.

"Certainly. Can I ask you a favor?"

"Sure, anything."

"Can I have four tickets to your next fight for my husband, my two children, and myself?" She blushed, averting her eyes. "We are such big fans!"

"No problem, I'll be happy to get you tickets," Vinnie replied gratefully. "Thank you so much." He hugged her, and she patted him on the back.

"Of course, Vinnie. It's what I do. Rest up, and we'll talk soon."

He headed back to Mary's room to let her know he'd be resting in the doctor's sleeping quarters.

She blinked her tired eyes and said, "Okay, Vinnie, I'm glad. You look like you haven't slept in days."

He kissed her hand, then her lips. "My next fight is coming up, and I'll have to start training hard soon. But I promise when I finish my training each day, I'll come here to be with you as long as you're at the hospital."

"I love you, Vinnie."

"I love you, too, Mary. I'll be just down the hall if you need me." He kissed Mary goodnight, and stepped out of the room.

CHAPTER 21

ROAD TO RECOVERY

Vinnie awoke looking at the clock on the nightstand. It was nine in the morning. He took a quick shower, shaved, and rushed down the hall toward SICU. He noticed his mother walking down the hall with Mario and Maria.

"Vinnie!" Mario and Maria ran over, hugging their older brother, and Vinnie embraced his mother.

"Hey, Mom," Vinnie said. "You didn't tell me you were coming."

"Mary seems much better this morning than she did last night," Incoranata said, gently rubbing her son's back.

"You were here last night?" Vinnie asked, surprised.

"Yes, I arrived late. I was very concerned about Mary's condition and arranged for Whitey to stay with Mario and Maria. From what the doctors were allowed to tell me, it sounds like Mary is doing just fine. I asked how much longer she'll need to stay, and they think if she keeps improving, she'll be up and out of here within seven to ten days. She will need bed rest for another week or so, to get her strength back. Someone should stay with Mary to cook for her and make sure she takes her medicine." Incoranata smiled, putting her arms around her younger children. "That's why I think it's a good idea for Mary to stay at our home, and I can nurse her back to health. I'm sure you'll agree to that, right, Vinnie?"

"Yes, Mama! Thank you for offering your help, it means a great deal to me." He hugged her again and kissed her on the cheek.

"Oh, of course, my son. It's the least I can do. I love you, and I love Mary, too." She stepped back, placing her hands on her boy's shoulders, then lovingly straightened his shirt. "One more thing. I also visited Marenzano. He is a tough old bird. He told me all about Mary, her mother, and stepfather, Jerry Vincente. On the news this morning, I heard the guy who shot Marenzano was caught. The state police raided his house. Someone named Trooper Walsh led them."

"I know Trooper Walsh. I met him here at the hospital yesterday, when he was investigating."

His mother nodded. "There's more. Are you ready for this? The man who shot Marenzano turns out to be Jerry Vincente's brother."

"Mama, that's unreal!"

She frowned, shaking her head. "It reminds me of the old times in Castelammare with your father. Too much fucking drama, it's like the soap operas I watch each day."

Vinnie chuckled. "Ma, no one forces you to watch them."

"This is true, but the soaps are addictive."

"Ma, what is your favorite soap opera?" Vinnie said, his arm around his mother as they walked down the hall.

"This thing of ours!" she retorted. "You know, our life is a never-ending soap opera. Look at everything that has happened since we arrived in Boston."

"Ma, this is true, and you are a very wise woman."

"Vinnie, before I go, I brought you a change of clothes and your gym bag." She handed him a duffel bag with his things inside.

"Thanks, Ma." He kissed his mother, brother, and sister goodbye.

"Everything will be okay, son." Incoranata kissed him again on the cheek.

"I know," Vinnie said assuredly. "I always pray to the Blessed Virgin Mary. She takes care of us."

"That's my boy. I will see you later."

His family waved to him as they went down the hall, then disappeared around a corner. Since he knew his girlfriend was improving, he decided to visit Marenzano first.

Upon reaching his room, Vinnie heard him yelling at two nurses, complaining about the hospital food. Vinnie shook his head, chuckling to himself as he stepped inside.

"Don Marenzano, you are recovering from a gunshot wound," Vinnie reminded him. "You shouldn't be yelling and getting yourself all upset."

"Vinnie!" Marenzano was sitting upright in bed, wearing a hospital gown. "You know something, the food sucks, but the nurses are beautiful." Both ladies rolled their eyes and laughed despite themselves. "Vinnie, this is Angela and Tammy."

"It's good to meet you," Vinnie said, shaking both their hands.

"It's great meeting such a handsome hunk of a man like yourself," Tammy joked, winking and tossing her auburn locks to the side.

"You must be married or have a girlfriend," Angela flirted.

With that remark, Marenzano interjected. "Cool it, girls. He is engaged to my daughter."

"Oh, too bad," Angela said, shrugging. "All the good ones are taken." Both women laughed again.

They finished taking Marenzano's vitals, and Tammy said, "Well, I think we are finished here. You're doing well, Salvatore. He's all yours, Vinnie."

On her way out, Angela murmured, "If there is anything you need, Vinnie, do not hesitate to use the call button and ask for Angela." She winked.

"What about me?" Tammy said, nudging her friend.

Vinnie laughed. "I'll keep that in mind."

"You'll keep *what* in mind?" Marenzano shouted. "It better be my daughter, Mary, you're keeping in mind."

Vinnie shook his head once they were alone. "Relax, Don Marenzano, you'll get your blood pressure up. I'm surprised you didn't pick up on what those scheming nurses were trying to do. I think Angela was trying to piss you off by getting you jealous. I think she really has the hots for you."

Marenzano relaxed. "I hope you're right," he said, grinning.

"What about your wife?"

"Okay, Vinnie, sit down." Marenzano sighed, visibly irritated at the mention of his wife. "I have some things to discuss with you. After your visit with Mary, I want you to call my chef at my restaurant on Hanover Street. Instruct him to prepare my usual meal and deliver it to my room. Also, cook enough food for twenty-five staff members in the SICU, and include twelve bottles of my best wine, compliments of Salvatore Marenzano. I want to show my appreciation for saving my daughter's life and mine, too." He paused. "Hey, did you hear Jerry Vincente's brother was the one who shot me? I guess he expected me to die, didn't think he'd get caught."

"I know, I saw my mother in the hall and she filled me in on everything. The hospital security was increased over the whole thing, all the staff members are freaked out."

"The FEDS got him this morning and put the prick in protective custody at an undisclosed safe house. They found out there's a million dollar price on his head and they suspect I had something to do with it."

"Did you?"

Marenzano looked annoyed. "Fuck, Vinnie, when did I have the time? I just got out of recovery a few hours ago. I can multi-task, but not that good."

"That's true," Vinnie agreed, realizing there was no way he could have orchestrated a hit on Jerry Vincente's brother.

"One more thing I need to talk to you about," Marenzano continued. "It's kind of delicate, but I need you to do me a favor. My wife and Mary's mother will be here. I haven't seen them yet."

Vinnie balked. "Oh, my God, I wouldn't want to be in your shoes!" He leaned back in the cushioned chair he was sitting in. "On the other hand, if the shoe fits, wear it."

"Okay, wise guy, close the door, because I don't want anyone else to hear this." Vinnie jumped up and shut the door, and Marenzano motioned him closer, telling him to sit by his bedside. Vinnie leaned forward, and Marenzano whispered in his ear, "I think my room is bugged…"

Out in the hall, Angela and Tammy were preparing the med cart. Tammy eyed Angela reproachfully.

"I think you pissed off Salvatore Marenzano."

"I think so, too," Angela said, brushing her raven black hair out of her eyes.

"Why did you want to piss him off? Sometimes I just don't get you."

Angela frowned and said nothing. There was a brief pause. Tammy put her hands on her hips. Her full lips turned up in a devilish smile.

"You like him, don't you?" Tammy said.

Angela only smiled shyly, and continued her work.

Back in Marenzano's room, he finished his conversation with Vinnie.

"And make sure Vito brings the sweeping devices."

Suddenly, there was a knock at the door. It was Marenzano's wife, Philamenia, and Mary's mother, Gina. Philamenia saw her husband for the first time since he'd been shot. She raised a small, manicured hand to her mouth and began to cry.

Embracing him, she sobbed, "Salvatore, when I said you should meet me at the hospital, I didn't mean like this."

Mary's mother, who hadn't seen him in years, grumbled and crossed her arms over her chest. "Don't expect *me* to cry."

"Well, some things never change," Marenzano said scornfully as he held his wife close.

Gina laughed and shook her head, shrugging off her disdain. "You look the same, except for the hole in your chest. It suits you."

"Gee, thanks!"

Vinnie listened with interest, his lips rising into a smirk. The banter didn't seem to bother Philamenia, who tucked her head against her husband and kissed him gently on the cheek.

"Are you going to die?" Gina asked sarcastically.

"No, I am too tough to die! It will take more than one bullet to stop me."

"Same old Salvatore, your ego is bigger than your head. Since I am talking about heads, do you still have one between your legs?"

"You'll never have the chance to find out again!" He sneered.

Philamenia finally had it. She straightened up and snapped, "That's enough! Don't you have any respect for one another?"

"No!" They both shouted in unison.

Vinnie was surprised when they all started laughing. It seemed Philamenia and Gina were getting along quite well. Gina went to Salvatore's bedside to embrace him and kiss him on the forehead.

"You know I didn't mean any of it, and I was only trying to bust your balls."

"Thank God!" Philamenia exclaimed, relieved.

Vinnie grinned and cleared his throat, already liking Gina. "I'm Vinnie."

Gina turned and snapped a smart-assed reply. "I knew that!"

"How did you know?" Vinnie asked.

"You're the only good looking guy in the room," she joked. "But the truth is, Mary showed me dozens of pictures of the two of you together."

"Thank you for the compliment," Vinnie said respectfully. "I need to go to Mary's room now and check on her."

Gina embraced him and kissed him on the cheek. Vinnie turned to Philamenia, and hugged and kissed her goodbye.

"Nice to see you, Vinnie," Philamenia said, squeezing his hand. "I wish it were under better circumstances."

Vinnie nodded. Then he leaned over Marenzano to kiss him on the forehead. "I prayed to the Blessed Mother for your speedy recovery."

"Thank you, you're a good guy."

As Vinnie walked to the door, he quickly turned and glanced at Marenzano. The two men locked eyes for a moment. Vinnie looked at both women, then grinned as he closed the door behind him.

Once he'd arrived at Mary's room, she seemed agitated. She was sitting in bed frowning, her eyes red-rimmed as if she'd been crying.

"What's wrong?" Vinnie asked, perplexed.

"Why didn't you tell me my father was shot?"

"Who told you?" Vinnie asked, grimacing.

"My mother and Philamenia."

"The nurses and doctors advised me not to tell you, due to your serious condition." Vinnie sat on the edge of the bed and took her hand. "The doctors felt it would be life threatening if you learned about your father being shot. You need to rest and get better, too, baby."

"Well, I guess you didn't have any choice." She relaxed and caressed his hand. "I'll forgive you if you give me a kiss."

They both laughed. "I think I can do that," Vinnie said. He slipped his arms around her, pulling her close, mindful of her injuries. Their kiss grew passionate, deep, and loving. Mary whimpered when he pulled away.

"When can I see my father?" she asked softly, leaning back against the pillow.

"When one of you is strong enough to be moved," Vinnie replied, consoling her.

He stayed with her for over an hour, and they talked.

"I have some things to do with your dad," he said after a while. "He gave me some errands to run, and asked me to do a couple of favors for him."

"What favors?" she asks, narrowing her eyes worriedly.

"Don't ask," Vinnie said firmly. She looked unhappy about his request, but said nothing. "I will return early this evening after my workout, so I can spend more time with you. Please get some rest." Vinnie kissed her goodbye, more passionately this time. "I love you, baby. Sleep well."

CHAPTER 22

SNATCH AND RIDICULE

Several weeks later, Mary was finally discharged from Mass General. But Marenzano was still recovering in the hospital, due to an infection which occurred after his surgery. Mary remained at Vinnie's home under his mother's loving care. She was visited daily by her mother, Gina, who helped Incoranata care for her. Their assistance gave Vinnie the opportunity to get into shape for his upcoming fight, which was slated to take place in two weeks.

After Vinnie's vigorous workout at the gym, Whitey invited him to have lunch at the local diner. While they ate, Whitey reminisced about the good old times growing up in Marenzano's home. Vinnie was intrigued, and opened up to Whitey by sharing some of his family stories. Their conversation ended with Vinnie expressing his concern about Marenzano's recovery.

Whitey shook his head, digging into his dessert. "He'll be all right. And…"

"And what?" Vinnie pressed, when Whitey said nothing.

"Well, I think we might see changes in Don Marenzano. Changes some people might think impossible."

"You mean…after everything that's happened…"

"I think you see what I'm getting at. Salvatore Marenzano is not the same man after his daughter was shot."

"I agree."

"But…that man can handle anything. According to his doctors this morning, they said he should be released within seventy-two hours."

"That's good to hear, I feel better now," Vinnie said, relieved. The waitress came and took his empty plate, and he thanked her.

"If his wound didn't become infected, he probably would have been released before Mary," Whitey added. He polished off his cake and slid the dish across the table. "It was good having lunch with you, but I need to get back to the gym. I'll see you tomorrow." He dragged his aging body out of the booth and stood.

"Yes, I need to get home to see Mary," Vinnie said. "Do you want a ride back to the gym?"

"No, the sun is shining and I'll enjoy the walk back."

"Okay, see you later." Vinnie paid the bill, and left the diner.

Whitey stepped lightly on the sidewalk, his hands in his pockets. One block before reaching the gym, he was suddenly grabbed and hurled into a black van by three masked assailants. Before he could scream, they placed a hood over Whitey's head and the van sped off down the street.

Whitey fought against them, his heart pounding, but they held him firmly.

"Relax, old man. You won't be harmed," a man's voice assured him. "As long as you cooperate and listen, you'll be just fine. Got that?"

"Yes, yes," Whitey said, the fear evident in his voice.

"We know all about you and your association with Salvatore Marenzano." The voice spoke harshly. "All we want you to do is pass some information to him."

"Why in the hell did you have to snatch me off the street and rough me up?" Whitey shouted. "I didn't do a damn thing."

The assailants laughed. "We didn't rough you up, what the fuck are you talking about?"

"Well, you picked me up like a fifty pound sack of potatoes and slung me into the van," Whitey retorted. "I can't even fucking see you with this hood over my head."

"If you call that roughing somebody up, what would you call it if we really whacked you around? It's not our fault you are the same weight as a sack of potatoes." They snickered.

"Take this goddamned hood off me, untie my hands and feet, come to the gym with me, and I'll take you on in the ring. Then I'll show you what a fifty pound sack of potatoes can do!"

"Shut up and listen, old man. Okay, this is the message we want you to give Marenzano. We know he was visited numerous times by the FEDS and the state police. We have many concerns about what was discussed regarding Marenzano and his daughter Mary's gunshot wounds, the hanging of Mary's stepfather, and the van found in New York with the men in it who were burned alive.

"We hope Marenzano had enough brains to keep his mouth shut while being questioned. It would be a real shame if some little bird flew into the window of the FBI Headquarters with a note attached to its leg revealing who the real mastermind was behind the van explosion and the fake suicide. In other words, presuming Marenzano plays ball, he has nothing to worry about. But if we find out he's a rat, we will take everyone who is close to him down one by one, starting with his daughter. *Capisce?* Now stick that in your sack of potatoes and deliver it to him."

"Stop the van," another voice yelled out.

Without ceremony, Whitey was thrown out at the curb before the van came to a complete stop.

"Oh, hope we weren't too rough, Mr. Potato!" A door slammed, tires squealed, and the men made their getaway.

Whitey's shoulder stung, and he knew he'd been scratched up in the fall. He took the hood off his head, rolled it up, and put it in his pocket. He'd been thrown near the government center subway station. He clambered to his feet, his whole body aching, and decided to take the train to park street and switch to the Redline train to the Mass General to deliver the message. On the train, he tried to relax in the torn, uncomfortable seat, but he was edgy and nervous the entire time.

When he arrived at the hospital, Whitey limped into Marenzano's room, rubbing his shoulder. He hadn't looked in a mirror, but he guessed he looked bad, because the Don's eyes widened when he saw him.

"What the fuck happened to you?"

Whitey tugged the hood out of his pocket and tossed it on Marenzano's bed.

"I was abducted."

Marenzano placed a finger over his lips, and beckoned Whitey closer, motioning for him to whisper in his ear.

Once he'd explained everything, Marenzano said, "Go downstairs and get checked out by the emergency room. You look like hell. Afterward, go home to rest and get back to the gym first thing in the morning. Vinnie's fight is right around the corner. I'm sorry you were roughed up."

Whitey cringed. "Don't use that word in front of me ever again," he snapped, touching the tender bruise on his face.

"Wow, I didn't know you were so sensitive. You have plenty of spunk left in you for a fifty pound sack of potatoes." Marenzano cackled.

"It's not funny," Whitey said, distressed. "That's enough, I'm leaving after that remark."

Marenzano flashed a grin and shouted after him, "What a fucking pussy!"

The next morning, a team of physicians woke Marenzano, headed by a beautiful neurosurgeon with long wavy brown hair and dark eyes. She was about thirty-five years old and had a body that would put the Playboy centerfold out of business.

"Good morning," she intoned, her voice soft and low, like sugar melting in hot coffee. "I'm Doctor Nancy Martinelli, and I'm the new doctor in charge of your case."

"My case?" he snapped. "You sound more like a prosecutor than a doctor."

Some of the doctors around Martinelli chuckled and exchanged amused glances, since Don Marenzano was known to be in and out of court. Dr. Martinelli just sighed and shook her head.

"Well, Mr. Marenzano, you have certainly caught the eye of my team," she said, raising her eyebrows. "They may find you very entertaining and intriguing, but I can assure you I do not! In fact, I think you are self-centered, egotistical, ruthless, and unscrupulous. Would you like me to go on?"

"Yes, please continue. I am finding this very amusing," Marenzano said, challenging her.

She couldn't help but crack a wry smile. "You know, the only good thing I can say about you is, while you were suffering from your gunshot wound, you seemed more preoccupied with your daughter's well-being than yours."

"See, I'm not all bad."

Dr. Martinelli smiled softly and continued her examination with the help of her colleagues.

Afterward, he asked, "When am I getting out of here?"

"How about tomorrow?" Dr. Martinelli suggested. "Is that soon enough for you?"

"Yes, I am sick of this place."

"All right then, I will prepare your discharge papers tomorrow morning, and by noon you will be out of here." The team of doctors stepped out of the room first, and Dr. Martinelli turned and asked, "Is it true you are a marked man?" She grinned as she shut the door behind her.

"You fucking cunt," he shouted furiously. "We'll see who's marked and it won't be me, baby!"

CHAPTER 23

SECRET IDENTITY

Vinnie arrived at the hospital the following morning to pick up Marenzano.

"It's about fucking time," Marenzano snapped, already out of bed and dressed. "Help me get my shit together and get me out of here."

Suddenly, Dr. Martinelli stepped into the middle of the hallway, her hands on her hips. "Salvatore, where do you think you're going?"

"It's noon, and I am getting ready to go home," he retorted. "You are supposed to have my discharge papers ready."

"The discharge papers are ready, but you need to sign them."

"Give me a pen, and I will sign the papers now."

"Salvatore, I don't see any reason to keep you any longer."

"Thank you, Dr. Martinelli, it's been real," he remarked, raising his eyebrows.

"No, Mr. Marenzano, it might have been real for you, but not for me." She shook her head.

"The next time I come to this joint, I will personally request your services."

"Mr. Marenzano, go blow smoke up someone else's ass, not mine," Dr. Martinelli replied. "Now, go home." She left the room, her heels clicking on the floor.

As they walked down the hall, Marenzano turned to Vinnie and said, "Can you believe how that bitch talks to me?"

Vinnie chuckled. "I think she likes you."

"Ha, Ha!" Marenzano shook his head, irritated.

"Forget about it," Vinnie said, mimicking the Don. "It's time for you to go home to your wife. I'm sure she has a lot to talk to you about, like Mary's mother Gina."

Marenzano smacked his forehead with the palm of his hand. "Oh no, I almost forgot about that, you had to remind me."

"I'd like to be a fly on the wall for that."

"No, you wouldn't, 'cause I would flatten you like a fly," Marenzano warned.

When he arrived home, Marenzano reluctantly opened the front door to find Philamenia waiting to greet him.

"Salvatore, you're here!" She embraced and kissed him, telling him she was glad he was alive and well.

Marenzano hugged her close and kissed her gently on the forehead, but he knew what was coming. Within twenty minutes, she had begun badgering him about Gina. Feeling like a mouse trapped in a cage, Marenzano paced his house, arguing back and forth with his wife for the next few hours.

A long while later, Marenzano stood in the kitchen while Philamenia threw clean pots and pans into the cupboards and slammed doors. She went upstairs, giving him a few minutes of peace, then returned with two packed bags.

"Where do you think you're going?" Marenzano said, exasperated, shoving his hands into the pockets of his slacks.

"I'm going to my sister's house for a few days, so I can think things out. I'm glad you're okay, Salvatore, and surprisingly I like Gina a lot, but I'm still pissed at you for what you did to me all those years ago."

"Yeah, go ahead to your sister's house, but don't expect me to drive you," he shouted harshly.

"Don't worry, I'll call a cab," Philamenia snapped, since she had never learned to drive.

After she'd made the call, several minutes went by and neither of them uttered a word. Marenzano listened to the clock ticking on the wall of the living room, and waited.

When the cab arrived and his wife had left, Marenzano yelled at the top of his lungs, "I can't believe she just fucking left me here alone like this."

He slumped down on the couch in the living room and dialed his cell phone. When the person on the other line answered, he said, "We need to meet now. My wife took off to her sister's for a few days, so the timing is perfect. Let's go hunting at the usual place."

The voice at the other end asked, "Are you sure you are up to this?"

"We have no choice, it's urgent."

Marenzano hung up the phone and packed a bag, then left for the long drive to New Hampshire. Forty-five minutes into the trip, his cell phone rang. He looked at the caller ID. It was Philamenia, but he decided not to answer. He was afraid of getting into another confrontation with her. Marenzano drove on, the phone stopped ringing, and he drifted into his own thoughts as the scenery whizzed by.

Philamenia began to worry when her husband didn't answer.

"Damn it, Salvatore, just when I am calling to apologize, to come home and take care of you, you don't pick up the phone," she mumbled to herself.

"Why don't you just leave him alone?" her sister whined. "It'll serve him right to be on his own a while."

"Oh, I can't. I'm going to find him!" Philamenia exclaimed.

She took a cab home, then began to panic when he wasn't there. He'd almost died, and now he was gone. She fretted, worried something might have happened to him. She decided to call the hospital emergency room to find out if he'd been brought back with a relapse. After the intensive surgery he'd been through, it was possible.

"No, Mrs. Marenzano, I'm sorry…he isn't here," a member of the staff assured her.

Next, Philamenia called the gym, but no one had seen or heard from him. Then she began dialing his restaurants, and everyone he knew. After an hour of calling around town, she couldn't find him anywhere. She broke down in the kitchen, leaning against the counter, her face flushed and her eyes brimming with tears.

"It's all my fault!" Philamenia sobbed and pulled out her rosary beads, desperately praying to the Blessed Virgin Mary to find her husband safe and unharmed. When she finished her prayers and calmed down, she said aloud, "I bet I know where the son of a bitch is!"

Without delay, she called another cab to drive her to Gina's house. Philamenia knocked hard on the oak door and Gina opened the door to greet her.

"Philamenia, this is a surprise!"

"I was in the neighborhood and thought I would drop by," Philamenia lied, smiling warmly.

"Come in, I'll make some coffee," Gina said courteously.

As she went inside, Philamenia glanced around for any sign of her husband, but saw nothing. The two women chatted for about an hour, and she became convinced Salvatore hadn't been there at all. Of course, she did not reveal the real reason for her visit.

After a while, Philamenia grabbed her purse and said, "Well, Gina, I've got to finish my shopping at the mall. It's been lovely, though."

Gina nodded knowingly. "Ah, I know the real reason you came to see me!"

Philamenia gulped, turning pale. "Oh?"

"So you could have an excuse to go shopping!" Gina exclaimed, patting her on the back. "I'll see you later. Have fun!"

"Oh, oh…yes. Thank you!"

Marenzano arrived at the cabin in New Hampshire, and patiently awaited the arrival of his friend.
When his cell phone rang, the voice on the other end said, "I am just down the road from the cabin. Hope you brought some food and beer."

"I copy that," Marenzano replied, then hung up.

He went into the cabin, turned the lights on, and threw some wood in the fireplace. Then he heard knocking at the door

"Who's there?" he called out.

"Who the fuck do you think it is? Open the door."

Marenzano let him in, and the two men started laughing and embraced each other.

"Don't squeeze too hard, I haven't fully recovered yet." Marenzano stepped aside, shutting the door, and added, "Come, sit and have a beer. Wait 'til you see what I brought to eat, but it's not kosher."

"Thank God," his friend replied.

"Look what I got! I bought some great Boston spucky rolls, Italian dry salami, provolone cheese, capacollo, prosciutto, mortadella, stuffed peppers, meat balls, calamari, and your favorite, braciole. It's food for a king!" Marenzano sat across from him in a straight-backed wooden chair and folded his hands in his lap. "So, Weinstein, did I convince everyone at the FBI Holding Center that I hate Jews?"

Weinstein grinned and adjusted his thin-rimmed glasses. "Yes, if I didn't know you better, you would have convinced me. However, tell me something, do you really like those Irish cops?"

"Okay, let's not get me going now on the Irish."

Weinstein chuckled. "Salvatore, I was worried about you, buddy. Are you going to be all right?"

Marenzano nodded. "I am getting stronger and stronger as each day goes by."

"Good, I'm glad. Now, what was so urgent you needed to meet right away?" Weinstein asked, taking a long gulp from his beer, and both men ate, enjoying the food.

"Whitey was snatched off the street and thrown into a van—"

"Hold on, I know all about it," Weinstein said, raising a hand.

"Already?" Marenzano asked, perplexed.

"Yeah, already."

"How's that possible?"

"Our intelligence on the street is great! Now, tell me something I don't already know."

"Three Islamic terrorists are meeting at the Caribe Lounge in Downtown Boston at one in the morning. A connection was made with some prominent Providence people from Federal Hill," Marenzano explained.

"Why the hell are the wise guys meeting with Islamic terrorists in a Boston strip club?"

Marenzano shrugged. "The strange thing is, my guys were not invited."

"That's weird. What exactly are they looking to buy?"

"C4 explosives, wire, nitro, and computer chips."

"What's the target?"

"Boston South Station."

Weinstein cringed. "When is this buy going down?"

"During their meeting at the Caribe Lounge."

"Is there anything else I should know about?" Weinstein took another swig from his beer and finished the bottle.

"Yeah, my guy Vinnie is fighting next Saturday night."

"I wouldn't miss it for the world!" Weinstein declared, grinning. "On another note, there is nobody up the ladder that knows anything about you or our relationship, not even the President of the United States. Marenzano, you have been in charge of the Death Squad under the U.S. Attorney's office with four other Death Squad agents. None of you know each other's identities. That's the way I prefer to keep it for the time being. I'm sure we understand one another, Special Agent Marenzano. There is one thing I want to ask you before we go. Is it true?" Weinstein stood from his chair, and Marenzano followed him to the door.

"Is what true?"

"Did you really cut your mother's fingers off to get her rings?"

After hearing Weinstein's question, Marenzano glared at him and said nothing.

"Why don't you answer me?" Weinstein wanted to know.

Marenzano continued to stare into his eyes, projecting evil. "I'm going home now, my wife has been calling me and wondering where I am. I hope you enjoyed the Italian food I brought to our meeting."

"Yes, I always enjoy the spread, thank you."

"If you want me to continue bringing the Italian cuisine, don't ask me questions concerning my mother ever again," Marenzano said sharply.

Without another word, the men left the cabin and got into their separate vehicles. Right before Weinstein drove off, he put his window down and called out to Marenzano.

"One more question. What happened to your devil's ring you always wear?"

Again, Marenzano stared at Weinstein in such a way he seemed to cast a glow in the dark, as though he were the Prince of Darkness himself.

CHAPTER 24

PAYBACK IS A BITCH

During Marenzano's trip back to Boston, his cell phone rang.

"Salvatore, are you all right?" Philamenia asked breathlessly. "I was frantic when you didn't answer before."

"Yes, I'm all right," he said, agitated, still upset with her.

"I've been calling you for hours and you didn't answer your phone. I was worried sick about you."

"You weren't worried about me when you left to run off to your sister's."

"I'm sorry, Sal. When I came to my senses and realized how wrong I was to leave you alone, I returned home. Not finding you home upset me and I thought the worst. Where did you go?"

"I drove up to New Hampshire."

"Why?" she asked eagerly.

"No reason, just to blow off some steam and clear my head."

"Are you still in New Hampshire?"

"Yes, but I am in my car driving back to Boston as we speak."

"How long will it take you to drive home?"

"I'll be home in an hour."

"Do you want me to cook you something to eat?" Philamenia asked, sounding distressed.

"No, I already stopped and had a bite."

"Salvatore, there is one more thing I want to discuss with you before you arrive." She paused, then continued. "I was shopping at the mall across from Gina's condo and decided to visit her."

"Why the hell did you go to a mall by Gina's condo, when there are other malls closer to home?" Marenzano asked angrily. When she didn't reply, he snapped, "Answer me, I want to know the truth."

"The truth is, I thought you went to visit Gina, since you were infuriated with me." Before he could say anything, she spoke hurriedly. "I know it was wrong, I'm sorry."

"I haven't laid eyes on this woman for years until you showed up at the hospital with her," Marenzano retorted. "Furthermore, I don't appreciate your bringing her with you to my hospital room. Gina is nothing but a sarcastic bitch. She always was and she always will be." He sighed heavily. "Philamenia, I think it's best that you and I don't bring up the past anymore. To be honest with you, I realize I'm not the best husband in the world, but I love you. Besides, you are the best fuck and blow job I ever had."

She laughed uproariously on the other line. "I know! Hurry up and come home, I have something special in mind for you."

After she said that, Marenzano pushed the accelerator to the floor, bringing the speedometer up to ninety miles per hour, because he knew exactly what she was thinking.

"Philamenia, I told you I'd be home in an hour, but make that a half-hour!"

The following week flew by as Vinnie trained in the gym for his next fight. Mary was getting better, and Marenzano had a smile on his face every day.

Soon, it was Friday night and Vinnie's family, including Mary, Marenzano, and Philamenia, were all sitting ringside waiting for Vinnie and his opponent to walk up to the ring with their entourage.

Eight men approached the row of seats where Marenzano was seated. It was the New York crew, who he'd promised front row seats to. One of the men signaled to Marenzano that he needed to speak to him. Marenzano stood, made his way through the crowd, and stepped into an aisle.

The man leaned forward and whispered in his ear. "What about the girls you promised us?"

"No problem, we will be joining them after the fight when my wife and family go home."

"Thank you, Don Marenzano, I knew you would not disappoint us. I will pass the word to the commission and I'm sure they will be pleased."

"So, why did you guys really take me up on my offer?" Marenzano asked jokingly. "Was it the fight or the girls?"

"Don Marenzano, with due respect, it was kind of a toss-up between the two, but I'm leaning more toward the girls."

"I respect your honesty." Both men laughed.

"Don Marenzano, we will see you later…after Vinnie wins the fight!"

"That's what I like to hear, a positive attitude."

They both returned to their seats. No sooner had Don Marenzano sat down, Gina came down the aisle accompanied by four other women, all dolled up and dressed to kill.

Philamenia glared at Marenzano. "How did they get ringside seats?"

Incoranata turned to Philamenia and patted her on the hand. "Don't worry, it wasn't Salvatore. He had nothing to do with it. My son was the culprit, he was sweet-talked by Gina for ringside seats. After all, she is going to be Vinnie's mother-in-law."

Philamenia shot her a dirty look, not finding her comment amusing.

Gina greeted everyone with a wide smile and introduced her friends. "Everyone, this is Susan, Stephanie, Roberta, and Leslie. We're all single girls out for a good time!"

Philamenia seemed particularly irritated when Gina winked. She turned to her husband again and sneered.

"What's wrong? I had nothing to do with this," he said, trying to defend himself, but she continued to give him dirty looks.

Suddenly, Philamenia burst out laughing, and so did the rest of the family. She stood up and turned toward the girls, continuing to laugh and grin. Gina and her girlfriends seemed outraged, as it appeared Philamenia was laughing at them.

Stephanie put her hands on her hips and said, "Come on, bitch, do you want to fight?"

Marenzano jumped up and threw his hands in the air. "What the fuck is wrong with you people?"

At that moment, Gina and her girlfriends burst out laughing, too, and they each gave Philamenia a high five.

Gina shouted out, "The joke is on you, Salvatore!"

"What do you mean?" he asked, bewildered.

"I mean your wife confessed about why she really came to visit me. I assured her there is nothing between the two of us and hasn't been for years."

"I hope you all had your fun," Marenzano said, sitting back down. "Payback is a bitch and that goes for all of you, especially my wife and Gina, the ring leader."

At that moment, the announcer rang the bell and the ladies sat down. *"I am Steve Kelly, your announcer. Tonight there will be fifteen rounds of professional boxing here at the Tropicana Casino and Resort. From Atlantic City, New Jersey, at six feet tall and weighing in at two hundred and four pounds, our top contender for the Heavyweight Championship, Juan Frisco Alvarez, with twenty-five wins and two losses."* The crowd cheered with such exuberance that people couldn't hear themselves talk. *"Here he is now, coming into the ring, Juan Frisco Alvarez. His opponent is now approaching the ring. This man needs no introduction. At six-foot-one, weighing in at two hundred pounds with a two inch reach advantage. He is originally from Castellammare del Golfo, Sicily. Now making his home in Boston, Massachusetts, the one, the only, Vinnie the Sicilian Fighting Machine Russo."* The crowd shrieked with delight. *"Let me introduce our referee for the night, Charles Romano."*

The referee stepped up and said, "Okay you two, you know the rules, no hitting behind the head and no hitting below the belt. I want a clean fight. Touch gloves, and return to your corners!"

CHAPTER 25

ONLY THE STRONG SURVIVE

The bell went off and the men came out fighting.

"Vinnie, the Sicilian Fighting Machine, comes out with a flurry of left and right punches to the face of Juan Frisco Alvarez," the announcer shrieked. "Alvarez is stung by the hits thrown by the Sicilian Fighting Machine. Alvarez comes back with a powerful left hook to Vinnie's face. The referee steps in and flags Alvarez back to his corner and starts giving Vinnie the ten count. One, two, three, and Vinnie staggers to his knees! Four, five, six, Vinnie grabs the corner post and he is back on his feet."

The referee lifted three fingers and asked Vinnie, "How many fingers do I have up?"

"Three," he said, then flew forward.

The announcer continued to shout, and the crowd screamed. "Alvarez comes out again with a flurry of punches to Vinnie's head and body. Vinnie doesn't look good. He has a deep cut over his right eye, which is bleeding profusely. The bell rings and both fighters go back to their corners."

The doctor quickly examined Vinnie's right eye.

Whitey leaned over him and said, "We need to cut your eye."

"No!" Vinnie shouted. "Roll it and paste it."

"If he hits you in the right eye again and you're bleeding too much, we will have to stop the fight," Whitey reminded him.

Vinnie replied sharply, "It's not going to happen. Alvarez is going down for the count in this round."

"I hope you're right, otherwise I am throwing in the towel," Whitey said.

"The bell rings! Vinnie comes out with an upper cut and a left hook, which sends Alvarez clear across the ring." The crowd jumped out, pumping their fists into the air. *"Vinnie runs toward Alvarez and continues to hit him with punches to his midsection. Alvarez can't even get off one punch to Vinnie, the Sicilian Fighting Machine. Alvarez is knocked down for the count. The referee orders Vinnie to his corner. One, two, three, and Alvarez is up!"*

Vinnie pivoted to face his mother and signaled to her that Alvarez was going down now.

"The referee finishes his count, and tells the men to continue to fight. Alvarez begins throwing left and right punches to Vinnie's midsection and head, but can't seem to connect with one blow. Vinnie is taunting Alvarez, folks, laughing right in his face, as he begins to shuffle his feet!"

Vinnie yelled out, "I told everyone you are going down in two, as you look at your shoe."

Alvarez, not being too bright, glanced toward his feet and Vinnie hit him with an upper cut. The crowd screamed out hysterically, shouting, "Vinnie, Vinnie, Vinnie!"

"Ladies and Gentlemen, we were scheduled for a fifteen round event, but Alvarez went down in two when he looked at his shoe!"

The spectators roared, and the announcer gave the judge's ruling. Judge Mike Delaney ruled 26 to 0 Russo. Judge George Becket ruled in Russo's favor, 26 to 0, and Judge Silvio De Charra 20 to 6 in favor of Russo.

A unanimous decision, a new world contender for the Heavyweight Championship, Vinnie *the Sicilian Fighting Machine* Russo. Meanwhile, Alvarez was knocked unconscious and he was receiving medical attention.

Salvatore Marenzano took the microphone and said, "My fighter, Vinnie, will be the next Heavyweight Champion of the World!" The fans were fired up. "I think tonight's show was of epic performance and extraordinary. With that in mind, I hereby rename him, Vinnie, *the Animal, the Sicilian Fighting Machine*, Russo."

The crowd went wild. Some of the women were throwing their undergarments, bras and thongs into the ring, hoping to get Vinnie's attention. His physique was so well defined, his body so well muscled, that he was offered a contract right in the ring to model men's underwear. It was from a fashion designer for a five million dollar contract.

Marenzano raised a hand. "As Vinnie's manager, any contract will be considered upon review by our law firm." He turned to Whitey. "Take Vinnie to the emergency room to have his right eye examined. After the doctor releases him, you can both attend the victory party at Incoranata's house. If there is any problem, let me know."

Marenzano went to his wife and hugged and kissed her. "I'll join you in a few hours at Vinnie's party. I have something important to discuss with the New York crew."

"I understand and I will see you later," Philamenia said, kissing him on the cheek before they parted ways.

Mary joined Vinnie in the locker room, and he noticed right away that she seemed worried and distant.

"Mary, Is there something wrong?" he asked, brushing the hair out of her eyes.

"Yes, you are very perceptive. How did you know?"

"I am very perceptive when it comes to you. I can see it in your face, so spit it out."

She frowned and finally admitted, "I wasn't very happy when women started throwing their bras and thongs with their phone numbers at you. Instead of a boxer, the women were treating you like a male stripper."

"I can't help it, I'm so pretty!" he joked. "Male strippers make tons of money, maybe I can do that, too."

Mary didn't like his joke, even though she'd been a stripper once herself. Or, perhaps it was *because* she'd been a stripper that the joke irritated her. Pissed off, she punched him in the arm.

"Ouch!" Vinnie yelled out.

Mary winced. "Oh, I'm so sorry, I forgot Alvarez gave you a beating in the first round, almost winning the fight." Her voice was edged with sarcasm.

"You're kind of hitting below the belt now." They both laughed.

"Vinnie, what do you have in that paper bag?" Mary asked inquisitively.

"Oh nothing, just dirty clothes. I'm bringing them home for my mother to wash."

"Don't give them to your mother, I'll wash them for you," Mary said, trying to be helpful.

"No, it's not necessary, you're still recovering from your gunshot wound."

"Okay, but I'll bring them home to your mother for you, since you are going to the hospital." Vinnie didn't want her to have the bag, but she took it anyway. "I will see you at your house later." She turned and sauntered out of the locker room.

After she'd left, Mary was curious about what was in the bag, especially since Vinnie had been so reluctant to let her have it. She peeked inside and couldn't believe what she found.

In the bag were the bras and thongs with women's phone numbers written on them in marker. There was even one thong with a picture resume attached to it.

No wonder he didn't want me to have this bag.

"Okay, Vinnie, the Animal, the Sicilian Fighting Machine Russo, paybacks are a bitch!"

CHAPTER 26

DON'T GET CAUGHT WITH YOUR PANTS DOWN

At ringside, Marenzano made a quick call on his cell.

"Carlo, is it done?"

"Yes, Don Marenzano."

"Video and audio, correct?"

"Ten four," Carlo affirmed. "One more thing, all the girls are here and it is snowing outside, boss."

"How many inches have fallen so far?"

"Sixteen inches and much more on the way."

Marenzano hung up the phone and walked over to his New York associates. "Don Chico, everything is in place, including the women."

"Everything is in place including the fringe bennies?" Don Chico asked.

"Yes, even the fringe bennies are on ice."

With that, Marenzano and his New York associates hopped in the limo to take off on a short trip to Beverly, Massachusetts. The limo driver pulled up to thirty-foot high gates with an electrified fence. When the gates opened, he drove the crew up a hill to a circular driveway that ended in front of a huge twenty bedroom mansion.

Don Chico balked, his eyes widening in surprise. "Holy shit, who the hell lives here?"

"A very close friend of ours," Don Marenzano replied.

"A friend of ours? What I want to know is, how the fuck does someone who's a friend of ours make more money than the Head of the Commission?"

Marenzano interjected. "When he made money with us, he didn't blow it, like you and I. He invested it into companies such as AIG, Freddie Mac, and Fannie Mae."

"What is he, a fucking politician?" Don Chico wondered.

"No, I told you he's with us. We don't have politicians with us, they can't be trusted. After all, remember that big scandal with Freddie Mac and Fannie Mae during the presidential election?"

"So, what's the big mystery? Just tell me who it is!" They climbed out of the limo.

"It's Jean Claude De Martino. He controls all the drug moves in Canada."

"Touché!" Don Chico said, impressed. "He *has* done very well for himself."

At the front door, they were invited inside by two gorgeous nude girls. One of them was carrying a tray of glasses filled with champagne.

Don Chico looked the girls up and down, admiring their full perky breasts and round bottoms. "Will Jean Claude De Martino be joining us this evening?" he asked.

"No, he is out of the country in Switzerland for two weeks. He conveys his hospitality to us with these words, *my house is your house*."

"You know something, Don Marenzano."

"What's that?"

"I like the way you do things," Don Chico said. "I think I would like to wash some of my clothes with you and Jean Claude De Martino. Let's say, I am very interested in expanding my empire."

The two girls led them into a huge den with a pool table and a bar.

"Of course, Don Chico, but enjoy yourself now," Marenzano suggested. "You and your associates have the whole weekend to fuck, suck, drink, and get high."

Marenzano crossed the room and grabbed the doorknobs to fifteen-foot double doors. Don Chico and his associates looked inside with amazement.

Beyond the comparatively small den was a living room that had to be at least three thousand five-hundred square feet, with the hottest women on the East coast waiting for them. Twenty-five feature strippers were made available to the New York commission, compliments of Salvatore Marenzano.

Don Chico looked Marenzano in the eyes and said, "You and I have a big future together. We are going to be bigger, richer, and stronger than U.S. Steel, now that our president has finally opened up trade between Cuba and the United States again. We will pick up where Hyman Roth was instrumental in opening up Las Vegas gambling casinos and hotels in the fifties. Now is the time to move on this, because our economy has improved dramatically since the last election."

"Don Chico, I like the way you do business."

The men embraced and kissed each other on the cheeks. They agreed to start a new merger between the New York crime family and the New England organized crime family.

Then, Marenzano excused himself and explained he needed to make a phone call to his wife, letting her know he would leave shortly to join her at Vinnie's party. After that, he phoned Weinstein.

"It's me. Everything is in place and running, including video and audio."

"Great, I can't wait to see the video and listen to the audio," Weinstein remarked. Both men laughed. "Don Chico is no fool!"

"I know," Marenzano agreed.

"That is why my video and audio surveillance equipment is impervious to any kind of sweeping devices Don Chico may have. This is the same type of surveillance the Navy Seals and CIA use. Example, when catching Bin Laden!"

"You need not say anymore," Marenzano said, understanding how high tech the surveillance system was.

"Well, congratulations on Vinnie's win and enjoy the victory party!"

"Thanks, we'll talk later."

Don Marenzano returned to the living room to find that every man including Don Chico had been stripped naked of their garments by the girls, leaving only their shoes and socks.

It's so tempting to stay with these girls, Marenzano thought. *But the sight of the commission's bodies being so out of shape and flabby makes me want to puke.*

He hurriedly said his goodbyes and departed.

During his drive back to Boston, he called up to his limo driver.

"Ciro, pull over, I need to take a piss."

The car pulled to the side of the road, and Marenzano stepped into the wooded area to relieve himself. While he was out there, he decided to call Weinstein.

"Is something wrong?" Weinstein asked.

"No, I just stopped to take a piss."

"So, you had to call me. What makes you think of me while you're taking a piss?" When Marenzano laughed, Weinstein added, "What are you laughing about, are you drinking?"

"No."

"Then what the hell is so humorous?"

"I'll tell you what's so humorous. I was thinking about when you guys watch the videos of these fucking *mamalouks* with their clothes off and flabby skin on their bodies hanging down to the floor. I couldn't help but share this with you."

"You know something, Salvatore, you have a weird sense of humor."

Suddenly, Marenzano yelled out, "Ouch!"

"What happened?"

"I caught my dick on my pants zipper."

Weinstein burst out laughing, and Marenzano finally removed the skin of his dick from the zipper, but in the process got urine all over his pants. He could still hear Weinstein laughing hysterically over the phone.

"Sal, are you all right now? Have you safely gotten your dick back in your pants?"

"Fuck you!" Agitated, Marenzano hung up on Weinstein.

He climbed back in the limo and told his driver to take him home first.

"Boss, aren't you running late already?" Ciro asked.

"Mind your fucking business and just take me back to my fucking house."

"What's the matter, boss, why are you yelling at me?"

"I had a little accident, shut the fuck up."

"What did you do, boss, pee yourself?" Ciro started laughing. "Ah, everyone pisses themselves sometimes. No need to be embarrassed. I've done it to myself plenty of times. Forget about it!"

CHAPTER 27

BROWN BAG IT

After a quick shower and a change of clothes, Marenzano headed to Vinnie's victory party, where he was greeted at the door by Philamenia. She'd had a few drinks and was feeling no pain. She embraced her husband and kissed him, sticking her tongue halfway down his esophagus, while waving a pair of thongs in front of his face.

"You're shit-faced," Marenzano noted, disappointed with her behavior.

"Yes, I am, and you're going to enjoy yourself when I get you home."

"Where did you get the thongs?"

"From Vinnie's grab bag," Philamenia replied.

Marenzano nodded. "Oh, that's from all the women's bras and panties they threw into the ring at him."

"That's right, and Mary has the bag."

"Does he know?"

"Oh, yes, she took the bag from him in the locker room." Philamenia giggled.

"What was Mary's reaction?"

"Paybacks are a bitch!"

Marenzano laughed heartily. "That's my girl. So, Mary has the bag, Vinnie knows, and he probably told her they were dirty gym clothes. She must have offered to wash them. Vinnie figured she wouldn't open the bag, but she did. Mary hasn't let on that she looked in the bag, but is acting cool about the situation for now. Am I right?"

"You're one hundred percent right!" Philamenia declared. "You are so smart, my Salvatore."

"Thank you, and you are so drunk, my dearest Philamenia." He put his arm around his wife and said, "Let's go and join the party."

When he made his appearance, his friends and family cheered for him. He signaled everyone to lift their glasses of champagne to toast Vinnie on his victory.

"I hereby propose this toast to Vinnie, the Animal, the Sicilian Fighting Machine, Russo." Everyone whooped and hollered. "I also give a toast to his trainer, Whitey, and his entourage, who have made this win possible tonight. I know how much work this young man has put into winning this fight, and it paid off. This was not an easy achievement. There were extenuating circumstances that interrupted his flow of concentration and training.

"First, my daughter Mary was shot and shortly after, I caught a bullet myself. Despite this, Vinnie's strength and stamina prevailed. Vinnie should be commended for keeping his head together despite the stress and pressure he was under. I toast again—to my future son-in-law, and to my beautiful daughter, Mary. To the next Heavyweight Champion of the World, Vinnie, the Animal, the Sicilian Fighting Machine, Russo."

Everyone clapped and drank their champagne, and Marenzano embraced Vinnie and his daughter to commemorate a job well done. Vinnie took a second glass of champagne and proposed a toast to Don Marenzano.

"I'm not great at making speeches, so I will make this very short," Vinnie said. "Don Marenzano, you have been a wonderful manager and quite generous to my family, but one thing stands out more than anything about you. Since my father has been absent during the last few years, you have been like a father to me. Although you will never replace him, for my father is number one in my life and will always be. You will have to take second place, but as my future father-in-law, you are number one in my book.

"To my future wife, Mary, you will always be number one. To my fantastic family, my father, Vinchenzo, my mother, Incoranata, my brother, Mario, my sister, Maria, and most of all, my older brother, Dominick, who died several years ago in a car bombing. I love you, Dominick. I know you must be in Heaven watching over us. If it wasn't for you teaching me how to box, I would not be where I am today." Tears brimmed in Vinnie's eyes. "I have a final request. Would everyone please put their glasses down and join me in prayer to the Blessed Virgin Mary."

Together, everyone bowed their heads and recited a Hail Mary. At the end of the prayer, they all rejoiced, and Vinnie yelled out, "Let's party! There is plenty to eat and drink for everyone."

"Wait a minute, not so fast!" Marenzano shouted. "I believe my daughter has something to share with you."

At that moment, Mary held up a brown paper bag and said, "Your mother was too busy to wash your clothes, so I decided I would wash them for you, but look what I found in the bag instead."

Shock registered on Vinnie's face and every person in the room began to laugh. They were already aware of what Mary had discovered. She reached in and pulled out a double-D bra. "This is big enough for both you and my father. Permit me to show you what else is in here…thongs and bras with telephone numbers, and pictures attached. Wow, look at this!" Mary raised a card up in the air. "A bimbo gave up her driver's license to make sure Vinnie could locate her. She is either stupid, desperate, or both."

Vinnie interjected, puffing out his chest. "She is neither. I'm just irresistible."

Mary scoffed and dumped the contents of the bag over his head, then laughed at how he looked with dirty underwear hanging over his face. Soon, even Vinnie was laughing, pulling the thongs off and tossing them on the ground.

Mary embraced him and kissed him passionately. "Vinnie, I decided to keep all the undergarments in the bag, and when you become the Heavyweight Champion of the World, we can auction the items off as memorabilia."

Vinnie chuckled at her ingenuity. "What if I don't become the Heavyweight Champion of the World?" he asked curiously, flashing a grin.

"Then I'll have to pimp you off to all these women who threw their bras and thongs at you."

"We'll have to make a living somehow." Vinnie won the last round, as usual. "It sounds like it would be more fun making a living that way."

Mary began throwing playful punches at Vinnie and they both laughed.

"All right, enough! The food is ready, come and *mangiare*," Marenzano announced.

The victory party lasted for hours, and the guests ate, drank, laughed, and danced the night away.

CHAPTER 28

SUCH A DEAL

Early in the morning, Whitey was opening the door to the gym. As soon as he stepped inside, the phone started ringing. He ran across the floor, cursing, trying to answer it in time.

"Marenzano's Boxing Gym, Whitey speaking." He gasped before adding, "Who's calling?"

"It's Mickey La Blanc. Is Marenzano there?"

"No, he isn't here yet."

"What time do you expect him?"

"He should be coming in the door any minute. Do you want to leave a message?"

"Yeah, tell him I have a great offer to propose," La Blanc said.

"What kind of offer are you talking about?"

"Tell him I got a deal for his guy Vinnie to fight the reigning Heavyweight Champion of the World, my fighter Sugie *the Executioner* Lamar."

"Wait a minute, Mr. La Blanc, he's just coming in." Whitey held the phone away from his mouth and called out, "Hey, boss, you have a phone call from Mickey La Blanc."

"Okay, I'll take the call in my office."

"Mr. La Blanc, he will be taking your call in his office, so I'll place you on hold for a moment," Whitey said.

Moments later, he hung up after Marenzano had picked up the call. He stood there for a moment, wishing he could listen in on their conversation.

"Sugie Lamar," he mumbled to himself, shaking his head. "Vinnie will wipe the floor with that guy."

Marenzano sat down in his chair and picked up the phone. "Hey, Mickey La Blanc, It's been a long time since we spoke." Relaxing, he kicked his feet up on the desk.

"Yes, it has been a long time. I know you're a busy man, so I'll cut to the chase. I'm offering you the chance for your fighter Vinnie to fight my guy for the Heavyweight Championship of the World at Caesars Palace in Las Vegas on May twenty-fifth of this year."

"What's in it for Vinnie?"

"Ten million dollars if he wins, with all the amenities that come with it."

"Give me an example of your amenities," Marenzano said, wanting the best deal for his fighter.

"Five national TV commercials and product endorsements, plus some more bonuses. I'll have it all spelled out in his contract," La Blanc explained. "If he loses, he gets one million and no bennies."

"What is your guy getting if he wins?"

"My guy will get the same exact deal as your fighter, if he wins or loses, but my guy is not going to lose!"

"That remains to be seen," Marenzano replied firmly.

La Blanc laughed dryly.

"I have one more question for you that you failed to bring up," Marenzano said, cutting him short.

"What would that be?"

"Our cut of the pay-per-view TV."

"Twenty-eight percent for you, if your guy wins, or two percent if he loses, and the same for us."

"You have a deal." Marenzano did his best not to show his enthusiasm. "Put it in writing, I'll have my attorneys look everything over, and if we all agree we will set a date for signing the contracts. Make sure the pay-per-view representatives are there at the meeting with their attorneys to sign, as well. By the way, Mickey, no games! *Capisce?*"

"*Capisce*, Don Marenzano!"

"Afterward, we will have a press conference with our fighters and release the date for the Heavyweight Championship of the World."

When Marenzano hung up, he yelled out to Whitey. "We struck it big! Vinnie will fight Sugie *the Executioner* Lamar for the Heavyweight Championship of the World."

Ecstatic, Whitey let out a loud whoop. Tears fell from his eyes. Marenzano embraced Whitey, becoming emotional himself while he shouted, "We did it, we did it!"

"Yes, we did it, boss, didn't we?"

"Listen, Whitey, listen to me very carefully, no one and I mean *no one* is to know about this, understand? Pick up the phone, call Vinnie, and tell him to get his ass in this gym by noon today. If he wants to know why, just say I was insistent about seeing him."

"I'm on it," Whitey said, heading for the phone.

Vinnie walked in promptly at noon and spotted Whitey walking across the gym.

"Hey, Whitey, what's up?"

"Come with me, he is waiting in his office for us," Whitey said, putting his arm around Vinnie and leading him up the stairs.

Marenzano ushered them in and sat behind his desk. "Take a seat, both of you," the Don said. He stared into Vinnie's eyes, then slammed his hand hard on the desk.

Nervous, Vinnie startled and said, "Did I do something wrong, Don Marenzano?"

He continued to stare into Vinnie's eyes, worrying him.

"What the fuck," Vinnie mumbled. "Are you going to have me wacked or something?"

Marenzano slowly rose from his chair and pulled the gun out of his holster. He pointed it at Vinnie's head without uttering a word, just staring at him intensely. If he hadn't just gone to the bathroom, Vinnie might've wet himself. He trembled, sweating profusely, as Marenzano steadily lowered his gun and slipped it back in the holster.

He walked toward Vinnie and suddenly grabbed him, kissing him on each cheek. Then he held him at arm's length and shouted at the top of his lungs, "We did it, Vinnie, we did it!" as he shook him back and forth vigorously.

Whitey joined in, clapping and rejoicing, until finally Vinnie couldn't take it anymore and he yelled out, "What the fuck did we do? Someone please tell me what the fuck is going on!"

"We got you a shot at the Heavyweight Championship of the World with the reigning Heavyweight Champion, Sugie *the Executioner* Lamar at Caesars Palace in Las Vegas on May twenty-fifth of this year."

"Oh my God, that's fantastic news." Vinnie ran his hand through his hair, a wide smile crossing his face. "I thought I was going to be wacked."

The two jokers started laughing hysterically.

"Yeah, it's really amusing to you, but I was scared shitless," Vinnie retorted, pissed off. "I can't believe I finally have a shot at the Heavyweight Championship of the World!"

He hugged both men, and they all laughed and cheered. Marenzano wiped his eyes and said, "Okay, let's all calm down, I want you both to listen carefully." He stepped back behind his desk and sat down. "Here are the rules. Neither one of you are to discuss this with anyone, not even your families." He gave Vinnie a pointed look. "Not even Mary. It doesn't leave this room. I don't want this leaking out until everything is signed, sealed, and delivered. *Capisce?*"

"*Capisce*, Don Marenzano," both Whitey and Vinnie agreed.

"Now that we understand each other, the two of you can get to work. I have to go to a very special luncheon date." He flashed a grin and headed for the door.

"What's her name?" Vinnie asked, chuckling.

"Don't be a smart ass!" Then, in Italian, Marenzano said, "You mind your business and I'll mind mine. Have a great day, boys."

CHAPTER 29

UNDERCOVER

Marenzano was to meet Weinstein at the usual location. He climbed in his Cadillac and got on interstate I-95, headed for New Hampshire. Upon arrival, Weinstein set up the slide projector, and the audio and video equipment, displaying the wild party with the five heads of the commission.

Weinstein began with the slide projector. "I need you to identify the five heads of the commission for me, since they all look different with their clothes off." They both burst out laughing. "Okay, who's this guy on the sofa with the hot blonde?"

"He's Don Chico, who runs New York City and heads the commission for the five families."

"That's what I thought, and the other guy who looks like he's nine months pregnant standing with the sexy brunette with the big boobs?"

"It's Don Genaro Bertolli, he runs Brooklyn." Marenzano chuckled and scratched his chin.

"Is this who I think it is?" Weinstein rolled his eyes.

"Yes. It's Michael Franchase, he runs New Jersey, including AC."

"He's the only one in decent shape out of the whole group," Weinstein noted. "Take a look at this guy coming in the door all dressed up at six in the morning with two suitcases in his hands."

"Oh shit! That's Jean Claude De Martino, the owner of the house," Marenzano exclaimed, astounded by his early arrival.

"Wait until I show you the video of what happens to Jean Claude De Martino after he puts his suitcases down. Salvatore, I hope you're ready for this!"

As the video played, Marenzano watched what the heads of the families did and said. Halfway through, he asked Weinstein to stop the video for a minute.

"You know," Marenzano began, "if we make thousands of copies of this video and sell it, just imagine the millions of dollars we could rake in. Your FBI warnings about making illegal copies could be put at the beginning of each DVD."

Weinstein roared with laughter until his side ached. "I hate to burst your bubble, Marenzano, but that's against the law and everything I stand for. As you Italians say, forget about it!"

"Go ahead and start the video again."

Weinstein hit the play button. "Sal, who is this guy who has a face only a mother could love?"

"He's Frank Cataldo, who runs Philly."

"The guy with the three broads all over him, what's his name?"

"That's Peter Champa, he is in charge of Queens."

"Okay, Sal, we are coming to the part where Jean Claude De Martino enters the house and drops his suitcases in awe." They watched as Martino was quickly joined by two naked chicks who wasted no time in seducing him and removing his clothes.

"What's his part in all this?" Weinstein wanted to know.

"Simple, he owns many legitimate businesses in the U.S. and Canada. The boys need somewhere to wash their clothes."

"Yeah, I'm sure he does an excellent job doing the laundry."

"Now you got it, Weinstein!"

"Salvatore, after watching and listening to your *goombas*, what did you surmise from all of it?"

"For one thing, I found out who my real friends are, and who my enemies are. Now I know who I can trust and who I can't. Was all the evidence we gathered substantial enough for the bureau?"

"I have enough here to put these guys away for the rest of their lives. However, we need to gather more intelligence to find out who will roll over on who."

The men shook hands and went their separate ways, until their next encounter.

CHAPTER 30

MEETING OF THE MINDS

Early in the morning, Marenzano and his wife were fast asleep when the phone rang, startling them. The clock read seven.

"Who the fuck is calling me this early?" Marenzano snapped, sitting up.

Philamenia tugged a pillow over her head. "Well, answer the fucking phone and you'll find out!"

He picked it up and spoke in an agitated voice. "This better be important, since you woke us up from a sound sleep."

"It's Mickey La Blanc, I wanted to let you know that I just dropped off the contract in a large envelope at your front door, inside the screen door. I apologize calling you this early, but I'm on my way to the airport to catch a flight for West Palm Beach, Florida. I have an appointment with Bobby Brown this afternoon."

"Is he still alive?" Marenzano joked.

"Yes, I know he's been around for ages, but he is quite alive and continues to do promotions, talking up a storm."

"I remember his hair standing up straight, like he stuck his finger in an electrical socket," Marenzano said, laughing and yawning at the same time. "Give the old gizzard my regards."

"Will do. Now, make sure you give the contract to your attorney today."

"Yes, I can deliver it to him this afternoon. I can assure you, I am as anxious as you are to get this contract signed and announce the big event at the press conference. When do you return?"

"My meeting is just for the weekend, so I'll see you on Monday."

"Okay, have a good and safe trip."

After he hung up, he headed downstairs to retrieve the envelope, and Philamenia began making breakfast while Marenzano shaved and showered. As the couple ate their eggs and toast, Philamenia asked, "What's in the envelope?"

"Some papers I need to bring to my attorney."

"Is everything all right, Sal?"

"Yes, everything is fine." She would find out soon enough.

After breakfast, Marenzano drove to downtown Boston to the law office and met with attorney Paul De Angelo to go over the contract for the Heavyweight Championship.

Paul nodded, seemingly pleased. "On the surface, everything seems in order, however, it is a lengthy contract, and I would like to take it home over the weekend to examine every detail carefully."

"Do that," Marenzano said, shaking his hand.

"I'll call you on Monday morning," Paul said, slipping the papers back in the envelope.

"Not too early, this La Blanc guy called me at fucking seven in the morning and woke up my wife and I."

"Okay, how about after ten?"

"That sounds good. Paul, just one more thing. La Blanc flew to Florida this morning to have a meeting with Bobby Brown, the promoter."

Paul laughed and shook his head. "Well, the meeting could be either a good thing or a bad thing."

"We'll see."

Marenzano left and headed back home. He'd promised to take Philamenia to their cabin in New Hampshire for a quiet, romantic weekend. On Monday morning, they headed back to Boston. While driving home, Sal received the promised phone call from his attorney.

"I went over the contract extensively and it's a good deal!"

"That's excellent news," Marenzano said. "What's the next step?"

"I intend to reach out to La Blanc and his attorney, advising them that we agree to the terms of the contract, and we can set the date for signing it."

"Great, call me back when you have the date and time."

Then he called Vinnie and spoke as cryptically possible. "Everything looks good, I will notify you when I have more info." He hung up and turned to his wife. "How about going to the North End for lunch?"

"Perfect, I wasn't in the mood to cook anyway," she replied, delighted.

She didn't ask what he'd been talking about on the phone, and he was relieved.

A couple of days passed, and Marenzano was in his office doing paperwork when someone knocked on the door.

"Who's there?" he shouted.

"It's Paul De Angelo."

Marenzano opened the door and invited him in. "Hi, Paul, how are you? Would you like something to drink?"

"No, thanks."

"So, what's up?"

"We set the meeting for Friday at my law office for two in the afternoon. Is that agreeable to you?"

"Yes, that's fine, Vinnie and I will arrive together."

"Sal, I will have my associate, William Driscoll, with me at the meeting. La Blanc will be there with his attorney and two representatives from pay-per-view along with their attorney."

"Okay, that's how I like things to go," Marenzano said, leaning against his desk.

"Well, since everything works for you, I'm taking you to lunch this time," Paul said, opening the door to leave.

"Fair enough, where are we going for lunch?"

"There's a brand new Syrian restaurant which opened in the Back Bay. I've already been there, and the food is absolutely delicious."

They arrived at the restaurant and were escorted to their table. The hostess handed them a menu, and in the interim, a very well dressed Syrian man walked over to their table to greet them.

"I am glad to see you again, Mr. De Angelo," he said, nodding.

"How are you, Mohammed?"

"I am great!"

"How is business?"

"Business is very good, thank you," he boasted.

"Mohammed, I would like to introduce you to my close friend, Salvatore Marenzano."

"Good to meet you, Don Marenzano."

"So, you've heard about me," he replied with surprise.

"Your reputation precedes you."

They all laughed good-naturedly.

"Don Marenzano, you and I have a great deal in common," Mohammed continued. "Let's just say, we have the same interests and may walk the same paths. Someday, I will come to visit you and we can talk some more."

"I am always interested in doing business with someone who can make me money," Marenzano said frankly.

Mohammed smiled. "Lunch is on the house! Allow me to order my special cuisine for you."

They both thanked him for his hospitality, and Marenzano and his attorney enjoyed exotic Syrian dishes and imported alcohol, making it an incredible luncheon.

At two o'clock on Friday, Marenzano and Vinnie arrived at the law firm. They were met by Paul and his associate, William Driscoll, who led them to the conference room. Mickey La Blanc was there with his fighter, Sugie *the Executioner* Lamar, his attorney, and two representatives from pay-per-view, accompanied by their attorney. Everyone was seated, awaiting their arrival.

Paul introduced Marenzano and Vinnie to the group.

The Executioner rose from his seat, an imposing, tall man. He pointed threateningly in Vinnie's direction. "You don't have a chance to win."

"Wrong!" Vinnie retorted, standing up to him.

"I will *execute* you in the ring!"

"Don't be so sure of that," Marenzano interrupted, standing between them. "Okay that's enough, save it for the press conference."

All the appropriate parties signed the contracts and shook hands, excited for the upcoming fight. The press conference would take place in two weeks. The meeting ended, and Marenzano and Vinnie headed back to the gym.

CHAPTER 31

WHAT GOES AROUND, COMES AROUND

The press conference was set up at the Airport Hilton Hotel in East Boston. A multitude of media trucks and vans congregated outside the Hilton, filling the vast parking lot. Inside the hotel, an abundance of reporters and photographers representing TV news networks, newspapers, and magazines from all over the world, were packed in the conference room.

Cameras began flashing when Vinnie *the Animal, the Sicilian Fighting Machine* Russo entered the room, accompanied by Salvatore Marenzano, and his trainer, Whitey. They walked toward the huge table and sat down in front of the microphones.

The media frenzy kept a close eye on the Heavyweight Champion of the World, Sugie *the Executioner* Lamar, with his manager Mickey La Blanc and trainer Joe Brown. Cameras were rolling, and pictures were being snapped, while an array of flashing lights blinded Vinnie and forced him to blink and squint.

The news reporters shouted out questions, and it was hard to follow what they were saying. Everyone was talking at once, causing the conference room to go in complete pandemonium.

Ultimately, Marenzano stood up and raised his hands. "Everyone, please be quiet for a moment. We need to conduct this press conference systematically. Just raise your hand, and when you're called upon, you can ask your question." Marenzano glanced around, then pointed at someone in the back. "Okay, the woman in the blue dress, what is your question?"

"Hi, I'm Linda Blank from channel four, and I have a question for Sugie. When you begin your training, will you have to train harder than you ever did before?"

"Shit, he's nobody special." Sugie glared down the table toward Vinnie. "I'm gonna whip his ass in three, then hang him on the tree."

The crowd burst out in laughter. "Mr. Lamar, when you say *in three*, are you referring to three minutes or the third round?"

"I'm referring to three minutes, when I intend to pulverize this Italian and send his butt back to Sicily, where all the other grease balls come from."

Some of the people in the crowd seemed amused, others cringed at the reference. Vinnie's face turned red with anger, and he jumped out of his seat to lunge at Sugie. He was quickly restrained by Marenzano and Whitey, who held him tightly as he tried to pull forward toward Sugie.

Sugie Lamar invited it, beckoning Vinnie forward, and taunting, "Okay, Marenzano, let your boy go! I'll do him right here and in front of all these cameras, so we don't have to wait."

Mickey La Blanc jumped from his chair and yelled, "Now, now, boys, there will be no fighting today. Besides, Pay-Per-View is not here. We don't want to lose all that revenue and sponsorship money."

A burst of laughter came from the crowd. Next, Rudy Constanza, a reporter from the Boston Herald, had a question for Vinnie. "What do you have to say for yourself regarding the comments from your opponent, Sugie Lamar?"

Vinnie stood from his chair and walked calmly to Mike, staring into his eyes. The reporter leaned back, seemingly intimidated.

"He's dead meat!" Vinnie growled.

"What do you mean exactly?" Mike asked.

Vinnie continued to stare at the reporter without uttering a word. Then, he turned on his heel and headed back to his seat.

"I believe I know the answer, Vinnie," Constanza shouted. Vinnie turned and looked at him. Constanza snickered and said, "What are you going to do, have Sugie wacked?"

The crowd went silent. Someone in the back of the room coughed, then blew their nose.

Marenzano stood and shouted, "*Nobody* is going to get wacked around here." He glared at the reporter. "My fighter, Vinnie, will teach Sugie Lamar a lesson in the ring, the day of the fight, not before. Sugie will get the beating of his life, I guarantee it! He won't be able to walk out of the ring on his own accord, he will be carried out on a stretcher. This press conference is now over." Marenzano looked toward La Blanc.

"Yes, the press conference is over," La Blanc affirmed, "so no more questions."

It hadn't gone as well as they'd expected. Sugie Lamar's distasteful comment had infuriated Vinnie, and it was obvious to the crowd that he was already considering ways of getting back at Sugie in the ring. But the reporter's comment had been even more unnerving, and Marenzano wasn't about to let that slide. The last thing they needed was bad press, especially at a time like this.

The news media didn't bother to hide the fact that they were disgruntled as they were told to vacate the premises. Marenzano stepped down from behind the table and waded through the crowd. People stepped aside for him, nodding respectfully or looking to the ground. They didn't want to get in his way.

With a few short steps, he'd caught up to the reporter, Rudy Constanza, and tapped him roughly on the shoulder.

When the reporter turned and opened his mouth to say something, Marenzano stopped him by asking, "Did you record the audio?"

"Yes," Rudy said, looking both perplexed and worried.

"Do me a favor and play it back for me."

As the audio played, Marenzano snatched the recorder and pulled out the disc.

"What are you doing?" Rudy demanded. "Give it back to me, it's private property."

"In just a minute. First, you are going to listen to me," Marenzano commanded, leaning in close enough the man could smell his breath. "Remember what you said about me having Sugie wacked? I assure you, the only one that's gonna get wacked is *you* if you don't curb your wise remarks!" Marenzano handed him the recorder and disc. "Now get the fuck out of here, you weasel."

The reporter left the room in a hurry, trembling and looking as if he'd peed his pants. Marenzano slipped his hands into his pockets and shook his head, chuckling to himself.

Early the next morning, Vinnie ran up the steps to Marenzano's office and burst in, forgetting to knock. "Have you seen the newspaper, we made the front page!" he exclaimed.

"No, let me see the paper." He took the Boston Herald from Vinnie and unfolded it. He glanced down at it, then back up at Vinnie. "By the way, try not to rush in like a fucking elephant next time, you almost gave me a heart attack." He turned back to the headline, and read the article. When he was finished, he dropped the paper on his ink blotter and burst out laughing.

"What did you say to this reporter to have him do a complete turnaround?" Vinnie wanted to know, as he leaned against the desk.

"I just told that *mamaluke* that the only one who's gonna get wacked around here is him if he doesn't cut the shit."

"What else did you say?"

"I told him to get the fuck out of there."

Vinnie laughed, his hand on his belly. "Come on, let's go to breakfast to celebrate. I'm buying."

They decided to walk to the diner, and talked along the way. Marenzano spotted a newspaper machine, with the Boston Herald displayed through the clear plastic.

"Hang on a minute, Vinnie." He placed coins in the machine and opened the door, removing all the newspapers.

Vinnie watched him tuck the entire stack under his arm. "Don Marenzano, you only paid for one newspaper," he said, concerned.

"Fuck the Boston Herald," Marenzano snapped. "Payback is a bitch."

They walked into the diner and sat at a booth. He dropped the pile of papers on the table.

"Watch this." Marenzano stood up and shouted, "Extra, extra, read all about it! Read the front page of today's Herald. Come and meet the next Heavyweight Champion of the World, Vinnie *the Animal* Russo. Get your free autographed copy of the Boston Herald and meet Vinnie in person."

Excited diners left their tables and swarmed over to Vinnie. Surrounded by people, he signed the papers and handed them off to his fans. Some people snapped photos of Vinnie with their cell phones, and had their picture taken with him. It was an unexpected joyful event for everyone.

Marenzano only shook his head and chuckled, clearly impressed with his own clever gag.

CHAPTER 32

A FIGHT TO THE TOP

Weeks went by quickly, and Vinnie rose early each morning, executing his vigorous training program. He began with grueling miles of road work. His training routine included running up and down the Harvard Stadium stairs, as before, across Storrow Drive and over the Charles River into Cambridge, until arriving at Bunker Hill and navigating the streets of Charlestown.

He cooled down by walking at a leisurely pace back to the gym, then showered to refresh himself, ending the morning with a meal at his favorite diner.

At the diner, a stringent diet meal was prepared by a special chef hired by Marenzano. After his lunch, he returned to the gym to relax and take a short nap. When Vinnie awoke, he got ready for the rest of his training with Whitey, hit the heavy bag, and practiced his timing with the speed bag, jumping rope, and doing three minute rounds with six different sparing partners. It was a full day, after which he headed home to eat dinner and relax.

Even with his busy schedule, he found time to spend with his family and Mary. The grueling pace continued as Vinnie prepared for the Heavyweight Championship. The next morning, he had a short visit with Marenzano and Whitey up in the office.

Marenzano reclined in his chair, and Whitey leaned on the desk. Vinnie listened attentively from where he sat.

"You've got three days before the fight," Whitey said, "so we're stopping the strenuous training program."

Marenzano nodded. "You're ready. And you're going to win this!"

Vinnie was in the best shape of his life both physically and mentally. "What should I do to get ready?" he asked nervously.

"Just relax," Whitey told him. "Don't train anymore, just stick to your diet. Take it easy."

Vinnie nodded. "I will."

Later that afternoon, Vinnie was enjoying some time alone at his house. There was a knock at the door. When Vinnie answered it, he was surprised by the man who was standing there.

"Hello, Grandmaster Wooten. How are you?"

"I am well, thank you."

"What can I do for you, sir?"

"Well, since your fight is scheduled for three days from now, I want to show you something that will help you, if that's all right with you."

"Of course, come inside." Vinnie stepped aside and ushered Grandmaster Wooten into the living room. He shrugged off his jacket, and the two of them sat across from each other in comfortable armchairs. "What are you going to show me?"

Grandmaster Wooten nodded and stood. "Vinnie, I want you to watch me carefully. This exercise will help you greatly if you use it." He demonstrated a very special exercise in Tai Chi which was known to relax the body. Then, he showed Vinnie another martial art exercise in Qigong to help him find his inner strength. Vinnie tried it, and Grandmaster Wooten coached him.

Finally, Vinnie couldn't help but ask a question that was bugging him. "Grandmaster Wooten, why are you doing this for me?"

"Easy." He shrugged. "I like you, Vinnie, and I think you have a lot of talent. I thought you might benefit from this. It's something you won't learn from Whitey, and I thought it might give you a boost up."

"Thank you so much," Vinnie said gratefully. "Even after that first try, it's unbelievable, I can actually feel the difference."

"Good. Now, I want you to practice with me for thirty minutes. Is that all right?"

"Yes, definitely! I want to learn all I can."

At the conclusion of the session, Vinnie thanked the Grandmaster for his secret tips. "I know this will help me, and I promise to practice the movements of Tai Chi and Qigong every day including the day of the fight," Vinnie declared.

"No need to make any promises," the Grandmaster said, stepping toward the front door. "I'm just glad I was able to help. It has been great seeing you, and good luck with the fight. I will be there cheering you on!" Before he left, he added, "There's one more thing I need to tell you. This might sound very strange." He frowned, as if worried what Vinnie might think.

"Please, tell me," Vinnie urged him.

"I had a dream a couple of nights ago, and you were in it. There was a woman's voice and she told me you would need my guidance. That's the real reason I'm here."

"Did you see the woman's face in your dream?"

"No, but there was something very unique and sacred about her voice." He thought for a moment. "It's odd, I can still hear her voice in my head. This is why I was compelled to visit you. You must think I'm weird." The Grandmaster laughed worriedly.

"Not at all." Vinnie thought of the Blessed Virgin Mary, and made the sign of the cross. He embraced Grandmaster Wooten, then stepped back. "I know who spoke to you in your dream."

Grandmaster Wooten's eyes widened in curiosity. "Please, enlighten me!"

"I'd rather explain everything after the fight."

"Okay, but this is going to bug me until you tell me." The Grandmaster chuckled. "Looks like we have something in common. We're both a little out there, eh?"

Vinnie laughed. "Maybe."

"*Ciao*, Vinnie, I will see you in Las Vegas at the fight."

"*Ciao*, and thank you again, Grandmaster Wooten." Vinnie waved to him, and watched him depart.

In Las Vegas on the morning of the big fight, Vinnie stayed huddled beneath his warm blankets in the hotel room, thinking about Grandmaster Wooten's fantastic dream. The day went by fast, and soon Vinnie was being escorted to the locker room at Caesars Palace for preparations before his championship fight. He was accompanied by Marenzano, Whitey, the towel man, cut man, and their doctor. The physician examined him, and determined he was one hundred percent fit to fight.

He spent some of his free time practicing the moves Grandmaster Wooten had shown him. As he made the necessary hand movements, concentrating on his breathing, he saw Whitey watching him. The confusion on his trainer's face was clear. Finally, Whitey stepped closer, peering at Vinnie.

"Okay, I'll bite," he said, crossing his arms over his chest. "What the hell are you doing?"

"I'm practicing my Tai Chi breathing exercises and Qigong inner strength focus ability," Vinnie explained, smirking at Whitey's bemusement.

Whitey rolled his eyes. "Well, cut the crap and get over here, I need to tape your hands." He eyed him, adding, "Get rid of your chop suey bullshit!"

Vinnie shook his head, laughing. "It comes in handy. You'll see."

Soon, everyone else had left the room to give Vinnie time to chill out, except Whitey. Vinnie stepped into the restroom, leaving the door partially open. Peeking out, he grinned in amusement when he saw Whitey standing in front of a mirror, mimicking his Tai Chi and Qigong movements.

When he emerged from the restroom, Whitey immediately acted as if he hadn't been doing anything, and Vinnie did his best to suppress a wry smile.

"I'm going to lay down and rest, Whitey."

"Good, chill out, and I will be back soon," Whitey replied.

Thirty minutes passed, and Vinnie's entourage arrived to escort him to the ring. The crowd broke out in shouts and screams, rising from their seats and pumping their fists into the air. The atmosphere was charged, causing Vinnie's excitement to increase tenfold. The floor vibrated as spectators stomped their feet on the stands. Bras and panties flew through the air as women screamed Vinnie's name.

"Vinnie, Vinnie, Vinnie!"

When they reached ringside, the crowd was roaring and chanting. As the current champion entered the arena, the crowd quieted and watched raptly. The huge spotlights crossed the room and focused on Sugie *the Executioner* Lamar, the reigning Heavyweight Champion of the World, accompanied by his entourage. His fans went ballistic and chanted, "Sugie, Sugie!"

They stomped their feet as he strutted through the arena and into the ring, raising his arms in the air.

The announcer pulled down the microphone, and his voice echoed throughout the room. *"Ladies and gentlemen, welcome to Caesars Palace, Las Vegas, with a crowd capacity of fifty-six thousand people.*

"On hand for super fight number three, the reigning Heavyweight Champion of the World, Sugie the Executioner Lamar, six feet tall and weighing in at two hundred and twenty-three pounds. His challenger, Vinnie the Animal, the Sicilian Fighting Machine Russo, six-foot-one and weighing in at two hundred and eight pounds.

"Our referee tonight will be Mark Tabata, and the five judges from left to right are Mike Donnelly, Irving Shapiro, Richard Weiner, Joe Nettie, and Jose Gonzalez. Let's not forget our fifteen gorgeous card girls, one for each round."

The crowd cheered for the sexy girls, scantily clad, who waved and smiled, winking fetchingly at the men nearest them.

Without warning, Sugie stepped forward, and the announcer shouted, *"What's going on? Sugie, get back in your corner."*

Sugie waved a hand in annoyance. "I just want to talk to Vinnie," he said, shrugging his massive shoulders.

Sugie rushed over to Vinnie's corner and threw confetti over his head. The crowd burst into uproarious laughter.

"You're going down in three!" Sugie shouted, stepping back.

"You are dead meat," Vinnie yelled.

Everyone in Vinnie's corner jumped in the ring to restrain him, while Sugie stepped close and taunted him, then jumped back again.

The referee jumped between them, his eyes narrowed. "Sugie, get back in your corner, or you will be fined ten thousand dollars!"

The threat did the trick, and the reigning champion returned to his corner.

The announcer shouted, *"The bell rings and the fight is underway! Vinnie the Animal Russo charges at the champion, Sugie the Executioner Lamar with a flurry of punches to his head. Sugie is pushed into the corner, and Vinnie works him with upper cuts to the abdomen and arms. You can see Vinnie's anger as he grabs Lamar out of the corner into the middle of the ring!"* The crowd shrieked. *"Wow, folks, the referee is warning Russo not to repeat that stunt or he will lose a point! The fighters resume with Lamar finally waking up and sending a left hook to Vinnie's head, knocking him to the floor.*

"Blood is dripping down the side of his face and the referee starts his ten count. Vinnie slowly staggers up on the ropes and stands straight. The referee's asking him if he's all right to continue, and he's nodding yes, folks!

"The fight continues, and Vinnie is quickly struck with another left hook to his head, starting the ten count again. Vinnie gets up, and again the referee is checking on him. He's okay! But blood is still dripping from his head." The noise in the arena was almost deafening as Vinnie's fans rooted for him.

"There are only sixty seconds left in the first round. Vinnie charges with a right upper cut to the jaw, picking his whole body six inches off the floor, knocking Sugie out cold. What an amazing triumph, Vinnie's right upper cut was a bombshell of a blow!"

In the ring, Vinnie tugged out his mouthpiece as Sugie awoke. He bent over the fallen fighter and sneered.

"You were number one and you did not take me out in three." Again, Vinnie's fans were stomping their feet and shouting. "I took you out in one, and now *I'm* number one!"

Marenzano went to Vinnie and handed him some confetti to sprinkle over Sugie Lamar. They laughed, proud of the victory.

Vinnie "the Animal" Russo versus
Sugie "the Executioner" Lamar

"Now, it's my turn to be the Heavyweight Champion of the World," Vinnie exclaimed, throwing his arms into the air.

The referee took the microphone and made his announcement. "By unanimous decision, our five judges have ruled a knock out in the first round by Vinnie *the Animal* Russo, the new Heavyweight Champion of the World." He turned to the winner. "Vinnie, on behalf of the Nevada State Gaming Commission, I hereby present you with the World Heavyweight Championship belt."

The announcer shouted excitedly, *"Vinnie holds the championship belt in the air and the crowd cheers—pandemonium!"*

The referee handed Vinnie the microphone. "First, I want to thank my family, my trainers, and all the people in my life who made this possible." He felt his heart swell with pride as he clutched the belt, his gaze scanning the crowd. "Without you, I would not have accomplished this victory. A special thanks to my trainer, Whitey, who stuck by me from day one. My manager, Salvatore Marenzano—without him, none of this would have been possible. Dad, if you are watching from wherever you are, I love you! There is one more person I need to thank, and she is my girlfriend, Mary, who's here tonight at ringside. Mary, stand up, so I can see you."

Mary rose, tears of happiness streaming down her cheeks.

Vinnie had been planning this moment, rehearsing it in his head, but none of his dreams compared to the energy of the crowd, the emotions filling him with joy, and the excitement he felt standing before thousands of people, about to proclaim his love to the woman of his dreams.

"Mary." He listened as the crowd hushed, growing quiet. "Will you marry me?"

Mary covered her mouth, smiling and laughing through her tears. "Yes, yes, I will!"

She ran into the ring and wrapped her arms around Vinnie and kissed him. Breaking away from her soft lips, Vinnie turned to Whitey and asked, "Where's the thing?"

"What thing?"

"You know, *the thing!*" All around them, people were clapping and whistling as Vinnie held Mary close.

"Oh, *that* thing, I left it locked up in the office safe."

Vinnie gasped, and his jaw dropped. "Whitey, what the hell…?"

Whitey grinned, showing off his crooked yellowed teeth, then waved a hand nonchalantly. "Oh, I forgot, it's right here in my pocket."

Vinnie shook his head, then laughed as Whitey handed him the ring. He slipped the ring on her finger, then kissed her gently on the lips.

"I love you," he exclaimed.

Rather than answer, she pressed her body against his and kissed him passionately, not seeming to care about the sweat or the blood. The fans cheered enthusiastically, and even Marenzano had a few tears in his eyes. Vinnie waved to the crowd, thanking them, just before the Caesars Palace security escorted him safely to his locker room.

It had been an amazing fight. Not only had he secured the championship, but he'd also gotten engaged to the love of his life.

Nothing could be better than this.

CHAPTER 33

IN THE DARK OF AN ALLEY

In the locker room, Marenzano opened a large bottle of champagne to celebrate Vinnie's win and his engagement to Mary.

He raised his glass in a toast. "Salute to the new Heavyweight Champion of the World."

Everyone raised their glass. "*Gendon*," they intoned, "May you live a hundred years!"

Marenzano had reserved the ballroom at Caesars to celebrate Vinnie's victory, attendance by invitation only. Family and friends returned to their hotels to dress for the victory party. Marenzano and Whitey hung back with Vinnie.

Vinnie could still hear the screaming of the crowd in his head; it was an echo that refused to relent. He didn't mind. This was the best night of his life.

Marenzano placed a hand on Vinnie's shoulder, then hugged him. "I'm very proud of you," he said, stepping back and looking at him admiringly.

Whitey nodded in agreement. "Kid, you were a real fighting machine out there. You showed that big mouth who's the boss and made me very proud of you, too. Now, hop in the shower and I'll rub you down when you get out. I can't wait to see you in your fancy tuxedo."

"Thank you both," Vinnie said, before he turned and headed for the shower.

Glancing behind him, he had a sensation the two men were talking about him; he felt as if they were hiding something from him, but he wasn't sure what it was.

Once he'd received his rubdown, he put on his tuxedo.

When he emerged, Whitey whistled and said, "Wow, you look like a million dollars in your tux, and you've got your own millions to go with it."

"Thanks, Whitey." Vinnie adjusted his jacket and added, "Now I need to get to the party and meet Mary."

"Not so fast, kid! I am under strict orders from the boss to keep you here until he returns."

"Why?" Vinnie asked, frowning. In the back of his mind, he realized they had some sort of surprise for him. *I wonder what it could be?*

As if answering his thoughts, Whitey said, "I guess you'll find out when he gets here and you stop asking so many questions."

Vinnie narrowed his eyes, looking irritated. "But—"

"But nothing! Just because you're the Heavyweight Champion of the World, it doesn't mean you don't have to listen to me anymore. I am still the boss! So, sit down and have another meatball and glass of champagne with me."

Suddenly, there was a knock at the door. "Who is it?" Whitey snapped.

"It's me, Marenzano, open the fucking door!"

Vinnie laughed. "That's him, all right."

Marenzano stepped in first, then raised a hand and said, "Vinnie, someone's here to see you." He peeked around the corner to someone Vinnie couldn't see yet, then nodded for him to come inside.

Vinchenzo Depasquale walked in, grinning happily, dressed neatly in a suit for Vinnie's party.

Vinnie's eyes widened and he ran forward to hug his father. "Dad, oh my God, you're here!"

Vinchenzo held him at arm's length and looked into his eyes. "I wouldn't miss your championship fight for anything in the world. I am blessed, and so proud to have a son like you."

Vinnie embraced his father, and Vinchenzo kissed him on both cheeks.

"Salvatore." Vinchenzo turned to the Don and opened his arms. "Thank you for everything you have done for my family." Next, he turned to Whitey and said, "Whitey, you have trained my son well, and I am indebted to you."

"It's been my pleasure, he is very talented," Whitey said with admiration.

"Dad, how are things in Sicily?"

"The war is finally over," Vinchenzo replied, appearing relieved. "You can remain living in Boston for now, but soon you will have to return to Sicily. Remember the promise you made?"

"Yes, Dad."

"You have approximately eighteen months to return home to Sicily." He patted him on the back. "I know you are eager to meet Mary at your victory party. Marenzano, Whitey, and myself have business to discuss, so we will meet you in the ballroom."

Vinnie turned to head out, and Marenzano called out, "Wait, Vinnie, before you go, make sure you go out the back exit door to avoid the crowds, or you'll never get out of here."

Vinnie nodded, and headed down the hall toward the rear exit. After shoving on the door and stepping out into the balmy evening, the darkness was a stark contrast from the bright lights of the building behind him. The door clicked shut, and he was alone. Shadows fell around him as he stepped onto the dirt and cracked cement.

For a moment, he paused, enjoying the solitude. Glancing into the sky, he noted the rising moon; he wasn't sure what time it was, but he knew he had to get moving.

As he turned to walk down the alley, he was startled by a man dressed in casual slacks and a button-up shirt.

"Russo, good fight." The man didn't sound sincere, and there was something about him Vinnie didn't like. As he reached out to shake the man's hand, the stranger refused to reciprocate, and Vinnie stepped back nervously.

"Who are you?" he asked, taking a second to check his exit from the alleyway, and make sure he could leave quickly if he needed to.

"I am the MMA Champion of the World, Jimmy Doherty, and I can kick your ass!" the man snapped.

Vinnie's eyes widened in surprise. "I'm sure you can, but I'm on the way to my victory party." He sidestepped the man and headed toward the mouth of the alley, but Doherty jumped in front of him, grabbed his arm, and wasted no time slapping him across the face.

In an attempt to protect himself, Vinnie immediately took a defensive stance, as Doherty swung around in a spinning hook kick to the head, and quickly grappled Vinnie to the ground.

In the ring, Vinnie was unstoppable, but now he wasn't so sure of himself. He'd been attacked in the dark, and he wasn't prepared. When Doherty grabbed him with both arms in a strangle hold, he couldn't fight back, and the world seemed to spin.

He struggled to break free, but it was too late. The alley grew darker, and his eyes fluttered shut, just before he was dropped unconscious against the cold cement.

After enjoying the exciting fight, Grandmaster John Wooten was walking outside in the warm, dry Las Vegas evening, glancing up at the stars in the sky and watching the city come alive. He was lost in thought, when he suddenly spotted a man running out of the dark alley nearest him.

John followed boxing closely, and had always loved the sport, so when he saw the man's face, he knew immediately that it was Jimmy Doherty, the MMA Heavyweight Champion. There was no mistaking the man's bulky features and chiseled, hard expression.

There wasn't much going on along this street, which was tucked away from the action of Vegas, behind the casinos. John wondered why the man had been running, and why he was out here. As he stepped up to the mouth of the alley and peered into the shadows, he spotted a broken form lying on the ground, his face on the dirt.

At first, he thought it might be a bum, but as he rushed into the alley, he realized the man was wearing what looked like a nice suit. When he turned the body on its side, he saw it was Vinnie, badly beaten, his face marred with bruises, stained by the dirt and grime of the alley.

"Holy shit," he hissed under his breath, immediately retrieving his cell phone from the pocket of his light jacket. He dialed 911, and explained the situation as he knelt over Vinnie.

The police and ambulance arrived in minutes, and John waved them into the alley.

"This way!"

"Do you know this man?" a paramedic asked.

"Yes, it's Vinnie Russo, the new Heavyweight Champion."

A cop walked up to John, scratching at his chin. "I know who he is, I was working detail at ringside," the officer explained. He and John stepped back as the paramedics did their job. "What's your name?" the cop asked.

"My name is John Wooten. And you, officer?" The two men shook hands.

"I am Sergeant Sam Varga of the Las Vegas Sheriff's Department." The sergeant nodded toward Vinnie's broken body as they lifted him onto a gurney. "Mr. Wooten, how could this happen to him? Did you see anything?"

"Yes, sir. The man I saw running from the alley was Jimmy Doherty, the MMA Heavyweight Champion of the World. Doherty would have used his martial art expertise by kicking and punching Vinnie's body and head. He would have exceptional martial art abilities to fuck up and overpower…even a Heavyweight Champion Boxer."

Sergeant Varga nodded and continued to question John, even as the ambulance pulled away, racing Vinnie to the nearest Emergency Room.

"I appreciate your help, Mr. Wooten. I'm so glad you were here to witness this. You'll need to stop by the police station for a signed written statement."

"I'll be glad to do that, but first I need to notify his family. I know they're in the Caesars ballroom at Vinnie's victory party, and they're expecting him. I was headed there myself when this happened."

The sergeant nodded. "I need to accompany you, so you can point out his family and introduce me to them. I'll explain what happened." He paused, shaking his head. "Vinnie could have died here tonight."

John looked around at the now empty alley, shocked that a professional fighter would do such a thing. "His family will be devastated," John said, more to himself than to the sergeant, as the two men walked somberly out of the alley.

CHAPTER 34

ONLY GOD KNOWS

John arrived at the party with Sergeant Varga, both men wishing they didn't have to deliver such unhappy news.

John scanned the crowd of people, and pointed to the right. "I see Vinnie's manager, Salvatore Marenzano."

"All right, let's go talk to him. You can introduce us," the sergeant suggested.

After wading through the crowds of people, John stepped up to Marenzano, who was enjoying a drink with a few of his colleagues.

"Excuse me, Mr. Marenzano, I'm sorry to interrupt. This is Sergeant Varga from the Las Vegas Sheriff's Department. He has something he needs to tell you."

Marenzano nodded curtly. "Hello, Sergeant, how can I help you?"

"It's good to meet you, sir, but I'm afraid I have some bad news about your fighter, Vinnie."

Marenzano was good at remaining stoic, but when his left eye twitched slightly and the corner of his mouth turned down in a frown, it was clear he was worried. "Bad news, what bad news?"

"Vinnie was found in an alley unconscious, badly beaten," Varga explained.

Marenzano's eyes widened and his fingers tightened around his empty glass. He turned and handed the glass to a passing waiter, who nodded and walked on.

"It couldn't have been from the fight," Marenzano mumbled. "He hardly had a scratch on him."

"I agree, I was on detail duty at ringside and saw the entire fight," Varga explained. "While Mr. Wooten was walking by, he identified Jimmy Doherty running out of the alley."

"Yes," John affirmed. "I ran into the alley and noticed it was Vinnie on the ground and quickly called 911."

Marenzano ran a hand over the side of his head. "Shit."

The news caused Marenzano to reel where he stood. It seemed as if only moments had passed since Vinnie had been handed the championship belt; now, he was unconscious, and God only knew how bad it was. Marenzano lost interest in the revelry around him. After all, without Vinnie, the party was nothing.

He thought back to the moment he'd encouraged him to go out the back way, through the alley. His attacker had anticipated that, and had been waiting for him. Marenzano couldn't help but think if Vinnie had gone out the front and battled the crowds and excited fans, he wouldn't have ended up in the hospital. He knew it wouldn't help matters to blame himself; after all, if Vinnie's attacker was determined to corner him, he would've managed it in another setting. But he continued to return to the thought, dragging himself through a million versions of *if*.

"Now I need to speak to his family," Varga said, breaking Marenzano out of his reverie.

"Right. I'll bring you to them." Reluctantly, Marenzano led the way, and introduced Vinnie's parents to Sergeant Varga, so he could break the terrible news to them.

Marenzano's heart was heavy with emotion when he saw the expressions on the faces of Vinnie's parents. They were traumatized, unable to believe someone would commit such an atrocity against their son.

Incoranata froze for a moment before dropping the wine glass she'd been holding. It shattered on the floor as she covered her face and wept. Mary wrapped her arms around her, and the two women consoled each other.

The party stilled. The music stopped.

Vinchenzo hugged his wife, kissed her, and looked deep into her eyes for a long moment, whispering something Marenzano couldn't hear.

Then, Marenzano put an arm around him, and said, "Come on, I'll have my limo drive your family to Sunrise Hospital." He signaled to one of his men, and said, "Go get Whitey and have him meet me at the limo."

"Yes, sir." The man rushed off to find Vinnie's trainer, while the party transformed into a somber event as word spread that Vinnie had been attacked and wouldn't be joining them.

Due to the mass hysteria over the attack, the family was escorted to a private waiting room. Incoranata was frenzied as her thoughts returned to Dominick; she was terrified she would lose Vinnie, too. She clawed at her husband's chest, tugging on his jacket, and shouting out in Italian, "My son, my son!"

Mario and Maria clung to their mother, crying, distraught. Mary leaned against her father, overcome with tears. Whitey slumped into a chair and sat with his arms leaning against his legs, his head hanging as he stared at the ground.

A priest entered the waiting room and introduced himself as Father Andrew Andolini. He was there to console the family and lead them in a prayer.

Incoranata calmed herself and listened to the priest's calming words. Over and over, she felt herself breaking on the inside, and wondered how she'd managed to handle this turbulent lifestyle for so long. The love of her family carried her, and her husband was her anchor to reality; she didn't know what she would do without him. She thought of Vinnie in the hospital bed, his body bruised and bloodied, and she wept harder.

"Hail Mary, full of grace, the lord is with thee…"

Following their prayers, Father Andolini bowed his head. "Vinnie is in God's hands now."

Maria wiped her tears away. "He is in the Blessed Virgin Mary's hands, too, and she will not let anything happen to him."

"You are right, Maria, you are so right," Father Andolini agreed.

Two hours passed, and one of the doctors entered the waiting room. He was a short man with mousy brown hair and a perpetual frown on his wrinkled face. "Hello, I am Dr. Polsky." He glanced around at the small group. "Who are the parents of Vinnie Russo?"

"We are the parents." Vinchenzo stood.

Incoranata rose, leaning her trembling body against her husband as she prepared herself for the worst.

"We have completed the surgery on your son and I have some good news and bad news."

"Tell us the bad news first."

"Your son is still in a coma," the doctor said gravely.

Incoranata gasped. "Oh, God…"

"He suffered a right side vertebral artery dissection, which is one of four arteries that supply blood flow to the brain." The doctor spoke slowly, as if mindful of Incoranata's panicked state. "The right artery occluded, preventing blood circulation to the brain, subsequently causing a pin hole bleed. The good news is the operation was successful in stopping the bleed in his brain. He also suffered a couple of broken bones. The truth is, I don't know how long he will remain in a coma. It's too early to make an accurate prognosis. I will keep you posted of any changes in his condition. All you can do now is pray."

Incoranata shuddered and continued to weep, muttering to herself.

I cannot lose another son. Please, God…don't let me lose another child.

"Can we see him?" Vinchenzo asked, wrapping his arms around his wife to keep her steady.

"No, he is still in the recovery room. Once he is placed in the intensive care unit, you can see him. The next seventy-two hours are very crucial, so please be patient."

"Thank you, Dr. Polsky."

"You're welcome. You will hear from me soon." The doctor excused himself and left, stepping quietly down the cavernous hall.

Vinchenzo turned and beckoned to Marenzano. "Come here, I want to talk to you." He looked into his wife's eyes. "Incoranata, will you be all right? I'll only be gone a moment." He wiped the tears from her cheeks with his fingers, and brushed her hair away from her eyes.

She nodded. "Mm-hm."

"Good. Be right back." He helped her gently into a seat, tucking her shawl around her body.

With a quick glance back at his wife, he stepped out in the hall with Marenzano on his heels. Turning to make sure they were alone, he kept his voice low so they wouldn't be heard. "I would like you to find out everything you can about this guy, Jimmy Doherty, and I mean everything," Vinchenzo murmured. "Do me a favor and set up a meeting for us with our connection in Vegas. Start off by obtaining information, find out if this guy is connected. Don't do anything to anyone without clearing it with me first, and that's an order."

Marenzano nodded. "You got it." He placed his hand on Vinchenzo's shoulder. "Don't you worry. We'll get this guy."

"Oh, I'm not worried. I *know* we'll get him." The sensation coursing through Vinchenzo's veins was predatory. No one could hurt his son—or anyone he loved—and get away with it.

No one.

CHAPTER 35

PENTHOUSE CONNECTION

Early the next morning, Vinchenzo met Marenzano for breakfast in the hospital cafeteria. Before eating, they stood by the station in the corner where the condiments, napkins, and utensils were displayed. Vinchenzo was meticulous and slow at stirring the sugar into his coffee. Both men made it appear as though they were enjoying nothing more than casual small-talk.

"Here's what I found out from our contacts," Marenzano said quietly. He nodded to a nearby table, where they placed their coffees before getting their breakfast trays. "This Doherty character is owned by Frankie De Nucci." He kept his voice at a low whisper as they headed back to the table with their trays.

"It figures." Vinchenzo shook his head, grimacing. He sat down and dug into his eggs and bacon, forcing himself to eat despite his unrest. "Something always has to get in our way and make things more difficult. I am the Boss of Bosses, and whether he is with us or not, this guy is going to pay one way or another."

"I agree," Marenzano said between bites. "I already set up a meeting for us with Frankie at his casino penthouse apartment. I spoke to Wooten and he will come with us for back-up."

"Is he with us?" Vinchenzo inquired, disbelieving.

"Not really, he's an independent, and the only guy I trust outside of our family. Besides, he is the toughest and strongest mother fucker I have ever met. He is also your son Mario's Jujutsu instructor."

Vinchenzo grinned. "That's why Mario goes around the house performing his Kung Fu movements."

"Grandmaster Wooten and I have had our differences in the past, but he has always been there when we needed him, no matter what!" Marenzano took a moment to finish the last of his eggs. He shoveled sausage into his mouth with gusto, then frowned in distaste. "This food sucks. Not like at my restaurant."

Chuckling, Vinchenzo said, "Okay, Sal, from now on Wooten is with us. I'm convinced."

Marenzano glanced up and nodded toward the entrance to the cafeteria. "Speak of the devil, here he is."

After breakfast, the three men left for their appointment with Frankie, arrived at the casino, and headed straight for the penthouse. They were met by four of Frankie's goons, one of which immediately pulled out a gun, brandishing it at them.

John was quick to react; he grabbed the gun out of the man's hands and aimed it between his eyes.

"Stop the bullshit!" Vinchenzo growled. "Wooten, give the man his gun back…and you, put your gun away where it belongs." He glared at the four goons. "Do you know who I am? I am Don Depasquale from Sicily."

The four goons glanced at one another, and the man who appeared to be leading them immediately apologized. "Don Depasquale, I'm so sorry, you are welcome of course."

"That's better." Vinchenzo shoved past them when they opened the door, which was ornately decorated with a design of golden vines along the frame.

The goon turned to Grandmaster Wooten, his eyes narrowed, and said, "How'd you get that gun from me so fast?"

John leaned in close, jabbing the man in the chest with his index finger. "If you pull your gun out again, I will shove it straight up your ass and pull the trigger, unloading a round of ammunition until it comes out of the tip of your dick."

"Sorry I asked!"

Frankie De Nucci greeted the men and introduced one of his captains, Nick Pellagrini. He ordered his goons to wait outside the door.

Frankie placed a reassuring hand on Don Depasquale's shoulder. "Vinchenzo, let me apologize for my fighter Jimmy Doherty's actions, which were unjustified and all because of his ego and jealousy."

"What the fuck did my son ever do to him?"

"Nothing, you have a right to do whatever you see fit."

"You're damn right I do!" Vinchenzo retorted.

"What do you want done about this unfortunate situation?" Frankie asked, cocking his head.

"I'll tell you what I want." He glared threateningly at Frankie. "If my son dies or never wakes up from his coma, your fighter will die by my own hands and you will lose all your control of Vegas. You will no longer be allowed to earn from this family or any other family for life, *capisce?*"

"*Capisce*, Don Depasquale. And if your son fully recovers?" he asked, clearly probing for more information.

"Frankie, I'll make this interesting for you. If my son lives and fully recovers, Grandmaster Wooten will exclusively train Vinnie to have a professional match with your fighter, Doherty, for the MMA World Championship. You will personally put up one hundred million dollars, winner take all, and only then will I allow you to stay in Vegas."

"What if Vinnie should lose?"

John Wooten crossed his arms over his massive chest. "He won't lose, I'll see to that. Vinnie will give your fighter the worst beating he has ever experienced in his career."

"Vinchenzo, I know you are upset," Frankie began delicately, "and you have every right to feel this way, but aren't you being a little unreasonable?"

"Unreasonable!" Vinchenzo pulled his gun out of its holster and shoved it in Frankie's mouth. "Do you still think I am unreasonable?"

Frankie shook his head, his eyes wide and terrified, sweat beading on his forehead.

"You have no rights or say in this matter any longer." Vinchenzo shoved the gun at him harder, making him flinch. "It is what it is." Then he pulled his gun out and put it away.

Nick, Frankie's captain, reached for his own gun, but John quickly subdued him, swinging him around and hanging the helpless man by his feet over the edge of the balcony.

Marenzano cackled, his hand on his stomach. "Look, Nick pissed himself!"

"Frankie, now that we all understand each other, you will not make another move in this town without consulting Wooten. He will report everything to me. Do we all agree?"

"Yes, Don Depasquale." Frankie nodded, wringing his hands, his gaze cast toward the ground.

John threw Nick onto the plush carpeting, and the man stayed there as if afraid to move.

"Good, this meeting is over!" Vinchenzo turned toward the door. "I need to return to the hospital and be with my son."

The trio left the penthouse, laughing about the events of their meeting. While driving to the Sunrise Hospital, Vinchenzo turned to Wooten and said, "When we arrive, Marenzano will introduce you to three of our zips. Remember, you guys need to keep a close eye on Frankie and his crew. But don't kill anyone."

"Okay, but can I hang someone over the balcony until he pisses himself?" John asked, giggling.

They all laughed. Don Depasquale turned to Marenzano, grinning. "Wooten will fit in our family just fine, he's insane!"

CHAPTER 36

DREAM OR REALITY

Back at the hospital, Vinchenzo went to his wife, who had exhausted herself crying, her arms wrapped around her body as she sat, defeated, in the cushioned chair.

"Has anyone heard from the doctor about Vinnie?" Vinchenzo asked, his face etched with worry.

"No." Incoranata rubbed her tired eyes. "Please find out something."

Vinchenzo headed for the nurse's station and spoke to Carol, the nurse assigned to Vinnie's case. "I'd just like to know if there have been any changes in my son's condition."

"Yes, but you need to speak to Dr. Polsky. He can explain your son's prognosis." She glanced down the hall and added, "I see him now. How's that for timing?"

Vinchenzo flagged down the doctor, who smiled warmly. "Dr. Polsky, has there been any improvement in my son, Vinnie Russo?"

"Yes, but, I prefer to talk to everyone in your family and your friends at one time," the doctor said, placing a comforting hand on Vinchenzo's shoulder.

When Dr. Polsky approached the waiting room, Incoranata sat up straight, then rose from her chair, tissues clutched in her quivering hand. Vinchenzo put his arm around her, steadying her.

The doctor folded his hands before him. "I am sure you're all very concerned about Vinnie's present health and well-being," he began. "He is now out of recovery and in the ICU. Vinnie is still in a coma, but there is good news. His vital signs have improved and he is resting comfortably."

Marenzano stepped forward and said, "Excuse me, doctor, do you have any idea how long Vinnie may be in a coma?"

"No, I'm afraid not," he replied, shaking his head sadly.

"Can we visit him now?" Incoranata asked.

"Yes, but I have some specific rules you'll need to follow," the doctor said, raising a hand pointedly. "Only the immediate family, parents, and siblings will be allowed to see him now, and only for fifteen minute intervals."

Whitey grimaced, exchanging displeased glances with Marenzano and Mary.

Vinchenzo shook his head. "I would like his manager, Salvatore Marenzano, his wife, and their daughter, Mary, Vinnie's fiancée, as well as Vinnie's trainer, Whitey, to be allowed to visit with my son."

The doctor nodded. "They can see him starting tomorrow, but no one else." He glanced toward the young lady who stood near her father. "I will allow Mary to see him tonight with the family. It may do him wonders to hear her voice. I will have the nurse take you to Vinnie's room."

In the Intensive Care Unit, Carol, the nurse, paused by the door to Vinnie's room. "Now, I must warn you," she said, raising her hands emphatically, "Please control your emotions. No crying out. We believe a comatose patient can still hear you, so this kind of reaction can hinder your son's recovery. Always say encouraging things to him, such as 'I love you' or 'we are praying for you.' You can also reminisce about good times spent together. Now you may enter, but remember…only fifteen minutes at a time."

"Yes, we understand, and thank you," Vinchenzo agreed, eager to see his son.

Vinnie looked so much smaller in the hospital bed, hooked up to machines. There was a tube down his throat to help him breathe, and his arms were hooked up to all kinds of intravenous lines and monitors to record his vital signs, his pulse, respiration, and heartbeats.

Incoranata went to his side and kissed him on the forehead, whispering, "I love you."

She wept silently, tears falling down her face, trying her best to compose herself, remembering what the nurse had told them.

Vinchenzo held his hand. "Don't worry, my son, you will have a full recovery, I promise."

Little Maria and Mario kissed their brother and told him how much they loved him. Then, they both bowed their heads in prayer, reciting the Hail Mary.

Mary stood nearby, waiting anxiously, biting her bottom lip as she looked at her future husband laying there helpless. It broke her heart. Soon it was her turn, and Incoranata ushered her over, putting an arm around her to encourage her. Mary took a deep breath, letting the tears fall along her reddened cheeks.

"Go ahead, dear," Incoranata whispered.

Mary nodded, then hugged and kissed Vinnie gently. "I love you so very much, Vinnie, and I am waiting for you to open your eyes." She paused, almost as if she believed the first sound of her voice would awaken him, draw him out of his deep sleep and back into her arms. "I cherish the day when we get married…I…" She had to stop, bite her bottom lip again, and steady herself. Incoranata gently rubbed her back. "I think about it every day, about you…Vinnie." She stepped back, covering her mouth, and Incoranata hugged her close.

Mario looked up at his father, a book tucked under his arm. "Can I read a story to Vinnie?"

"You have a book with you? What's it called?"

Mario held it up so Vinchenzo could see the cover. It was emblazoned with the image of a strongman lifting the back end of a truck. Vinchenzo nodded approvingly.

"*The Adventures of John Wooten, World's Strongest Man, Master of Masters,*" Mario said excitedly.

Vinchenzo chuckled and tousled his son's hair. "Yes, of course you can." He looked impressed, glancing at the book again. Was there anything Wooten *didn't* get into?

Mario stepped close to Vinnie and began to read, relaying the fantastic tales of John's escapades. The family listened, watching raptly for any sign that Vinnie could hear them—a twitch of an eyelid, a finger, *anything*.

In the middle of the second short story, there was a light knock at the door. The nurse peeked in. "I'm afraid your fifteen minutes are up," she said, her voice soft and low.

"Can we just kiss Vinnie goodbye?" Incoranata asked, wringing her hands.

"Yes, most certainly," she replied, the expression on her face conveying a deep understanding for what they were going through.

Once they'd said their goodbyes, they left the room reluctantly, following the nurse back to the waiting area.

Her hands folded before her, Carol addressed them. "I'd like to make a suggestion. You all look so exhausted. I can tell you need some sleep, and you aren't going to help Vinnie by damaging your own health. Maybe you can take shifts being with Vinnie. This way, some of you can get a few hours of sleep. If there is any change, I will contact you. My prayers are with you."

The nurse departed, and the family exchanged uncomfortable glances.

"I want to stay," Incoranata blurted out.

"Me, too," Mary said, taking her hand to comfort her.

"Vinchenzo, dear, will you take the children back to the hotel?" Incoranata asked, nodding toward the young ones, who were already beginning to nod off in their seats.

"Of course." Vinchenzo roused them, and Incoranata and Mary walked them to the elevator.

On the way, they spotted double glass doors that opened into a small area with pews, and a beautiful altar that stood before stained glass windows depicting religious scenes.

"Oh, a chapel," Incoranata said, sounding relieved. "Before you leave, let's go in and pray for Vinnie." She took her husband's hand, and they went inside.

Kneeling before the altar, they recited one Hail Mary and one Our Father prayer. The ambiance in the chapel was overcoming, and they felt a sense of peace descend on them, as if the Virgin Mary herself were standing beside them, telling them everything would be all right.

Their son's health was in God's hands, and He would surely care for them all.

Back in the ICU, Dr. Polsky ordered a CT Scan for Vinnie, and had him transported downstairs for the test.

The nurse was waiting for him to be wheeled back to his room. Upon his return, Carol and another nurse washed him and changed his gown. Afterward, she dimmed the light and placed a small statue of the Blessed Virgin Mary on the night table next to his bed. The statue was close to Carol's heart; she always kept it on her desk. For some reason, she'd been compelled to bring it to him. She thought it might help somehow.

"You need the Virgin Mary more than I do right now," she whispered.

After Carol left the room, all was silent. For a long while, the dim lighting cast a soft glow over Vinnie. Soon, the light brightened, and a pale form appeared at the end of Vinnie's bed, clothed in white, her hands folded before her.

The Blessed Virgin Mary spoke, and there was no question Vinnie heard every word.

CHAPTER 37

A CLOUD OF LIGHT

In the morning, during Carol's hospital rounds, she went to check on Vinnie and noticed some miraculous changes in his appearance. It seemed as though all his cuts, scratches, and bruises had completely disappeared overnight. After making a thorough examination to ensure she wasn't imagining things, she rushed to the nurse's station and ordered one of the clerks to page Dr. Polsky.

She told the clerk to have the doctor meet her in Vinnie's room. Moments later, Dr. Polsky, along with a team of doctors, arrived.

"Carol, what seems to be the problem?"

"Well, Dr. Polsky, there's actually nothing wrong, which is why I called you here."

"I...I'm sorry, I'm not sure I understand," the doctor replied, perplexed.

"You need to see what I've discovered." She gestured to Vinnie's face. "Look here, on his face and head...he doesn't have any bumps or visible bruises." The doctors gathered around, and she pulled the sheets down to expose Vinnie's legs. The signs of the attack were virtually gone.

All the doctors gaped in surprise, and Dr. Polsky raised an eyebrow, leaning closer.

"Nurse, please untie the top of his gown."

The doctors were baffled as they gazed upon his torso, seeing no evidence of bruising anywhere on his body.

"It's a miracle," Carol whispered in amazement. "This is going to sound very strange, but—" She glanced nervously at the other doctors. "Last night, before I left, I placed my statue of the Virgin Mary by his bedside." She indicated the little statuette, its hands folded in prayer.

Dr. Polsky furrowed his brow. "Well, however it happened, it's quite apparent that something unexplainable has occurred. I would like to do a thorough examination."

"Yes, Doctor. Good idea."

During his examination, the doctor removed the breathing tubes, and Vinnie began to breathe on his own.

"Nurse, notify the family immediately. This is wonderful news."

She nodded excitedly and rushed off. Carol knew Incoranata and Mary were still at the hospital in the ICU waiting room. When she told them the news, tears of joy ran down their faces, and they hugged in excitement and relief. They were certain Vinnie would continue to recover from his coma and injuries with their faithful prayers.

After calling to notify the rest of the friends and family, everyone arrived in good spirits to talk to Vinnie, knowing he could hear them at last.

On the following afternoon, Mary was alone with Vinnie expressing her love to him, grasping his fingers tightly.

Since the attack, she had been mired in grief and fear. She knew she was lucky to have found the love of her life at such a young age, and she couldn't bear the thought of losing him. Like everyone else, she had been thinking of *if*—if this had happened, or if that had happened, might things have been different?

She shook her head, trying to expel those thoughts. Right now, Vinnie was here. He was going to wake up, and he needed her.

She sat there for a long time, thinking of their future together, when suddenly he responded by tightening his hand around her fingertips.

"Oh, Vinnie, can you hear me?" She gasped, overcome with joy. "Can you feel me touching you? Vinnie…Vinnie, please wake up and show me a sign you can hear me. I love you so very much, and I can't live without you."

Unexpectedly, his eyes began to tremble and his face showed obvious signs of a grimace, as tears slowly dripped down his face. Suddenly, his hand went limp and his expression disappeared along with his tears.

Mary shot up from her seat and ran to the nurse's station. "Nurse! Carol! Someone…come quickly!"

My Vinnie will be okay, she thought to herself. *I just know it.*

On the morning of the third day, Vinnie's family and close friends sat by his bedside, discussing his progress with Dr. Polsky.

John shook his head in wonderment, certain there was something special about Vinnie. He thought back to the dream he'd had, where a strange woman told him Vinnie needed his help. He had done as the woman asked, not questioning it.

His gaze shifted from Vinnie to the statue of the Blessed Virgin Mary on the bedside table. John was beginning to think divine intervention had played a part in the young man's recovery; surely, nothing so miraculous could be an accident.

The doctor shook his head, amazed by the rapid improvement. "I will need to run a battery of new tests, including another CT scan and MRI. I'll need everyone to leave the room so we can run the tests. It will take most of the day, so you may want to leave the hospital and come back in a few hours."

John stood with the family, wishing there was something he could do. He thought of his own son, Michael; he couldn't imagine anything like this happening to him. With a deep understanding of what they must be going through, John stuck close, ready to offer assistance in any way he could. He watched as Incoranata and Vinchenzo listened to the doctor, and solemnly nodded their understanding.

"Yes, Doctor," Vinchenzo said, putting his arm around his wife. "We'll return soon."

Everyone left. When the hall outside Vinnie's room was mostly empty, and he was alone, John glanced through the small window in the door, shaking his head.

"You'll be okay, Vinnie," he whispered. "I know it."

Moments later, when the room was empty, a haze of soft light manifested around Vinnie's bed. The Blessed Virgin Mary appeared, bowing her head, a halo of golden pulsing energy surrounding her ethereal form.

"Vinnie, open your eyes, for I am here as I promised. You have a long road ahead of you, and a short time to reach your goal, before you return to Castellammare del Golfo. When I ascend from your bedside, you will recover fully from your coma and critical injuries.

"John Wooten will be your guardian and guide here on earth, to help you on your path to success. Listen to his wisdom and teachings of his martial arts. You will become faster, stronger, and more knowledgeable than you could possibly imagine. I will not appear to you again until you return home to Castellammare. Remember your promise."

As the light diminished, Vinnie's eyes fluttered open. He didn't realize where he was at first as he glanced around at the clinical white walls, and heard voices and phones ringing somewhere outside the room. After a moment of clouded thought, he realized he was hearing the background noise of a hospital, and he slowly recalled the attack. He couldn't remember anything after that; his mind had gone totally blank.

He dragged his body into a sitting position, and when he moved his arm, he felt a slight tug against his skin. Glancing down, he realized he was hooked up to IVs. Careful not to pull on the wires, he forced himself to the edge of the bed and slowly sat up, his body weak and trembling.

He felt cold and numb at the same time, his thoughts slow and jumbled. The stark white linoleum was frigid beneath his feet. He went carefully to a nearby mirror and looked at himself, noticing his bruises and cuts were gone, replaced by healthy skin.

Turning to the door, Vinnie dragged the IV station along with him, happy to be out of bed. Without stopping to consider the consequences, he walked purposefully down the hall.

Shortly thereafter, Carol was on her usual rounds when she stepped into Vinnie's room and gasped upon seeing the empty bed. She ran back to the nurse's station and slammed her hand on the front desk, startling the clerk.

"Sara, did someone take Vinnie for his tests?"

She shook her head. "No, is something wrong?"

"Are you sure?" Carol leaned forward, her eyes wide.

"Yes, why?"

Running back to the room, an odd thought crossed her mind as she picked up the little statue of the Blessed Virgin Mary.

Oh my God, she thought. *It's as if he's ascended to Heaven.*

Turning on her heel, she gasped to find Vinnie standing there, holding onto his IV pole. She clapped a hand over her heart in shock.

"Were you looking for me?" Vinnie asked, his voice scratchy.

"It's a miracle!" Carol shouted, clutching the statue to her chest. "You're out of your coma and walking around. Vinnie, my name is Carol, and I have been taking care of you throughout your ordeal. I brought you my statue of the Virgin Mary to watch over you, and it seems to have done wonders for your recovery. I am so thrilled to see you out of your coma, but you must conserve your energy by getting back in bed."

She ushered him to the bedside, helping him climb in and get under the sheets. "I can tell you're still weak," she continued as she tucked him in. "You must rest! I will call your doctor so he can examine you further. He just scheduled tests for you, and he will be amazed at your recovery. Well, he's *already* amazed," she rambled on. "I mean, nothing like this has ever—"

"Where are my family and friends?" Vinnie asked worriedly.

"They left when the doctor advised them your tests would take a few hours. I will contact them immediately."

Within minutes, Dr. Polsky had learned the news, and was astonished with Vinnie's unbelievable recovery. He was to be moved out of the ICU, and he would discontinue the majority of his medication. A prominent specialist,

Dr. Harold Greenberg, was to fly in to investigate Vinnie's so-called miraculous recovery—for which there was no medical explanation.

Family and friends arrived back at the hospital and rushed to his side. Vinnie was overwhelmed by their love for him, and he was so relieved to see his parents.

Incoranata burst through the door, shouting, "My son, my son, you are a very lucky boy!" Tears streamed down her face as she kissed him. "We all kept praying for you, and we knew in our hearts that you would come out of the coma. I can't wait for you to come home!"

"Ma, I heard your prayers and words of encouragement, but I couldn't respond." Memories drifted back to him; it was as if he'd been frozen in the bed, unable to say a word, but still observing everything that happened around him.

Vinchenzo stood behind his wife with his hand on her shoulder. "We know you are a fighter in many ways, and we had faith in God you would pull out of your coma. I am very proud of you."

"I love you, Mom and Dad," Vinnie said tearfully, hugging both of them. "You are the greatest parents in the world."

Maria tugged on her father's hand. "It's a miracle, it's a miracle, Daddy!"

Vinchenzo lifted her into his arms and kissed her on the cheek. "Yes, Maria, it is a miracle." He sat her down on the bed next to Vinnie.

"I knew you would be all right, the Virgin Mary told me you would be," Maria announced.

Mario leaned over his brother to kiss and hug him.

"I love you guys, and missed you very much," Vinnie told them.

Mary rushed in the room and embraced Vinnie, kissing him lovingly. "Could you hear me when you were in a coma?"

"Yes, Mary, but I couldn't answer you. I wanted to tell you how much I love you."

"It is just as well you couldn't talk, since every time you open your mouth, you insert your foot," Marenzano interrupted. "You know, Vinnie, everyone, including myself, has been worried sick about you, but I have to be honest about one thing. For a moment, I did say to myself, I could save money on a wedding if he doesn't wake up from his coma."

"Well, Sal, if you feel that way, maybe we should run away and get married." Mary punched her father playfully in the arm. "Dad, you didn't really think that!"

Everyone laughed. "What about all the money you would lose from my fights?" Vinnie pointed out.

"You know, I'm just kidding with you," Marenzano said, waving his hand. "I'm glad you're all right, kid." Marenzano hugged him.

"Boy, do I miss training you," Whitey said, giving him a hug.

"I missed it, too, and can't wait to get back to the gym."

"That's my boy," Whitey said proudly, patting him on the shoulder.

The reunion was joyous; everyone in the room was chattering happily. Vinnie was still exhausted from his ordeal, but he knew he would heal. He hoped he could return to training soon.

Recalling his win before the incident in the alley, he was filled with pride once again. *That attacker may have beaten my body, but he can never destroy my spirit.*

Vinchenzo gestured for Marenzano to step out into the hall with him. Once they were alone in a less-traveled area, he murmured, "Listen, Sal, I want you to pick up Wooten and visit our friend at the casino penthouse. Let him know how fucking lucky he is that my son is out of his coma."

"No problem, I'll take care of it."

Vinchenzo nodded, clapping Marenzano on the shoulder as he departed. He noticed Dr. Polsky walk down the hall, heading for Vinnie's room. Vinchenzo followed him and listened closely.

"I'll be moving Vinnie out of the ICU and to a regular floor, and I've requested that the head of neurology at the Mass General Hospital oversee your son's case. First, I have some more tests to perform on him. Someone from transportation will be here momentarily to wheel him downstairs for his tests."

Everyone said their goodbyes to Vinnie, assuring him they would wait at the hospital to be at his bedside. Vinchenzo knew his son was in good hands, and had faith he would pull through and be better than ever.

At noon on the following day, Dr. Polsky and Dr. Greenberg entered Vinnie's room. His entire family and close friends were by his side as promised. Vinchenzo was pacing back and forth. When he saw the doctor, he shook his hand warmly.

"Hello, Dr. Polsky, how are you?"

"I'm just fine, how are you?" the doctor asked.

"I'm great now that my son is doing well." Vinchenzo breathed a sigh of relief, knowing everything would be fine.

This had been a trying time for Vinnie, and for the family, but things were finally beginning to look up. Vinchenzo would've never thought his son's championship fight would end this way, and fury continued to simmer within him whenever he considered Vinnie's attacker.

The doctor turned and nodded toward an older man standing nearby. "Let me introduce you to Dr. Harold Greenberg from the Mass General Hospital."

As Vinchenzo shook Dr. Greenberg's hand, he noticed how kind-looking he was; his watery blue eyes showed a welcoming disposition.

"I have good news for you about your son's CT scan and MRI, along with his blood work," Dr. Greenberg said. "I examined the results and have come to the conclusion there is absolutely no evidence of any trauma sustained during his attack. In my forty years of practice, I have not seen anything like this." The corners of his mouth crinkled upward in a warm smile. "I don't believe any of my colleagues have ever experienced it either."

"Can I ask you something?" Vinchenzo said, cocking his head.

"Yes, sir."

"If you cannot explain what happened to our son, who can?"

"Well, let's just say, your son is a miracle fighter. Seems as if Vinnie is up for anything, even a fight for his life. He's a strong young man," Dr. Greenberg replied with admiration. "As far as Dr. Polsky and I are concerned, your son can be discharged tomorrow morning."

"That's wonderful, Doctor, but will my son ever be able to fight again?"

"Yes, absolutely."

"How long will it be before he can?" Marenzano asked anxiously.

"I'll answer that question in thirty days at the Mass General, when I complete his follow-up examination. Vinnie, you're a lucky guy!"

Vinnie had been listening attentively from where he sat in his bed. He nodded, laughing. "Yes, doctor, I agree with you. I am a miracle fighter."

CHAPTER 38

BILL OF GOOD HEALTH

Thirty days passed, and Vinnie was pacing back and forth in Dr. Greenburg's waiting room at the Mass General to hear the doctor's evaluation from his new series of tests.

Finally, the receptionist stepped out into the waiting room and announced, "Vinnie, Dr. Greenburg will see you in his office now. It's down the hall, last door on the left."

"Thank you so much," Vinnie said, relieved.

When he entered the office, Dr. Greenberg spread his arms and exclaimed, "Vinnie, you look like a million-dollar man! What have you been doing for the last thirty days?"

"Well, to be honest, I've been training very hard," Vinnie explained as he took a seat.

"Tell me, what type of training have you been doing to get back into shape?"

"First, I took your advice not to engage in any sparring. I have been skipping rope, doing a great deal of roadwork, training on the heavy bag and speed bag, plus lifting weights."

The doctor shook his head, astonished. "Vinnie, how many hours a day are you training?"

"Three to four hours a day, five days a week, accompanied by a strict diet regime."

"That's wonderful. You'll be happy to hear your tests are all negative and your blood work is remarkable." He glanced down at the paperwork on his desk before removing his thin-rimmed spectacles. "As far as I am concerned, you can return to full contact boxing and martial arts. In your case, specifically Jujutsu."

"Doc, what made you pick Jujutsu?" Vinnie asked curiously.

"Grandmaster Wooten is my Jujutsu instructor and has been for many years. He's a close friend. His Jujutsu is as good as you're going to get anywhere in the world."

"Like you, Dr. Greenburg, you are the best neurologist in the country."

"I won't argue with you there," the doctor said, winking.

"So, Doc, has Grandmaster Wooten ever been one of your patients?"

"Yes, more times than I would like to admit. He's kind of a pain in the neck, if you know what I mean," he joked. "You're going to be fine, Vinnie. Go get 'em!"

"Thanks, Doc," Vinnie said, shaking his hand. "I'll make sure you have front row tickets for you and your family on fight night."

Vinnie left feeling reassured, and headed home. Upon his arrival, he found Marenzano and Whitey waiting for him in the kitchen, sitting at the table. The air was filled with the scents of bacon, eggs, and sausage.

"What are you guys doing here?" Vinnie asked, his stomach grumbling.

Incoranata stepped out of the living room and returned to her seat at the table, sipping her coffee. "They are having breakfast with me," she said cheerfully. "It is known I make the best breakfast in town. Sit down and eat with us. You can help yourself, everything is still hot on the stove."

Vinnie grinned. "Okay, when did I ever turn down my mother's cooking?"

He filled his plate and sat down, digging in.

"What did the doctor say?" Marenzano asked as he wiped his mouth with a napkin.

Vinnie handed him the medical authorization to return to fighting, and both he and Whitey were ecstatic.

"Eat up, kid, you're going to need it," Whitey said, finishing his toast. "Your *serious* training starts today! No more days off. You will train seven days a week, one day all boxing, the following day all martial arts, and you will be expected to put in anywhere from four to six hours a day for the next six months. You will be required to eat, sleep, train, and nothing else, *capisce?*"

Marenzano interjected, "Grandmaster Wooten said that as long as you're well, he wants you at his Dojo at one this afternoon. Looks like you're good to go, kid! Tomorrow morning, meet us at our gym at ten, got that?"

"Yes, sir!" Vinnie said excitedly.

Marenzano and Whitey finished their breakfast and excused themselves.

When Vinnie was alone with his mother, Incoranata took his empty plate to the sink. "Be careful with this martial arts, Vinnie," she warned. "You are out of your league right now. So you need to listen carefully to Grandmaster Wooten."

"Okay, Ma, don't worry," he said, hugging her close.

"Don't worry, you say, but I'm your mother," she retorted. "I was born to worry about you!"

Vinnie smiled warmly, kissing her on the cheek. "I was born to worry about you, too, Ma."

"Oh, Vinnie. *Ti voglio bene*. I love you."

CHAPTER 39

TRAINING AT THE DOJO

Warrior.

Vinnie arrived promptly at the Dojo, a little nervous about what was in store for him.

Grandmaster Wooten stepped aside, ushering him in. "Welcome to my humble Dojo. I would like you to meet some very close friends of mine."

A group of men were gathered together, talking amongst themselves. They turned when Vinnie walked in.

"This is Yuri Beznokof from Russia, a sambo master and Russian Collegiate Champion. Next to him, Mr. Yamamoto, who is an Olympic Judo Champion and Head Coach for Japan's National Judo Team. Also from Japan is Harry Yanagi, head of Butokokai, the world clearing house for Jujutsu in Japan. This is Mr. W.C. Kim from Korea, Master of Hapkido and Taekwondo.

"Beside him is Master Philipie from France, Master in Savate, French kick boxing, and this is Mr. Kwon Yu from Thailand, who is International Tai Boxing Champion. From the Philippines is Grandmaster Florando Galo, who is a Master in Filipino Stick and Knife Fighting. All of these men will be training you for thirty minutes each day, demonstrating their expertise in the martial arts of their country. Everyone, this is Vinnie."

Vinnie shook their hands in turn. "Good to meet you all."

"You'll be training for a total of three and a half hours per day," John continued. "Afterward, you will be studying with me for one hour so I can help you combine each of the different arts into your mixed martial arts training.

"Mixed martial arts is a full contact combat sport that allows the use of both striking and grappling techniques, both standing and on the ground, from a variety of other combat sports. When you have finished your martial arts training each day, you will be given an hour to eat, drink, and recuperate. Then, you will train with Whitey for your boxing, including cardio. Are you ready for this vigorous training regime?"

"Yes, I am, Grandmaster Wooten." Vinnie bowed out of respect and turned to speak to the group of distinguished masters. "I am honored to have the opportunity to meet and study with all of you." Then he bowed to the group of masters.

Grandmaster Wooten handed Vinnie his new Jujutsu gi with a white belt. "When you complete your training, it will be an honor to present you with a real black belt for your accomplishments. Now, go into the locker room and change into your gi."

Once Vinnie was prepared, he stepped on the mat and was greeted by Mr. Yamamoto, who wasted no time in executing an *Ippon Seoi Nage*, or one arm shoulder throw.

Startled and disoriented, Vinnie sat up on the mat and looked up at Mr. Yamamoto. "What just happened?"

"This is only a break in the iceberg," he warned, his accent heavy. "Are you okay, Vinnie?"

"Yes, but how did you do that?"

"Don't worry, you will learn fast enough," Mr. Yamamoto said, waving his hand. "Let me help you up."

As Mr. Yamamoto grabbed Vinnie to lift him off the mat, he surprised him again by throwing him with a technique called *Kotegaeshi*, wrist-turning, an Aikido move. Once more, Mr. Yamamoto offered his hand to Vinnie. This time, Vinnie declined, leaning away from his teacher.

"Thank you, but no thank you. I'll get up on my own."

Mr. Yamamoto laughed, the others with him, while Grandmaster Wooten looked on with amusement.

John Wooten

Incoranata already had dinner ready when Vinnie struggled into the house. She could tell how difficult it was for him to drag his aching body into the kitchen. She watched him slump into a seat, and gaped at him, clucking her tongue.

"Vinnie, you look like you've been hit by a train."

"Ma, you don't know the half of it!" He slumped down at the kitchen table, and his mother placed steaming bowls in front of everyone, inviting them to dig in.

"Do you want to watch a movie with me tonight?" Maria asked, bouncing in her chair as she began to eat.

"No, not tonight," Vinnie muttered, rubbing his eyes.

Mario grinned and added, "Do you want to practice Jujutsu with me? I bet that's more fun than a dumb movie." Maria stuck out her tongue at him.

The thought of more training only exhausted Vinnie more. "I'm sorry, I've had enough Jujutsu for one day."

"What did those people do to you?" Incoranata asked, rubbing her son's tender back. "You can't even pick up the fork to eat!"

"Vinnie, I will feed you," Mario suggested.

"No, thanks," Vinnie said, rolling his eyes. "When I finish eating, I'm going right to bed."

When the doorbell rang, Mario scrambled out of his seat and ran for the front door. "I'll get the door. It's Mary!"

When she entered the kitchen looking prettier than ever, Incoranata welcomed her. "I'm afraid our Vinnie is in a lot of pain today. He was worked over very hard during his training," she explained.

"Oh my God, Vinnie, you look like you were hit by a train!" Mary exclaimed, astonished.

"I know, my mom already told me the same thing." Vinnie sounded irritated, but he stood from his chair and leaned into Mary, breathing in the sweet scent of her shampoo. Her softness and welcoming touch made him want to curl up in her arms.

"Let's go upstairs and I will give you a massage," Mary suggested, taking his hand and leading him away.

In his bedroom, Vinnie slipped off his t-shirt and lay down on his stomach. Mary worked the knots out of his back the best she could, massaging his shoulders and occasionally placing delicate kisses on his skin. Soon, he was so relaxed he had fallen asleep, and he began snoring so loudly he sounded like a foghorn.

After kissing him gently on the cheek, Mary went downstairs and found Incoranata in the kitchen. "I think your son is out for the night." She hugged her future mother-in-law. "I'm going to leave now and visit my father."

"All right, dear. Thanks for being so sweet to my boy."

Incoranata was truly grateful. She thought of Dominick, and wished he were still alive. He would have been so proud of his brother. Somehow, she knew he was proud anyway—looking down on them from Heaven.

Three months later, Vinnie had adapted to his strenuous training regime, and was becoming quite the martial artist. But he had seen very little of Mary and his family, and it was bringing him down.

At the Dojo one day, after his training, he sat down on the floor to take a breather. Staring at the polished wood grain, he sighed heavily.

Grandmaster Wooten must have sensed the change in him. An uplifting social life was important for someone who worked as hard as Vinnie. He called him over one day to speak with him.

"Vinnie, starting this week, I'm giving you every Sunday off to spend with Mary and your family."

He didn't bother to hide his relief. "Thank you, Grandmaster, and my body and mind thank you, too."

He left that day feeling more relaxed than usual, knowing he would have plenty of time with his family—and the woman he loved.

CHAPTER 40

A WORD OF WISDOM

Marenzano called Vinnie to arrange a breakfast meeting to discuss a few things. He sounded pensive, and Vinnie hesitated, not sure if he should ask why. When he'd said 'a few things' he sounded worried, and it wasn't like Marenzano to worry.

Vinnie bit his lip. "Okay, where?"

"At the diner near my gym at ten."

"Sure."

Marenzano hung up before Vinnie could say goodbye.

When he arrived at the diner, he sat down in the booth across from the Don. It wasn't that busy, and the tables around them were empty. The waitress sashayed over, her auburn hair pulled back in a ponytail. She smiled flirtatiously at Vinnie and slipped a pencil out of her apron, her notepad in her hand.

"What can I getcha?" she asked, jutting her left hip to the side.

"Just coffee for now," Vinnie said, his voice quiet. When she'd left, he leaned on the table, clasping his hands before him. "So, what do you want to talk about?"

"Are you sure you are ready for the championship MMA fight?" Marenzano asked, after taking a sip from his steaming mug of coffee.

"Yes, I'm ready," Vinnie said firmly, wondering why Marenzano was asking. He figured his answer would be obvious. The waitress brought the coffee, and Vinnie ordered a simple breakfast.

"Then let me ask you this." Marenzano paused, leaning forward conspiratorially. "Has anyone *threatened* you?"

"No." Vinnie frowned worriedly. "Why?"

"I received some threatening phone calls…I don't know who it was." Marenzano shook his head, glancing around. The hostess had seated an elderly couple nearby, and the man was adjusting his hearing aid when the waitress asked him what he'd like to drink. There was no need to worry about them overhearing, that was for sure.

"What did he say?" Vinnie asked, concerned.

"He said, 'I want your fighter to take a dive in round two…or both of you are dead.'"

"What?" Vinnie hissed, clenching his fist on the table. "Do you have any idea who this might be, any at all?"

"No, but one thing is for sure." Marenzano lowered his voice. "It's not anyone *connected*."

"How can you be so sure about that?"

"Connected guys don't operate that way, Vinnie. Believe me, if it was an organized crime family, I would know where it was coming from and who we're dealing with. In other words, keep your eyes and ears open for anything unusual."

"No problem. I will."

The waitress brought their food, and the two men ate. But Vinnie couldn't enjoy his breakfast, which suddenly tasted like cardboard in his mouth. Who was out to get him? And *why?*

After breakfast, Salvatore walked Vinnie to his SUV. The two engaged in a heavy conversation, reminiscing about the past. Suddenly, Vinnie glanced at the roof across the street, where he saw a shining beam of light. He noticed a man unpacking and assembling what looked like a rifle with a scope.

Before he could say anything, a shot was fired just as Vinnie instinctively pulled Marenzano to the ground to avoid being hit. The two hit the pavement hard while more shots sounded overhead.

"Vinnie, stay down and don't move." Marenzano crawled across the sidewalk and took cover behind Vinnie's SUV, then unloaded a round of bullets at the assailant. They soon discovered Marenzano had hit him right between the eyes.

The police and FBI arrived at the scene moments later, and the identity of the shooter turned out to be the brother of the MMA champion, Jimmy Doherty, scheduled to fight Vinnie the following month. The same MMA champion who'd put Vinnie in a coma in Las Vegas.

His heart hammered in his chest as he climbed to his feet and rubbed his hand across his sweating brow. The brother was dead, but what of Jimmy Doherty?

Weeks went by, and after further investigation, the police and FBI decided there'd been no conspiracy and no accomplices. Kevin Doherty had planned and orchestrated the botched hit on his own.

It was two weeks before the fight, and after a grueling day of combat martial arts, Grandmaster Wooten sat down with Vinnie, along with the other masters.

"Vinnie, we are here to inform you that your fighting ability has been extraordinary," Grandmaster Wooten declared. "You are an elite fighting machine with skills beyond comprehension. Your training will end with the other masters today. However, I will continue to fine tune and critique your fighting skills for the next week. You resume your training here tomorrow."

"Thank you, Grandmaster Wooten," Vinnie replied, indebted to the master for his wisdom and martial art skills. He bowed before all the grandmasters, showing respect to them. They wished him good luck. "We will all be rooting for you in the front row seats at the MMA World Championship."

"Thank you, Grandmasters. I am humbled and honored for all your training."

Vinnie trained privately with Grandmaster Wooten for six hours each day for the entire week. It was exhausting, but Vinnie was happy to know he was finally ready.

"Now that the intensive training has finished, what have you learned?" John asked.

"Well, I have learned to be very humble, aggressive without malice…and it's not the winning, but *how* you win. I have had the opportunity to train with the best. This last week with you was incredible. With no disrespect, I believe even as old as you are, if you fought the MMA champion today, the fight would never go beyond the first round."

John laughed and clapped a hand on Vinnie's shoulder affectionately.

"Grandmaster, someday, you need to tell me about all the masters you have trained with over the years. If I go into this fight next Saturday night having absorbed only ten percent of what I have learned, I will come out a winner. If I win the MMA Championship of the World, you will know who the real champion is. That's you, sir."

"Thank you, Vinnie." The two men hugged, tears in their eyes.

Redirecting your opponent's force.

CHAPTER 41

PRESS CONFERENCE

Two stretch limos pulled up in front of Vinnie's house to take Vinnie and his entourage to the airport for his MMA fight in Las Vegas. He was accompanied by Marenzano and a few of his soldiers, plus Mary, Whitey, and a few other trainers. Their family and friends would follow later in the week.

Upon arrival in Vegas, they were all jet-lagged and exhausted. They decided to lay low in their hotel rooms. Vinnie and Mary laid down to take a nap together, cuddling close on the soft comforter.

"Vinnie, I'm worried," Mary whispered, nuzzling her head against his chest.

"Why's that, baby?"

She seemed almost annoyed that he didn't already know. "Vinnie, you were shot at. You could have been killed by Doherty's brother. Aren't you worried your opponent wants you dead?"

"Mary, I *know* he wants me dead. Believe me, I've thought about it." He clutched her close and kissed the top of her head. "I am a little worried. But the Grandmasters have taught me to train my mind, and I am staying focused. The most important thing is to keep my mind on the fight, and on winning. Nobody's going to shoot at me in the arena."

"But what about before or after. Vinnie—"

"Baby, don't worry. Please. Just pray. God and the Blessed Virgin Mary will make sure nothing happens to me."

Mary tugged her body closer to his, and was quiet.

The next day, Vinnie and his trainers started his light workout routine.

On Thursday, a press conference was scheduled at the MGM Hotel and Casino where the fight was being held. Just before the press conference, Vinnie strolled by the MGM Sports Bet and inquired what the odds were on his MMA fight scheduled for Saturday night. He was disappointed to see the odds were forty to one, in favor of Jimmy Doherty.

When Vinnie turned around, he noticed Marenzano standing behind him.

"They have me at forty to one in favor of Jimmy Doherty," Vinnie snapped, agitated.

"Look, Vinnie, that's *good* for us!" Marenzano put a fatherly arm around Vinnie's shoulder as they walked together.

"How can that be?"

"It's because he's going to lose and that's what's in our favor. I'm planning to put a bundle of cash on you to win, since I truly believe in you. There are others betting on you to win, and they are counting on you to pull it off. By the way, your father just arrived with a couple of zips from Sicily. Don't worry, we have everything under control."

"Yeah, I know, *forget about it!*" They both laughed.

At the press conference, both fighters were sitting next to their managers answering questions from reporters. A member of the press stood to address Jimmy Doherty.

"I'm Rick Cuttingham, reporter from the Las Vegas Sun. Sir, in what round do you think you will take down your opponent, Vinnie Russo?"

"My opponent? He's no opponent, he's a joke! He's only been studying martial arts for one year. I've been studying martial arts my entire life. I am a seasoned fighter with twenty-three wins and no loses. Saturday night, I plan to take this joker out in the first round. I'll break his neck in one and he'll look real dumb."

Everyone in the crowd snickered.

"I heard Vinnie Russo is a very religious guy and that's all well and good." Jimmy squared his jaw and narrowed his eyes, clenching a fist. His massive bicep bulged. "But he'll need more than a few prayers to beat me." He turned and glared at his opponent, but Vinnie just smiled good-naturedly in reply, and that seemed to irritate Jimmy even more.

Another journalist was recognized and stood to introduce himself. "I'm Mike Reynolds, sports writer for the Boston Herald. Vinnie, I know you and watched you train for the past year. The way I see it, you will give the champ a run for his money. If I were to bet on the fight, my money would be on you."

Vinnie nodded. "Please allow me to express my thanks to you and the Boston Herald, along with the people of Boston. I find Jimmy Doherty misguided in his life's quest. He has no virtues or respect for other people. He is the most self-centered and egotistical person I have ever met. He fights with anger and malice. On the other hand, I fight with technique, wisdom, and the grace of God." A hush passed over the crowd.

Vinnie stood up and walked over to Jimmy Doherty, unafraid. "Saturday night is my night," he told him. "The first round will be *my* round when I knock you out, you clown!"

Jimmy Doherty raised a fist, his face red as he yelled profanities at Vinnie, who returned to his place on the panel.

Rick Cuttingham raised his hand and asked, "Vinnie, are you saying that you will knock out Doherty in the first round and become the new MMA Heavyweight Champion of the World?"

"Yes, that's exactly what I am saying." The media was in a frenzy, and the crowd was in total disbelief.

Could he do it? They all wondered. Could he really knock out Jimmy Doherty in the first round? Everyone waited, wanting to know, but Vinnie was already certain. He had God on his side.

CHAPTER 42

TERROR IN THE RING

It was Saturday night at the MGM Hotel and Casino. Vinnie was in his locker room with Marenzano, Whitey, Grandmaster Wooten, and the other trainers.

"What's going through your mind right now? Are you nervous?" Marenzano asked.

"No, not at all."

"You're not the *least* bit nervous?" The Don seemed disbelieving.

"Look, Sal, I'm not going to admit to you or anyone else if I am nervous or not. One thing is for sure, Jimmy Doherty will not be the champ for much longer. I am not fighting him to be the MMA Heavyweight Champion, but to teach him humility and respect for other people. I don't have to prove anything. It's not how you win the fight, but *why* you win. I have no other motives."

Grandmaster Wooten had been listening in. The expression on his face showed his pride. "You have a good attitude. Now, let me prepare your mind and body with some Chi relaxing exercises."

Vinnie was nearly ready. Nothing could stop him now.

In Jimmy Doherty's locker room, the champ was loud and vociferous, pounding on the lockers with his fits. His trainers grabbed him and held him until he stilled.

"Calm down, Jimmy! You're wearing yourself out. You haven't even fought yet, you have to stay prepared. You're just going to injure yourself punching walls instead of your opponent."

"The only one that's going to get hurt is Vinnie Russo. I am going to kill him in the first round! I will finish what I started over a year ago in the alleyway. This time, I'll make sure he never wakes up," Jimmy growled.

A big man with beady brown eyes, the Las Vegas Mob Boss, stepped forward as Jimmy's trainers released him. He slapped Jimmy hard in the face and pointed one fat finger toward the fighter's pug nose.

"Don't let me hear you talk like that again," he snapped. "Maybe you *do* need to learn some humility."

Before Jimmy could shout a retort, there was a loud knock on the locker room door.

"Doherty, you're up!" a man's voice yelled out.

A group of security officers escorted Doherty, his manager, and his trainers down the hallway. Jimmy grabbed the hood of his robe while cameras flashed. One camera man broke through the security line to snap a quick picture of the back of Doherty's robe. It had a cemetery and head stone with Vinnie Russo's name on it, including his date of birth and his death, showing the date of the fight. The cameraman grimaced, apparently finding the robe offensive, before he stepped back and melted into the crowd.

Jimmy and his entourage entered the arena while the crowds cheered and shouted, "Doherty, Doherty!"

But when he entered the ring, and people began to read the back of his robe, loud *boos* sounded out. Despite this, Doherty remained composed with his usual arrogance and began bouncing around the ring and shadow boxing.

When Vinnie Russo strolled toward ringside, the audience turned their heads. He was accompanied by Marenzano, Grandmaster Wooten, and his trainers, along with their body guards. The crowd cheered fiercely and stomped their feet as he entered the ring. The back of his robe showed a picture of Mary, the Blessed Mother.

The announcer walked to the middle of the ring and the microphone dropped from the ceiling.

"Ladies and Gentlemen, may I have your attention please. Welcome to the MGM Grand Hotel and Casino in Las Vegas, Nevada, where we will be holding the World MMA Championship fight this evening. Now let me introduce to you the World MMA Champion Fighter with twenty-three wins, and no losses, Jimmy Doherty, at five-foot-eleven and two hundred and two pounds." Cheers mingled with loud booing as the crowd responded.

"I would now like to introduce to you our contender, Vinnie the Animal Russo, the World Heavyweight Boxing Champion turned MMA fighter. This will be Vinnie's first MMA fight, at six-foot-one and two hundred pounds." The crowd stomped their feet and chanted his name.

"We have a special guest in the ring tonight, who you all know, Grandmaster John Wooten. He has trained some of the best fighters in the world and he's had an undefeated career of fifty-six wins and no losses. He is one of the greatest men I've had the pleasure of knowing.

"Now, ladies and gentlemen, please stand for our national anthem."

Then, the fighters emerged from their corners when the bell rang. The MMA commentators began giving the play by play of the fight.

"Doherty rushes out and sends a flying kick to Vinnie's head, but he avoids impact by shooting into Doherty's legs." The crowd cheered. "Both men end up in a ground and pound match. Vinnie puts Doherty in a Sankaku Jime, a triangle Judo choke shimewaza, from the front using the legs in a figure-four position around the neck and arm. Doherty suddenly breaks away, but finds himself laying flat on his back mounted by Vinnie."

Vinnie Russo, the World Heavyweight Boxing Champion, versus Jimmy Doherty, the World MMA Heavyweight Champion

The referee stepped in, waving his arms. The men had spent too much time on the mat, and they quickly returned to a fighting stance.

"Vinnie is pushed into the corner ropes and Doherty begins to throw a flurry of punches to his rival's head. We are now three and a half minutes into the first round with only a minute and a half to go in round one. I think we're all wondering Vinnie the Animal Russo bit off more than he could chew!"

Vinnie lashed back at Doherty, aggressively pushing him back to the middle of the ring. He shot for Doherty's legs again and quickly mounted him, repeatedly throwing punches and elbow strikes to his face and head.

The excitement of the screaming crowd was palpable, the air thick with heat. Grandmaster Wooten pumped his fist into the air and shouted, loud enough for Vinnie to hear, "Take him out now, Vinnie, now!"

He lifted Doherty up, then threw him in the middle of the ring, quickly mounting him and putting him into a kamura Judo choke. Blood leaked from Doherty's mouth and nose, but when Vinnie glanced at the referee for instruction, the man shook his head, indicating the fight had not yet ended.

With only ten seconds remaining in the first round, Russo choked out his opponent and the referee ended the fight. The crowd was going wild, and it was too loud for anyone but the referee to hear what Vinnie said.

"Why didn't you end the fight sooner? I almost killed him!"

The announcer strolled to the center of the ring. *"Ladies and gentlemen, the judges have voted. Judge Joseph Manning has voted in favor of the challenger, Vinnie the Animal Russo, twenty-five to twenty-three."* The crowd screamed in delight. *"Judge Nicholas Baldwin voted in favor of our challenger, Vinnie Russo, twenty-six to twenty-two."* The crowd cheered. *"Judge Anthony Fargas voted in favor of our challenger, Vinnie Russo, twenty-five to twenty-one."*

It was a unanimous decision.

"We have a new MMA World Champion tonight, Vinnie the Animal Russo from Boston, Massachusetts."

Jimmy Doherty had struggled to his feet, but no one paid him any mind. Chaos broke out as Vinnie approached the microphone, and it was suddenly clear that Doherty wouldn't give up his title without more of a fight.

He'd been handed a gun concealed in a towel by someone nearby; the offender had melted into the crowd, and Doherty was raising the gun, his thick hand wrapped around the grip. The agony and torment of losing the fight was clear in his narrowed eyes, his gaze filled with hatred and misery, blood and sweat glistening around his nose and mouth.

Vinnie raised his hands, his heart pounding as a hush fell over the crowd. "You don't want to do this! You'll ruin your life, Jimmy. Do you want to spend the rest of your days behind bars?"

Body guards were at the ready, and policemen posted at the event were aiming for Doherty, ready to pull the trigger if they had to.

Jimmy blinked, gritting his teeth, which turned coppery at the touch of his own blood.

Without warning, he turned the gun on himself, pressing the muzzle against his temple. Before anyone could stop him, he pulled the trigger, and the bullet crashed through his skull and into his brain. For a brief moment, his body remained suspended there, and then he crumpled to the floor. People in the audience screamed, some left as quickly as they could.

A few closest to the ring vomited, but Vinnie just stood there frozen, his eyes wide open, staring at the scene before him as if hoping it was all just a dream.

One word echoed in his mind: *Pandemonium.*

CHAPTER 43

BACK IN BEAN TOWN

At Vinnie's Victory party, there were more news reporters than fans. The police and FBI were questioning everyone connected with the fight, trying to find out who concealed the gun in the towel. The media seemed to have more interest in Doherty's suicide than the new MMA champion. The victory party was short-lived, and Vinnie wasn't feeling very celebratory anyway.

The next morning, Vinnie, his family, and friends flew home to Boston. Upon arriving at Logan International Airport in East Boston, Vinnie was greeted by thousands of fans. After spending a couple of hours acknowledging best wishes, along with signing autographs, the Massachusetts State Police helped Vinnie and his entourage into their assigned limos, keeping the crowds at a safe distance. Vinnie, Mary, and Vinnie's family were in one limo, while Marenzano, Whitey, Grandmaster Wooten, and some of the body guards rode in the next limo. The third was reserved for the remaining trainers and Marenzano's crew.

Vinnie signaled to his limo driver to take them to orient heights in East Boston, where the Madonna Queen National Shrine overlooked Boston. At Vinnie's behest, they stopped to give thanks. Vinnie's heart filled with love, and he knew he would never be alone as long as he had the Blessed Mother in his life.

Back home, the family gathered around the kitchen table to discuss their upcoming trip back to Sicily. When the phone rang, Vinnie stood and crossed the room to answer it.

"Hey, Vinnie, it's Marenzano."

"Hi, Sal."

"Hey, listen, we all decided to accompany you and your family back to Sicily," Marenzano told him, his voice edged with excitement.

"That's great! Even Whitey?"

"Yes, even Whitey, and Grandmaster Wooten has also decided to come. I'll be bringing my wife as well. You trusted us to train and prepare you for the championship. Now, we want to help you in your quest. We can all meet at Logan Airport next week."

"Sounds like a plan!"

When Vinnie hung up the phone, he thought for a long time about Marenzano, and how much the man had changed. When he'd first met him, he'd been afraid of him, unsure if Marenzano was someone he could trust. Now, he was like another father to him, and he couldn't imagine accomplishing so much without him.

He didn't know if the stories about Marenzano were true, but by this point he'd all but forgotten them. It didn't matter anymore. The Don had become his manager, and his friend. In fact, he was family.

And soon, he and his family would return home to Sicily—and to the mountain where Vinnie had first seen the Blessed Virgin Mary.

Life was good.

CHAPTER 44

ARRIVAL IN CASTELLAMMARE DEL GOLFO

Following a long week of preparation, everyone met up at Logan Airport around one o'clock. After clearing airport security, the group sat down to have a leisurely lunch.

Vinnie leaned back in his chair after taking a bite of his chicken sandwich. "I still can't believe everything that's happened," he said, reaching to his right and taking Mary's hand. "The love of my life nearly died. I almost died. And I can't believe Jimmy Doherty is gone. All because he couldn't handle losing."

Vinnie glanced up and caught the sad gaze of his mother.

"Vinnie, that man Doherty was already broken inside before he met you. Remember that." She cocked her head to the side, pulling her button-up sweater over her white blouse. "If he was going to shoot himself, he would do it anyway, no matter what. Don't blame yourself for that."

"I don't, Ma."

Incoranata shook her head. "I know that look in your eye. A part of you thinks if you hadn't gotten in that ring—"

"Well, of course." Vinnie shrugged. "Of course I think if I hadn't gotten in that ring, Doherty might still be alive, but—"

"He would have killed himself no matter what," Marenzano interjected. "Don't give two shits about a man who didn't care about himself. It isn't worth it, Vinnie."

"The Don's right, kid," Grandmaster Wooten said. "He probably would have ended up in jail eventually if he'd lived. The guy was a ticking time bomb."

"The important thing is we're here," Maria piped in as she lifted her sandwich to her lips.

Grandmaster Wooten mussed her hair with his big hand and she looked up at him and grinned. "From the mouths of babes."

Everyone shared a lighthearted laugh, and the tension eased.

When their flight was announced, they headed to the gate, passing their tickets over to be scanned. Once they were all seated, and the plane took off, Marenzano finally glanced at his ticket and realized the flight number was 666. He balked, his face turning pale.

Marenzano leaned across the aisle and nudged Vinnie. "Hey, did you notice what our flight number is?"

"Yes, I did notice."

"Why didn't you tell me before I boarded?" Marenzano glanced down the aisle, a nervous expression on his face, as if he expected someone to lift a gun and start shooting, or reveal a bomb hidden under a jacket.

"I knew how damn superstitious you are." Vinnie shook his head, grinning. Beside him, Mary chuckled and interlaced her fingers with his. "I was afraid you'd refuse to get on."

"You're right!" He reached up and slammed his thumb on the call button for the flight attendant.

A middle-aged blonde with crow's feet at the corners of her bright blue eyes stepped along the aisle, placing her hand on the seat in front of Marenzano's. "May I help you, sir?"

"Yes, I need a martini!"

"Maybe you better give him a double." Vinnie smiled coyly.

When his drink arrived, Marenzano guzzled it, and Vinnie snickered as he watched him.

"Do you feel better now?"

"Shut the fuck up! I'll feel better when we get off this damn plane."

Finally, after an hour in flight, Marenzano slipped into a deep sleep.

Vinnie squeezed Mary's arm and nodded toward the Don. "Looks like our big baby is gonna be just fine."

"Vinnie, stop," Mary whispered, but she couldn't hide her musical laughter.

A long while went by in silence, when suddenly a bout of turbulence awoke Marenzano. He jolted forward, sweat beading over his eyes, which were wide with panic.

"What's happening? What's happening?" he exclaimed, clenching the armrests.

"Sal, don't freak out," Vinnie soothed. "It's only turbulence, you need to relax!"

"That's easy for you to say."

"Look at Maria and Mario, they're laughing about it." He was right. His siblings were acting as if they were on an amusement park ride, not a plane.

"This is fun!" Mario exclaimed.

When the turbulence subsided, Vinnie ordered another double martini for Marenzano. After a few drinks, he was out like a light again and slept through the dinner service. He finally awoke the next morning in time for breakfast and arrival in Rome. Upon landing, Marenzano made the sign of the cross to give thanks for a safe flight. Vinnie elbowed Mary so she could witness her father's religious gesture, something that was new to them both.

The plane had a scheduled stop in Rome, so they were able to do some sightseeing. They visited the Vatican, the Sistine Chapel, and the Colosseum. They relaxed and ate at some of Rome's finest restaurants.

Rome was wonderful, but they were all excited about their upcoming arrival in Sicily. Especially Marenzano, who commented that he'd be happy if he never saw another plane as long as he lived.

"I thought it was the flight number that bothered you, Dad," Mary said.

Marenzano shook his head, bleary-eyed. "Fuck, I don't know anymore."

Vinnie chuckled. "Well, you're on the ground now. Enjoy it while you can!"

Incoranata couldn't wait to see her husband.

The next morning, they flew into Palermo, Sicily, and were greeted by Vinchenzo and a few of his associates, along with Father Anthony and Father Vincent. Incoranata ran to her husband's waiting embrace, and he held her tight for a long moment.

"This way, my dear," he said, leading her and the others toward the cars.

There were three stretch limos waiting to take everyone to the new Depasquale estate. Upon arrival, Incoranata was speechless when she gazed upon her new home. She couldn't believe what she was seeing; it looked like a mansion.

Inside, a long winding staircase led to the upstairs bedrooms. Marble floors opened to a beautiful atrium with an indoor garden and a small fountain. The front windows were wide, letting in plenty of light. Everyone gawked, and Incoranata pressed a hand to her heart, gaping.

Vinchenzo took Incoranata's hand in his and said, "First, I would like to show my wife her modern, fully equipped kitchen and adjoining dining room which seats twenty-four people."

Incoranata squeaked. "What? Vinchenzo, my blood pressure cannot handle this!"

Everyone laughed. Grandmaster Wooten leaned over her shoulder and said, "I'll walk behind you. If you faint, I'll make sure you don't hit the floor."

She turned to him, suppressing a laugh, her eyes wide. "Well, thank you, I think!"

"Come." Vinchenzo led them to the kitchen, where white tiles gleamed, and the countertops were made of the finest material. An island in the center of the kitchen was flanked by stools, great for just hanging out while dinner was being cooked.

Vinchenzo led them through the house and talked as he went, his voice echoing in the cavernous hallway.

"Next is our recreation room with a pool table, poker tables, and a roulette table, and along the side of the room we have six computers. Our entertainment room has a full-screen movie theater. There's a popcorn machine and a full service bar with a deluxe refrigerator packed with plenty of pasta." They all laughed. "Oh, I almost forgot! We also have an espresso machine." Stepping through a wide entryway, Vinchenzo raised a hand and said, "This is our living room."

More wide windows invited the daylight into the room. In the center, a wide bay window housed a cozy sitting area. Built-in book cases lined the far wall, surrounding a fireplace and stone mantle. The furniture was soft and inviting, with couches facing each other, and a wide coffee table.

Incoranata gasped again. Behind her, her children *oohhed* and *ahhed*.

"It's so spacious and beautiful!" Incoranata said.

Maria ran over to one of the couches, her feet bouncing on the soft Persian rug. "It's comfy!" she exclaimed.

"Okay everyone, let's continue upstairs where we have twelve bedrooms, enough for you to choose from." Vinchenzo led the way. "Of course, the master suite is for Incoranata and myself."

When he opened the door to the bedroom, Incoranata was astonished. "This room was made for a queen."

"So, what's wrong with that? I'm a king and you're my queen."

They all laughed. The 'his' and 'hers' walk-in closets were the size of normal bedrooms. The bathroom was huge, equipped with a Jacuzzi, commode, and bidet.

Next, Vinchenzo took them to see Maria's room, decorated in pink and green with a canopy bed trimmed with ruffles. She had her own computer and shelves with stuffed animals.

Maria hugged her father tightly. "Thank you, Daddy! I feel like a princess."

"You are my princess," Vinchenzo exclaimed, kissing her on the cheek.

"Dad, where's my bedroom?" Mario shouted.

"Next to Maria's room. Come, I'll show you." Inside Mario's room was a computer with many video games, a baseball, glove and bat, a football, soccer ball, and a pair of Arnis fighting sticks used in Philippine martial arts, as well as a wooden training knife. A young man's dream room.

"Dad, thank you so much!" Mario said, bouncing on his heels. He couldn't decide what to do first.

"Vinnie, I'll show you your bedroom next," Vinchenzo said, putting his arm around his son.

Vinnie's room was decorated with framed posters and pictures of his fights. There was a king size bed with many pillows, and a computer and desk with a large leather chair. Boxing gloves, uniforms, and medals were displayed tastefully on nearly every surface.

"Mary, until you are married to my son, your bedroom is next to Vinnie's. Salvatore, you and your wife can sleep in the bedroom next to Mary's." He placed his hand on the Don's shoulder. "Marenzano, the help you have given my son and family has been greatly appreciated, and I am proud to call you my friend."

"Thank you, Vinchenzo. My wife and I appreciate you allowing us to stay here."

"It is my pleasure. Think nothing of it!" He turned to Vinnie's first and favorite trainer. "Whitey, this is your room," he said, stepping across the hall and opening a door.

"Wow, this is better than any four-star hotel," Whitey said, gaping.

"Whitey, you are a wise man," Vinchenzo said. "You helped build my son's character and self-esteem as a boxer. You are one hell of a boxing coach. As far as I'm concerned, you're a member of my family, too."

"Thank you so much, Don Depasquale. That means so much to me." Whitey's eyes moistened. He'd never known much in the way of family or friends, so having these people in his life was a great gift indeed.

Vinchenzo turned and nodded in the direction of the tall, imposing man standing beside Vinnie. "Grandmaster Wooten, you can sleep in the bedroom next to Whitney's. It's an honor to have you stay with us."

"Vinchenzo, you have outdone yourself, I am honored to be here." The Grandmaster bowed his head gratefully.

"It is nothing. I appreciate all you have done for my son, not only teaching him martial arts, but teaching him humility and honor."

"I enjoyed every moment of it."

"Now, everyone, please follow me downstairs and out to the back of the house," Vinchenzo said. "I have ten acres of land with electrified fences and security cameras, and there are ten members of my crew to run surveillance and secure my property twenty-four seven."

"There is more security here than Fort Knox," Marenzano joked.

"Yes, that's right, Salvatore. I am now stronger than U.S. Steel." Vinchenzo winked.

"I'll say you are!"

They crossed the lawn. It was a beautiful day, and the trees wavered in a slight breeze.

"Now, to continue on the tour, you'll see my stables in the back. I own a few race horses and built a race track for their training. I know Marenzano owns race horses as well."

"Over here, you can see I have a small wine vineyard and grow tomatoes along with other fresh vegetables which Incoranata will enjoy cooking."

Vinchenzo led them through the garden, inviting them to view a lovely shrine of the Virgin Mary he had built with running water streaming down a small hill. Vinnie's eyes widened and he felt a sense of peace. The spiritual presence here was clear. Vinchenzo had worked hard to make sure the spot was perfect and tranquil.

"Hey, Dad, what's under the canvas cover in front of the house? I noticed that as we drove up," Vinnie said curiously.

"Come, I'll show you now," Vinchenzo declared. "Mario, why don't you help me do the honors and pull the canvas off."

Once they had finished, a monumental statue of Vinnie boxing was revealed. The inscription read, *Vinnie Russo Depasquale, 2013, Heavyweight Boxing Champion of the World, and 2014 Heavyweight MMA Champion of the World.*

Vinnie's eyes watered and his chest tightened as pride welled up within him. "Dad, you didn't have to do this."

"You are my son," Vinchenzo said. "And you have succeeded beyond my best imaginings." He hugged him close. "I love you."

"I love you, too, Dad. Thank you."

Father Anthony raised his hands and said, "Let's go inside to celebrate and give a toast to Vinnie, the new Heavyweight MMA Champion of the World!"

In the house, they opened champagne and lifted their glasses in the air.

"*Gendon,*" everyone shouted. "May you live a hundred years!"

"Tomorrow, I will take everyone on a tour of Castellammare del Golfo," Father Anthony announced. "It is sure to be a beautiful day."

CHAPTER 45

MESSENGER OF GOD

Father Anthony arrived at Vinchenzo's estate early the next morning to escort Vinnie's friends and family on a tour of Castellammare del Golfo. The tour began at the gym where Vinnie had started training as a young man.

Vinnie could hardly believe seven years had passed since he'd first seen the Blessed Virgin Mary. Seven years since he'd left his home.

Next, they visited the church where the group attended a special mass dedicated to Vinnie. Afterward, they walked the path leading up to the mountainside where the Blessed Mother first appeared to both Vinnie and Father Anthony.

Soft loam pressed beneath their feet, and there was a chill in the air as Vinnie looked up at the naked trees. It was a breathtaking location chosen by the Virgin Mary to proclaim her seven incredible requests. In the seventh year, she promised to appear one last time after Vinnie's return home.

His heart pounded as he was filled with joy knowing he would see her again. He squeezed the hand of his true love, who was also eager to behold the sight. Together, they strolled into their future, honoring the Virgin Mary and the Lord God for their good fortune.

During their walk, Vinnie spoke of how he'd first heard the Virgin Mary's voice while in his bed at home. He revealed the details leading up to the miraculous vision of the Blessed Mother, and felt a chill crawl up his spine as he considered the fact he would soon behold her again.

"Father Anthony, remember this spot?" They stood on a grassy knoll, where large rocks were scattered across the landscape, and gnarled trees reached toward the sky. "This is where I asked the stranger for directions."

"Yes, I remember it well." Father Anthony nodded.

Suddenly, Vinnie heard a sharp intake of breath beside him.

"Mary, are you all right?" he asked, pulling her close.

"There, look!"

He turned to catch a glimpse of a man wearing a black cape and hood, carrying a wooden staff. All he could see was the man's hand, his fingers long and bony, his nails broken and bruised. Vinnie gasped, then slowly approached. The man lifted his head, revealing his weathered, wrinkled face and crystal blue eyes.

"Aren't you the same man who directed me toward the mountainside seven years ago?" Vinnie asked, even though he was certain he was.

The mysterious stranger didn't answer, but only pointed in the direction of the mountainside. Vinnie thanked him. As he turned to step away, the man lunged forward, lashing his staff toward Don Marenzano, who cried out and covered his face. A bright beam of light caught Marenzano's second devil ring—a desperate purchase he'd made after destroying the first—shattering it into pieces.

As Marenzano raised his head to look at the stranger, he vanished before his eyes.

Red-faced, Marenzano turned to Father Anthony, spit flying from between his lips as he shouted. "What the hell is going on here? Was that the devil?"

"No, Salvatore. You were touched by an angel to rid you of evil." Father Anthony bowed his head. "Come, follow me to the mountainside."

Vinnie was amazed to see thousands of people gathered and camped out to pay homage and pray with devotion to the Virgin Mary. The mountainside was thick with crowds, all waiting faithfully in anticipation to behold her miraculous appearance. Many religious believers had spiritual optimism for a miracle, and they hoped the Blessed Mother would cure them of their illnesses and crippling afflictions.

The crowds of people cheered as Father Anthony and Vinnie walked by the mountainside. A cold breeze caressed their faces, but it was invigorating, as if God Himself were gently touching them, reminding them of His presence. An old man stepped through the crowd, raising a wrinkled, trembling hand, and shouted out to Vinnie.

Vinnie stepped through the grass and took the old man's hand. "Yes, sir?"

"Do you remember me? I am Alberto Demasella. You grew up with my son, Angelo."

Vinnie grinned, knowing well the strong gaze that searched his eyes for recognition. "Yes, I remember you! How are you?"

"I am well, but my son Angelo is not. He suffers from a bad accident and is paralyzed from the waist down."

Shock and grief shuddered through Vinnie as he clasped a hand over his heart. "That's terrible, I am so sorry."

Mr. Demasella turned and beckoned to his wife. "Rosa, come, please bring Angelo down to greet Vinnie and Father Anthony."

Respectfully, the crowd parted as Rosa pushed Angelo in his wheelchair. Vinnie looked down at the saddened eyes of his once so cheerful and playful friend, his heart breaking for the young man.

"Hi, Vinnie. I missed you." Angelo's voice cracked, filled with relief to see his friend again.

"I missed you, too." Vinnie leaned forward and wrapped his arms around Angelo, hugging him close, as many memories returned to him of their times playing together as children, running through the grass, joking and laughing under the summer sun. A beautiful time, a time long since passed. Vinnie wondered what it was like to be unable to use one's legs, and he inwardly thanked God for his blessings. He released his friend, but continued to hold his hand.

Rosa's fingers tightened on the handles of the wheelchair, and her eyes brimmed with tears.

Mr. Demasella clasped his hands together, his lip quivering as he spoke. "Vinnie, I am here praying for a miracle, for the Virgin Mary to cure my son. Can you help me?"

"I can surely pray to the Blessed Mother. She will appear in a few days, just have faith." Vinnie squeezed Angelo's hand, then excused himself and continued to walk with the group.

Father Anthony reminded the people the Virgin Mary requested that seven tasks be completed in seven years, one per year.

Father Anthony's robes kissed the ground as he walked. "The first year, I spread the sacred word of the Blessed Mother," he said proudly. "In the second year, I received ten million dollars anonymously and bought construction equipment. In the third year, the townspeople worked to build twenty-six roads coming from all directions leading to the heavenly mountains. In the fourth year, the townspeople cultivated the land, and grew many organic and succulent crops to harvest. In the fifth year, they dug deep in the ground along the mountains and found an abundance of oil and other natural resources. During the sixth year, people from all over the world came here to pray and give homage to the Virgin Mary."

"Wonderful," Vinnie said, pleased. "Now, in the seventh year, she will appear to her faithful followers who have gathered to behold her coming. You have done great work, Father Anthony."

"Thank you, my son. I am ashamed that I didn't believe you when you first saw the Virgin Mary."

"Don't be." Vinnie paused, placing a hand on Father Anthony's shoulder. "You reacted the way anyone would have. But now we are seeing an incredible thing, and the truth of our faith is making a physical appearance. You yourself have seen it with your own eyes. That time wasn't that long ago, but it feels like ages. So much has changed." Vinnie turned to Mary, running a hand through her smooth, soft hair. She smiled bashfully, and nodded into his touch.

"I'm so proud of you, Vinnie," she whispered. "For all that you've accomplished. And I know we are following the path God has chosen for us."

Walking on, they breathed deep and enjoyed the beauty around them, cherishing the moment.

CHAPTER 46

A MATTER OF NATIONAL SECURITY

After their day-long journey ending at the breathtaking mountainside, Don Depasquale invited his friends back to his home where dinner awaited them. For the next couple of days, they wanted to get some rest and relaxation. Vinnie wanted to be alone with his sweetheart, Mary.

On the third day, Marenzano received a call on his cell from U. S. Attorney General David Weinstein. He stepped outside to take the call.

"Sal, I really need to speak to you, it's important."

"Yeah, no problem, but I'm sure you don't want to talk on the phone. I won't be back in Boston for another week." Marenzano tucked his jacket tighter around his body to defend against the chill in the air.

"It can't wait that long. That's why I flew to Palermo to meet with you."

"You're here?" Marenzano exclaimed in surprise. "Don't tell me the U.S. Attorney General's office is interested in the coming of the Virgin Mary."

"Why not? My office is always interested in the truth. Drive to Palermo and meet me at the Taste of Sicily Restaurant for dinner at six o'clock this evening."

"Okay, see you there." He ended the call, tucked his phone into his pocket, and went back in.

Don Marenzano arrived promptly at six, and Weinstein waved to him as he crossed the room from a corner table. He greeted Marenzano by shaking his hand, and led him to the back, where the waitress had already brought two glasses of water.

"Well, Weinstein, what's so important that you needed to fly to Sicily to speak to me?" It had to be good, that was for sure.

Weinstein laughed, his smile rising over a hint of five o'clock shadow. "It's because I missed you, Sal," he intoned, his voice tinged with sarcasm.

"Yeah, right. What the fuck is this about?"

The waitress stopped by, tucking a strand of hair behind her ear, and asked what they wanted. The two men ordered, then leaned toward each other and spoke conspiratorially.

"I have a deal to propose to you, Vinnie, Father Anthony, and Grandmaster Wooten," Weinstein explained. "Remember those indictments that were coming down on you and your crew?"

"What about them?"

"Well, I made the indictments go away *and* all the charges."

"Now you want something in return?" Marenzano growled in annoyance. This was nothing new. Just as he opened his mouth to ask how much the greedy bastard wanted, Weinstein stopped him.

"I want the four of you to be in charge of a new Federal Task Force implemented by the authority of the United States Attorney General's office on terrorism.

Marenzano frowned. He hadn't expected that. "Why us?"

"I have information on organized crime families with terrorist connections. I know you and the other old timers don't dabble in terrorism, and don't want any part of it. Father Anthony would be a good contact to keep here in Sicily."

"You're right." He paused, scratching his double chin. "I accept your offer, but I can only speak for myself. I can approach the other three, but I can't promise they'll say yes."

Weinstein sipped his water. "I have to confess I already reached out to Wooten, and he is on board with us. By the way, there's something you don't know about Wooten."

"What's that?" Marenzano didn't like *not knowing* things. As Don, it was his business to know everything on the guys he worked with, and since Wooten had become so close to Vinnie, he was certain he knew everything about him. The idea Wooten was hiding something troubled him deeply.

"He's CIA," Weinstein said without preamble.

"Son of a bitch!" Don Marenzano slammed a fist on the table, upsetting his water. The waitress promptly replaced the glass and brought appetizers. She hurried off, clearly made nervous by this irritated guest. "How long has Wooten been playing me?" Marenzano hissed.

"For a long time."

"If I could kick his ass, I would do it now."

"Let me persuade you not to go there with this guy."

"Yes, I know that." Marenzano shook his head, taking a deep breath in an attempt to calm down. "I've always liked Wooten, and he is one of the few rivals I respect. Are there any other surprises?"

"Yes, I also spoke to Father Anthony, and he's on board, too."

"Let me guess, you already asked Vinnie?"

"Father Anthony took care it, and Vinnie agreed."

"I see you were a busy man these last couple of days."

"Salvatore, look at it this way, you can think of yourselves as the miracle fighters against crime. This is a great opportunity for you." He plucked an appetizer off the dish and chewed it, washing it down with more water. "Don't be pissed at me, just be grateful."

Marenzano said nothing, only glared at Weinstein as they waited for their dinner.

CHAPTER 47

LADY OF THE MOUNTAIN

Sunday was a bright sunny day, and they all made the joyous trip to the mountainside. The breathtaking view displayed distant buildings and trees, and a mist rising over the valley. Suddenly, the bright sun was obscured by dark clouds. The mild temperature plummeted to below freezing within minutes.

"Look, it's snowing!" someone shouted.

The snowflakes were heavy and thick, covering the ground quickly. People huddled together and wrapped their jackets tighter around their bodies. As the morning passed, the people waited—and witnessed an incredible change in the weather as the temperature again rose, melting all the snow and drying up the ground.

"It's a sign!" A man lifted his arms toward the sky. "The Virgin Mary is coming!"

A gust of wind blew away the clouds, and the sun glowed, moving closer to the mountainside and turning a dark red. The color grew darker still the closer it came.

Again, the sky became black until they could see nothing more than circumference of the sun. Then, a beaming light shone directly over Vinnie and Father Anthony. Don Marenzano and Grandmaster Wooten were at their side, amazed. The people were numb and transfixed as they gazed upon the sky.

A voice echoed down to the devoted worshipers.

"I am the Virgin Mary, the Mother of God." She gradually began to appear, taking shape as the belief and faith of her followers brought her visitation to fruition.

"Men, women, and children of all races and creeds must come together to help one another, instead of having anger and hatred toward each other. The brutal fighting and killing needs to stop in your neighborhoods and in these dreadful wars. There is one God, and He loves all His people. I am here to give the world an abundance of food and natural resources which has depleted over the years.

"Now, look to the south side of the mountain, my people…"

Rocks crumbled and the earth shook, then water rapidly flowed out of the mountainside and into the valley below forming a lake.

"Those who are disabled and stricken with illness, go to the lake and immerse your body in the sacred water. Everyone who believes in me will be healed."

Vinnie's childhood friend, Angelo, was one of the first to submerge his body in the sacred lake with the help of his parents. Angelo and his family were overwhelmed with joyfulness when his paralyzed body was healed and he could walk again. Hundreds of believers flocked to the lake. Many others experienced the same miracle, and the crowds of people rejoiced.

The Blessed Mother spoke again. "Now, look to the north side of the mountain."

As the people stared upon the land, crops pushed speedily up through the soil into full mature plants. Green replaced brown dirt, as leaves and stalks grew thicker. There was an abundance of many different kinds of crops, all of them ready to be harvested. The worshipers gasped in amazement.

The Virgin Mary instructed her followers to look east of the mountains, and a loud rumbling echoed around them as black gold burst through the oil wells.

Then, the Blessed Mother told her followers, "Focus on the top of the mountain, my people."

Suddenly, lightning filled the sky and struck the mountaintop, carving out a beautiful sacred church where people of all religions could pray and worship.

The Virgin Mary now expressed her wishes to Father Anthony, Vinnie, Don Marenzano, and Grandmaster Wooten, making sure they were the only ones who could hear her. They felt her love surrounding them, like a soft blanket caressing their skin.

"I want you to know I will be at your side protecting you while you combat crime and evil in the world."

"Thank you, Blessed Mother, we will not disappoint you," Father Anthony assured her, his head bowed in reverence.

The Virgin Mary then addressed all her devoted followers. "Remember, I will be with you always. Pray and serve the Lord."

At that moment, a bright light appeared as the Blessed Mother ascended into heaven. The crowds of worshipers were elated.

The four men walked to the top of the mountain to see the spectacular church. As they walked, Vinnie asked Father Anthony, "Have you decided on a name for the church?"

"Yes, Lady of the Mountain," Father Anthony declared proudly.

"Good choice, I like it," Vinnie replied, euphoric.

After reaching the top, they gasped at the magnificent church in all its glory. They entered and walked to the side of the altar where a beautiful statue of Mary stood.

Kneeling down, they prayed to thank her for everything she had given the people of the world. While gazing upon the statue of Mary, her halo brightened and they felt her presence in the church—as well as within their hearts.

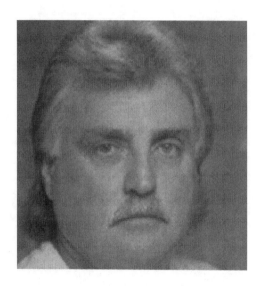

John Wooten holds 143 world records as the "World's Strongest Man." He has pulled a train, lifted an elephant, and lain on a bed of nails while two men with sledgehammers demolished concrete blocks on his chest. In addition to his feats of strength, Mr. Wooten is an actor, producer, screenplay writer, jujutsu grandmaster, and judo professor, and has earned black belts in aikido and karate.

Made in the USA
Charleston, SC
30 October 2015